MW00398938

Little
Hours

Little Hours

A NOVEL

Lil Copan

ONE BIRD BOOKS
FALMOUTH, MASSACHUSETTS

Cover Illustration Copyright © 2017 by Lil Copan
Cover Design by Kevin van der Leek Design Inc.
Typesetting/Interior Design by Klaas Wolterstorff / KWBookDesign
Design Consultant, Cover & Interior: Deborah Risë Mrantz

Manufactured in the United States of America

21 22 23 24 25 26 27 28   10 9 8 7 6 5 4 3 2 1

Print ISBN 978-1-7339200-7-0
eBook ISBN 978-1-7339200-8-7
Kindle edition available at amazon.com

For Kate, who introduced me to the Kitchen Table Writers.

And to the KTWs who introduced me to Marion,

and to Marion, who asked the questions in the first place

that gave rise to this book.

With a heart full of thanks.

And for Frankie.

Contents

Horarium

Bell to Rise—4:30

Matins—5:30, followed by Lectio Divina

Lauds—7:30, followed by Mass

Terce—10:00

Sext—12:30

None—3:30

Vespers—5:30

Compline—8:30

Prologue

March 23, 2003

Dear Sisters of St. Hildegard of Bingen,

I am married with two teenage children. I'm 42 years old. Today I got thinking that I'm like a religious Sister, working and praying through each day in a big cycle that seems ridiculously endless. But then I don't know too much about nuns.

Last week I drove to the south shore of Massachusetts and passed through the town of Weymouth. It wasn't really on my way anywhere. I stopped at Tom's Feed & Seed. Maybe what I need is another bird feeder, I said to myself. I left with one suet and two nyjer feeders and a book called Sister Bird's Small Guide to Small Birds.

Then this morning I brought the kids to school. Left there and drove over to the Quabbin Reservoir near where I live, and sat. Turned the car off. Turned the car on. Turned it off again.

The feeders and book were still on the front seat floor. I read the section "About the Finches" and then looked at the last page of the book:

The Sisters of Saint Hildegard of Bingen invite you to write us at Saint Hildegard Monastery, Plover Point, Weymouth, MA. We gladly respond to questions about the life of birds and/or the life of faith.

I'm writing this note now from my minivan, on the paper bag. So I wanted to ask about a couple of things—maybe my new interest in Catholic things is a calling? I'm a Baptist, so I'm not sure. And I have questions: Is there really birdwatching at the monastery? And, what do I do about my husband?

Maybe you can write to me. I'd like to know these things, other things, important things. Things about your monastery and how you live your lives. Maybe one day I could visit your little place in the world. I've always liked Gregorian chants.

Thank you,
Miriam

By Way of Introduction

7 April 2003
Feastday of St. Brynach

Dear Miriam,

Mother Lourdes, our Prioress, asked me to write to you.

First, I would like to respond to the questions you asked: In regard to the note, *Is there really birdwatching in the monastery?* Yes, there is birdwatching at monasteries. Well, at least, *our* monastery. I thought I would address that question first as you seemed ever so concerned.

Here, at our community of the Sisters of Saint Hildegard of Bingen (Bings, some call us), we have a small parcel of land: a meadow surrounded by marsh grasses on the edge of a mudflat, and many birds enjoy their stay here, and they flock to our statue of Saint Francis, unofficial patron saint of birds. I think it worth taking vows if only to come to our tiny nature reserve, and commune with Saint Francis and the singular egret or heron who visit our bayside garden and mudflats.

As to your other question: *What do I do about my husband?* This is probably your main question, and a troubling one. The question, maybe, entailed in your turning the car off, turning it on, not knowing what to do. I can't imagine that it is so simple as the annoying habit of balled-up socks flung under the bed that one must retrieve? Or the washing of dishes, or dutiful prayer for the soul of the one entrusted to your care? Is there more you might like to tell me of the shape of your life?

At various and frequent points in our lives we all necessarily question our places in the world. *Go. Stay. Wait. Get a bird feeder. Find a good book. Patience.* All of these speak to us at different times.

Though our lives are devoted wholly to Christ, we Sisters also are learning to live intimately. Waiting. Doing. Sometimes questioning our place in the world. Here we are all given, along with our rhythm of prayer and our lives of devotion, works that we must do to share in the life of the monastery. And dishes, as our Sister Anne will tell you, is her spiritual service, along with prayer.

And those balled-up socks under the bed, well, Sister Patrick Gertrude will convey, with a sigh that lets you know she's interested more in the *clean* part of *cleaning*, that this forms her myriad trials. She is the hunter and gatherer of laundry for our community—who, though given a heightened sense of smell from our Gracious Lord, has also been tested to the utmost in this matter.

Though birdwatching is an activity some of us take great joy in, it cannot be the bulk of our days. But Sister Bird (your first friend in this religious community) is the one whose occupation is all things ornithological. You may be familiar with her popular book, *Sister Bird's Bird Guide to New England Shore Birds: A Book for Birders.* (Might she have fit in one more *bird*?)

And as you have interest in our life here, you'll want to be introduced to Sister Farm, too. We call her this, though her full spiritual name is Sister Burgundofara, after the French saint. (You can see the necessity of a moniker.) She tends to the land here. If you are starting from the bayside in, there's the water, then the marsh grasses, then a wide stretch of grass, then the monastery garden, then a little henhouse & barn.

Here, Sister Farm tends to the 2 cows (Jerseys), and 30 hens (Buff Orpingtons), 7 Icelandic sheep, and one corpulent pig (of questionable origin). She daily tests the patience of Sister Patrick Gertrude, whose olfactory system takes offense to all matters farm.

Along with our work is the life of contemplative prayer—offering a listening spirit to God. We spend many hours in the stone chambers of our chapel, chanting the psalms and hearing the birds respond in kind from the outside. Praying with our small sisters, the birds, draws a heart close to our Lord as we watch the creatures live in simple praise.

With hopes that this letter finds you also watching your friends the birds, and, too, that your spirit finds a way to the place of peace in your heart that your letter suggests is your deep desire. (And with hopes that this letter attends to your other questions about monastic life.)

Yours,
Sister Athanasius, OSHB

20 April 2003

Dear Miriam,

That's the way it is in the world, isn't it? Your letter says so, exactly: *nervous, busy, lost, turned-about, people, children, spouses wanting to find understanding with each other, though only able to hurt themselves and each other with a series of quick sparks.*

You write how you struggle daily with this. Here, so quiet a monastery along the bay, with the unseen lapping of the incoming tide—we bring ourselves to connection with the world. We are away from the world, but we are not away. We experience the same struggles in a different context.

Sister Farm, as your letter inquired, struggles with this especially, finding the little barn to be her *true* altar, her joyous and quiet sacrifice to God and his scurrying and snorting and thick-uddered creatures.

But when she comes from her sanctuary of holy work to the chapel to pray what we call the Office, or the Hours, she sits next to Sr. Patrick Gertrude. Perhaps this seating arrangement is our Prioress's reminder to us that we may have our ecstatic smells or barnyard joys, but we must meet the other in the real world. The world where our habits rest inches from the other at prayer or sometimes touch, even when we cannot bear to offer each other the sign of peace, when we want our real peace to be somewhere else (me with my rambling thoughts or my pen) in this layered and prominent thing called Life With Others.

And so it is with you. And so it is with us as well.

And we attend to prayer. And we notice the way that the world shifts around us and shifts us around in it.

But, Miriam, come away from your troubles with me a moment with this: 2 darting, fast-winged killdeer flutter of a life surprised. And the snowy egret, a Holy Ghost presence, as I think of it (only showing up at divine whim and hardly when you'd expect it) comes to the bay infrequently but gracefully. And our hearts are warmed at the sight of this bird, who knows something of spiritual attention, inventiveness, and zig-zagging surprise.

Miriam, your last letter was dear, telling me of your days (oh, that constant rain!), your heart, your children, your husband, Franklin (and that awful flood in your basement)—and, of course, who wouldn't have a fight over a broken sump pump? Indeed, I would. That sort of pressure demands a good snarl between partners. I trust that all has worked itself out, that the sump is in place and that you had a lovely time of making up. In my early years and impassioned relationships, I knew the heat and dread and fire and fury of a good emotional brawl. And, too, the quiet grace of regained affection.

On another note, please do not apologize about short letters. You surely have little time, but I am glad that you say you enjoy my letters. But be forewarned: the others in the monastery—especially Sister Farm who likes a short sentence—find my parentheticals and asides and commas a sore distress. So you are brave, my dear, to read through all the loops and endure the commas.

Fondly,
Sister Athanasius

PS You asked about our habits. What color are they? Well, I'd like to say they look like Capuchin habits, after which cappuccino was named. Wouldn't that be lovely and decadent, to have a coffee-colored habit? Alas, our habits are what one might call *workman blue:* the color of mechanics coveralls or the blue of heavy industry work pants. It's not the prettiest of the habits, yet they are functional. And as I have been strictly disallowing myself coffee now for 8 years, 2 months, and 3 days, it's probably better that our habits do not serve as a call toward temptation. Sure defeat, it would be, to see a sea of coffee color every day.

5 May 2003

Miriam, dear—

A third letter from you. Surely we have entered into what can only be called in the old fashioned term, *a correspondence.* And I am a happy recipient of your letters.

I know what you mean, about the poets, the way that they remind you of the monastic life. And I wonder if we experience the poets trying to speak to ineffable things. And at the monastery, petty though I can find myself in a day, and troubled and lost and angry, the desire is toward ineffable things as well. And so I have discovered that you are a reader, and wish to hear what books form the piles you have on your end table.

My own readings show my interest in others' experience of the monastic life and why and how so many stay. And why some have felt compelled to leave. The Sisters here often accuse me of a talent toward the dark side. But books about struggle on levels spiritual and emotional are sobering and important books as well. They are like our occasional hawks or barn owls, calling into the night, giving voice or circling round the currents of the air. It's of little spiritual use to turn away from darker pictures in our lives, as they, too, tell the truth of it.

Here, I will continue, Miriam, with my little notes about the new friends you have taken interest in. There is Little Sister, also known as Sister Walburga, our youngest Sister (39) and our bossiest head of kitchen & bakery to date. After Matins, she enters the sacristy of the kitchen and barks outright a sentence of panic and demand, such as, "There *better* be enough eggs and flour in my kitchen"—as though the flour weren't in the pantry (in 50 lb. bags) and the eggs weren't within minutes of coming, as Sister Farm always leaves Matins to get the hens' morning offerings. Soon, though, Little Sister un-panics herself and settles into quotidian tasks. I believe she is a Sister with a private secret. But I can't guess what it is, or of what nature. As Sister Farm says about her, "She's like a poker player. She holds her cards tight and close."

You asked about what you called the "tiff" between Sisters Patrick Gertrude and Farm. Mentioning it within our community brings us either to high humor or to conflicted hearts. Sister Anne, the oldest here, despite frailty, her slips and falls, her knotting of the knees, her agonizingly slow progress down the hallways, often removes herself to the chapel, with quiet clicks of her rosary beads and supplication for the complexity of this tumult.

As our sacristan, Sister Patrick Gertrude has responsibility for preparing the chapel for prayer: flowers, vestments, books, candles, rubrics. One Lenten season, after her work, she began contemplating the passion and burial of Jesus and the burial spices enwrapping him in that dark stone tomb. Her olfactory gift came, full with tones and nuances. The trouble comes with a henhouse and adjoining bright red barn.

The barn hosts a variety of creaturely smells from its stalls and spaces: one stall reserved for a donkey, which despite Sister Farm's best efforts still hasn't found its way here. The others house sheep (for cheese and loveliest of wools), and one portly pig, which Sister Farm bought with the consideration toward food, but a poetic sensibility has settled upon us all and we think her RADIANT in the spirit of *Charlotte's Web*, so there will be no pork.

One day Sister Farm came to the laundry room to rid herself of the day's barn smells, just at the point when Sister Patrick Gertrude had shined and cleaned and rid the broad white room of odors other than the righteous ones. So a farmer's boots filled with muck, and straw sticking to the muck, and her blue coveralls that Sister Farm wears for work, which often reek not only of cigars and hog air and sheep but also of bodily odor for which she is renowned—and which she quickly corrects but not before she leaves her clothes at the drop-off point at the white tiles of the laundry room.

When two people have equal and opposite callings from Our Lord, a simple resolution seems distant, doesn't it, Miriam?

And now I have surely scared you off curiosity of the religious life. Still, whatever it is, this monastery is a real one, real spirit, real days, real wars, real faith. If you do visit at some point, know that we have 2 rooms that form our very small guesthouse. Sister Patrick Gertrude, along with being sacristan and cleaner and laundress, also attends to the details of the guest-house, so you will find the cut flowers of the season (now, daffodils from the garden), clean comfortable chairs, bookshelves, and icons in the corners.

Please do visit at some point, Miriam. There is no wife or mother or nurse (and you are all three!) who does not need at least a short retreat to unglue her soul from the pressing stages of life. Know that you are welcome to make a retreat here. A life can often feel covered by a wash of crises: watching your husband withholding a deep part of himself, watching children in newfound teen independence that comes disguised as anarchy. But still, I believe—am hopeful—that love is there, too, in crises, disguised or not, as it is in all of us.

Yours,
Sr. Athanasius

22 May 2003

My Dear,

You have written to me again. What delight.

First, as I know your heart beats a little faster at their mention: the birds. Our winged friends over the last months have been in full migrating pattern. Though we always see brants & eiders, grebes and gulls, this year we've had some other visitors, among them an alder flycatcher, a mourning warbler, and woodcocks, who are full of flight and sound and wild presence in mating season, and then retreat, shyly, who knows where.

And the red-throated loons with their sheeny throats lined with pinks seem thoughtful gifts of our Lord to us throughout this season.

I am writing late at night, after prayer, which brought me such unrest in my earnest petitions that I thought a cup of tea and a short letter to you might be the other form of prayer that brings peace.

I often think of young mothers, when babies voice their concerns in the deepest night, the way they drag their motherselves to their feet at 3 a.m. to quiet their young. And once, having attended to them, discover they cannot fall back to sleep, so soon the dawn comes and the house calls back into the rhythms of the day.

It is often the same, as I imagine it, with the late-night calls to prayer, which have such urgencies to be answered. Tonight, it was prayers for my dear Aunt Lorie who has had a stroke, and I feel so far distant from this woman who lives in London—the woman who introduced me to Emily Dickinson, Barton's Almond Kisses, and my first cup of coffee. Great unrest has kept my thoughts anxious and my heart displaced. Though sometimes we are given permission to go to be with friends or relatives, Mother Lourdes asked that I remain here. I know that finances are much to do with it: the farm, expenses. And try to make my peace with it. Still, not being there in person has its own weight.

These last nights I've asked for dispensation to remove myself to the chapel, praying that our Heavenly Father would bring peace to my aunt's heart and body, as well as to all who diligently seek God, but feel as though they can never, quite, find him.

Often as not another soul is in the chapel, hard at spiritual work in late nights: Sister Anne. You wonder, with a body so crooked, how she can adjust the laws of physics to stand, to walk. Still, slowly, painfully, she does. (Miriam, let's each resolve to have an extra glass of milk daily, shall we?)

Part of my work, along with secretarial work for Mother Lourdes, is caring for the needs of Sister Anne. But in the chapel, I always feel like she needs no aides, where she knows prayer to be true comfort, true bread. I sometimes watch as with a mystery, this life nearby that is like the poets you mention, speaking toward the ineffable.

Miriam, in some ways I am tempted to intimate that a cloistered life of unceasing prayer combined with the rhythms of work mix to create a "holiness." But, except for Sister Anne's journey, there are no such intimations to make. Early on, I had lingering hopes that the monastery fostered such grand things, and solved all manner of spiritual conundrums. Now, I think that perhaps the only thing the monastery solves is vocation: that is, if one is called here and one consents to follow that call, *wills* to follow that call, then a Sister is in a good place to form herself toward a certain spiritual work (whether or not we attend to that formation remains quite in the interior chambers of each Sister's spirit).

I've gotten so serious so suddenly. Perhaps late-night sorrows call for things serious, quiet, reflective? And though it has its turn, there should be a little fun in a letter, shouldn't there be? Then you will appreciate this exchange between Sister Patrick

Gertrude and Sister Farm earlier today. Dropping chunklets of manure from her boots in the mudroom, with Sister Patrick Gertrude looking on, Sister Farm said to her without looking up, "What?"

"Can any good come from that barn?"

"That's what they said about Nazareth," Sister Farm returned.

Miriam, I take cheer in knowing that the temptations that our own Lord faced were, as one of the biblical epistles says, *like unto our own.* And I like that we are being human right along with God's own Son, the Good that came from Nazareth.

And my own struggles ebb and flow, but still, the fact is, I myself am trying to be without coffee—yet vicariously enjoying yours along with you, as I think of you having a morning coffee when you write me a letter. If you're not a coffee drinker, Miriam, now would not be the best time to tell me.

Grateful for your letters, always,

Sr. Athanasius

5 June 2003

Miriam dear—

I have taken to slipping into late hours and with the all-day rains there have been clouds, so even the moon is no company tonight.

Sister Anne said something to me this morning, as I was pouring her a coffee in her Boston Red Sox mug, as I looked over her shoulder in the kitchen, looking at the *Boston Globe* sports section, listening to her early morning hums about baseball and such. Then she said to me, turning around, "It sounds basic, I know, but God's mercy and God's direction for each of us on our various paths are not given to limit us, but to offer sure footing." Then she turned back to the sports page, took a vigorous slurp of her coffee and said, "Let's hope this is a good, good year for our Red Sox."

No matter how many years I've lived the vowed life, I often feel like I am losing my footing. But maybe lost footing, Miriam, is a way to find the truth of our place in the world and with God? Maybe the result is simply finding a better ledge in the climb? Often when Sister Anne says something like this, it comes to me like Jesus' disciples after he told a parable. It was a story or teaching that always seemed appropriate, they just never knew quite how.

Do you remember when you wrote me asking about the vowed life? Perhaps the most appealing thing, after all, is birdwatching when you see Sister Bird go out after the prayer hour of Lauds (our second prayer hour, at 7:30) with her looking glasses and notebooks and guidebooks—what a rich little trail of enthusiasms she is.

And you, too, in the morning—I picture you at that oak table you told me about, looking at your sunny walls or out your picture window to some maples or sassafras or red pines nearby, a spot of dry dirt near your long driveway where the sparrows enjoy a dusty bath. Sister Farm can't abide house sparrows, those ruinous tenants near gardens and farms, but I like them, because they take comfort in living near people.

And with bird comments, I sign off.

Yours as ever,

Sister Athanasius

5 July 2003

Dear Miriam—

You wrote to me some weeks ago, wondering how one goes about the soul's journey. The phrase has stayed with me, and now I am revisiting your paragraph that introduced it:

> *Some days after working the night shift in the hospital, then at home, early morning, waiting to have a coffee (yes, I do drink coffee!) with Franklin, hearing him in the bathroom, clearing his throat, brushing, spitting. I wonder how the soul goes on a deep journey, when it feels like we are just in a regular tiring day.*

Today I am thinking more about this, watching Sister Anne wisp around, holding on to a walker. No one can bear to lose her—as some monasteries do—to such places as Our Sisters of St. Benedict Home (a rest home for old nuns mostly overfond of swearing, it seems). Mother Lourdes has a decided soft spot for anyone over eighty and Sister Anne stays. So, in her staying, and over the years, Sister Anne not only is my charge as she struggles with the excesses of age: swelling legs, enlarging bone spurs at each joint. Sister Anne is also my mentor, who taught me that *not* attending to spiritual work—once you've discovered what that work is—is to fall away from one's best knowledge.

She once told me how she attends to the days. In the dark early morning, as she dresses for Matins, our earliest prayer hour, she says to herself: "There is a quiet place for your soul at any given time of day, enter that quiet place as you work, walk, wait, and pray. It is all the Lord's presence. It can all be prayer." Miriam, do you know that little note in the Gospels about the poor widow who "did what she could?" That, too, is how I think Sister Anne holds her daily portion.

She begins with the first thing, the linens, the wool socks, the orthopedic shoes, which I make sure are near her bed. Then she shifts out of her bed, sits at the edge, hoists herself up and "begins in the quiet place."

Oh, I am led astray from my original thoughts, responding to your comment about the spiritual journey, but I am thinking that maybe Sister Anne speaks to it?

I have a great overfondness for little maxims, and keep a list of what I call Loose Rules, numbered and written in a notebook, my way of understanding things of a spiritual nature. One of my earliest (and I like to think most poetic) is Loose Rule #2: *The plovers know the holy as sand and small stones and a nest in their care.*

Sometimes a Loose Rule is discarded, when it doesn't hold up over time, or if I mention it to Sister Farm, who then fails to grasp any wisdom in it at all. But this one, despite Sister

Farm's insistence that LR#2 takes "too much time trying to say something easy," holds up. So perhaps you will find, too, that it speaks to the bond of what feels so much like daily life meeting the spiritual life.

And so go my letters, Miriam. And I am grateful that you take time in your busy schedule of night shifts and your "tired to the bones" self to correspond—what treasure to receive another letter written from your minivan—a very different road trip letter than the first you sent. Turning the car off, and on, and off. Which must pain you in its very memory.

And here you wrote, when you look for understanding, you look to the birds, as "maybe the birds tell all the truth of God." And so it is that I'll end my note on your own note about God. And I will go to sleep, and then seek to "begin the new day in that quiet place," as I know you do, too.

With fondness,
Sr. Athanasius

12 July 2003

Miriam, dear—

I am prone to ponder things of complexity and import, but then don't have the intellectual heft to do much of anything with it, like write a book on ethics or a philosophical tome. Within this religious community I sometimes feel how noticeable it is, each Sister with such a sense of a trade, an occupation. But I sometimes see myself as a filler.

Do you think, Miriam—as I have been considering this all day—that there is such a thing as holy stealing? Maybe all stealing has at the root a holy desire?

We all feel we need to own things—obtain things. Some of the great literatures of spiritual insight suggest this: Jean Valjean, stealing for bread. Though it was not according to God's holy law, still—and I have been accused of slippery theology and apostasy both—there's something hungry and true in the things we try to claim. The facts of it seem all wrong, but there's something right about it.

Perhaps someone steals someone else's identity to gain freedom in another country, running from political and religious persecution. This may be a holy stealing. And your daughter, stealing some CDs—as you wrote in your previous letter, so tired and sad it sounded. Maybe that is too? Looking for something to fill this space called adolescence?

I've got a little of that in me, too. A personal story, a stolen pea-green Berkeley edition of the Bible put out by the American Bible Society. It has been with me ever since I stole it. And to make matters spiritually worse, it was stolen from a missionary Sister in Venezuela, where I helped on a building project—all of us Sisters handing cement blocks down the line to Hermana Maria Natividad, who buttered the bricks and lined them up with a yellow plumb line. And nearby we heard the sounds from a local baseball stadium (which was one reason Sister Anne came along) that offered us a sense of the familiar, and another common bond. And in all that, I lifted Holy Writ.

And I felt wicked in the stealing from the Sisters. And, too, I have been grateful ever since to have a tiny book of the words of the Epistles of the apostles with me. And the words of Jesus, in the deeply inked red of the Gospel passages.

We are looking for something to fill our pockets. So maybe the stealings aren't holy in themselves, but seek to fill a hungry place within. What do you think, Miriam? What do you think for your daughter, who must be something extraordinary, to claim your heart and emotions in this way.

I learned a lovely word today: *lacunae*—the empty places in ourselves, these are the places these stealings hopefully will fill.

(late afternoon)

As simply as the clock flips over into the next hour or as easily as our prayers go from Vespers one hour to Compline the next, Sisters Farm and Patrick Gertrude continue at each other. Usually in a smolder, but sometimes toward a burn.

During Terce, in chanting the psalms, Sister Patrick Gertrude found great gusto for the imprecatory psalm, chanting with a little violence:

> . . . Dash the heads of mine enemies against the rocks by the waters. Let none of them prosper and your name, O God, be praised.
>
> The wicked have defiled your dwelling place, O Lord, defiled all the meeting places of thy people, O Lord. How long, O Lord, how long?
>
> Why do you withdraw your hand from me, even take your hand out of your bosom and destroy them.

Here, on one of those simple July days where the smells of the honeysuckle come around each corner and float along each bush mingled with the distinct smell of sun ripening the air and, too, the common smells of the life of the barn meet here on our little spit of land, both Sisters work heartily as unto the Lord and both are unable to rescue a softness for the situation.

After Terce, Sister Farm came alongside her and said, "I will remind you, Sister Patrick Gertrude, that our good Lord's first honorable dwelling and place of birth was a *stable*: donkeys, sheep. Onlooking animals. Yup," she said. As though that would suffice to quiet Sister Patrick Gertrude with this new insight as to the barn actually being a holy of holies.

And as you might expect of Sisters, someone must be in charge. Mother Lourdes, our Prioress, asked both Sisters into her office. And the sound that tears make reached the whole monastery, followed by quiet, heavy, and serious tones, then a red-eyed exit of the two Sisters. Then the serene and gray face of Mother Lourdes, coming after.

Sister Farm marked a barn-ripe path to her cell. Sister Patrick Gertrude to hers. Each, we were told, was to maintain silence. (Akin to any mother saying to a child: "If you can't say anything nice, don't say anything at all," I suppose).

Of course, into Lauds the next day, then Vespers—by the time we reached Compline we'd chanted at least three deprecatory psalms, and I was, in my own spirit, at war with these words.

A friend of mine, who is not part of a religious community, confessed to me when she came to our guesthouse and sat with us in our chapel as we chanted three psalms, read a Gospel passage and blessing, along with our bowing down before heaven at the *Glory Be's* where all of us find ourselves humbled and low, my friend said when she heard those psalms of righteous demolition, she considered them differently: "I think it's not so much that we want others to be dashed against the rocks of the shore as much as that we want God to raise *us* up from the rocks on the shore—to see our attempts at rightness and acknowledge us."

So I wondered if Mother Lourdes saw the irony of our fixed-hour prayers and the psalms of blood guilt in excess these days.

As you know, when entering an Order, we choose a new spiritual name, a saint's name that we hold near to us, a patron saint we hope to emulate or share some spiritually handed down gift with, a mantle.

So it's appropriate—in a hopeful way—that Mother Lourdes's name reflects the healing power of our Blessed Lady's appearance at Lourdes. We seem to be in need of a miracle, here caught between a barn, a laundry room, the psalms, and ourselves.

And so I will end this letter for now, Miriam dear, and wish you God's blessings and a little less tumult in our own house of dwelling.

Yours ever,
Sister Athanasius

PS Occasional quick-winged killdeer, good company along the bay these days. And the infrequent—but glorious—sight of the little blue heron in its white juvenile stage—of quiet disposition—who appears at low tide in the later hours, waiting in motionless quiet until quickly and respectfully attending to the evening schools of fish. I sometimes think of the quiet before and after the fish snack as grateful quiet prayers for the meal, the death of the fish, so that the noble member of the heron tribe may live. Even if it's not a prayer of thanks, it looks like one.

And there is the bird note for this week, and I will sign off with prayers for you and your daughter, both doing good spiritual work, in your different ways.

13 July 2003

Dear Miriam—

And now we know the cause of your tiredness. A new affront has come. In your letter (which I received as I went to mail my last letter) you wrote about Franklin's comment: "Miriam, he said, you look bad and you are acting worse. No one can make you happy. I'll fight you some more, if you want, but scooch over and give a kiss before the next round." And just with that, a moment after, the doctor's call.

Cancer.

I don't know what to write, wanting to say something of comfort, but of course, offering comfort would be false to what is going on, wouldn't it? But, Miriam, know that we will share your days with you, in prayers for healing and we are in the struggle with you. A strange feeling, isn't it, to see those around you who are well? For the ill inhabit a different wisdom, a thinner, decidedly aware, place. As I watch Sister Anne, she doesn't acknowledge the strangeness of illness, the way it separates her from others, the ones who are The Well. I think the surprise for me is that she treats her illness with a vibrancy that doesn't shimmer off or slow, even when she is failing.

But I often think that illness is like some small piece of your soul constantly gnawed on.

In a previous letter I wrote about the psalms, how they can excite, inflate, and then ease the heart—like you have said that your minivan, when you need it, houses a good cry or yell or scream. One of the psalms we prayed at None today—*Contend O Lord, with my contenders; war against that which wars against me*—rouses to both hope and anger, a sort of bleeding prayer to set things aright.

In this monastery there is little screaming, but Miriam, oh, screaming must be done. For me, the psalms, no matter how quietly I pray them, house my anger, my dread, my most awful moments. The psalms are my steam shop, which maybe is the one thing that allows us here to live in community with illness and hostilities and secrets and subtle wounds. They form the private interior place of great yellings at God.

Yours in dismay and prayer,
Sr. A—

PS Thinking it's better to end a letter with birds and prayer rather than dismay and prayer, so here's a note about Sister Bird's birdwatch this week: among the counted & noted are common loons, double-crested cormorants—with their ancient way of drying their wings, spread full out to the wind and sun—and osprey and American oystercatchers.

22 July 2003

Miriam dear,

I just received your letter, and now am sitting in the monastery garden near our statue of Saint Francis for a time of prayer, a conversation with the chipping sparrows (who are noisy and opinionated today), and, of course, a letter to you.

The breeze coming off from the slow tidal waters on the bay troubles the American elder shrubs nearby, and this afternoon has turned into a combined onrush of noise, salt, air wafts, and the quiet presence of Saint Francis in his stone-gray garb even as his cross, his Bible, his shoes, and his little bird creatures are.

And how are you, my dear? Your note was so quiet about your health; does that mean good news or waiting or resign? Know that prayers here continue, where the Sisters do not allow the face of God to look away, so constant are they. And you are writing, each letter written in short slices out of time, which you have taken to quiet your heart from the sometimes "grinding gears," as you describe it, of family life and work as a nurse, the frenzied carrying of others' burdens.

Know that every letter, Miriam, is a true gift. Appreciated and pondered.

Your note about coffee had me in stitches, you've got quite the sense of humor. Yes, now the numbers are added up and I have not been drinking coffee now for 8 years, 5 months, and 5 days. I'm told that if I went to a group like AA—or in this case, CA—I'd at least get a button and applause and a "Hello, Sister Athanasius" in chorus for my efforts. But no button, no applause. Though I fancy a sort of celebratory someday when the Sisters celebrate each other's efforts at overcoming great obstacles or learning to live with loss and finding great grace. Our triumphs are so quiet here, unnoticed. But here, now, I am hoping in the way one hopes vicariously, that you, my dear, brew a nice strong fully caffeinated mug with painted flowers or maybe green and yellow polka dots, and take one sip, then read a few lines of my letter until another sip calls your name. And so on.

Sister Patrick Gertrude noticed my caffeine joys, the coffee early and coffee late, and then early again. She notices things keenly, which makes her an excellent sacristan, of course, attending to humble details. And gifts offer, along with virtue, one's sorest vice, in direct tension. I know she thinks me weak and wished to make me, no doubt, spiritually rugged (but I rather pity the poor things—weaknesses—don't you?). Still, the longer view is discipline and when called into Mother Lourdes' office, she cleared the matter with a few decades of the rosary for me and an administrative cut to my craving, calling for the cessation of coffee entirely, "for your spiritual aid and physical well-being," she said.

My being overfond of the drink and overeager to find my way to coffee before a prayer hour, Mother Lourdes was wise in the decision.

Leadership is a tricky thing. In the Saint Hildegard of Bingen (Bing) tradition, balance within the hard spiritual work is sought so as not to diminish a Sister's spiritual joy. It is less about power than about proper adaptation to challenges.

When Little Sister came to us 5 years ago and sat under the tutelage of Sister Anne, the director of novices at the time, they had a lesson in dogmatics, some theological obfuscation that didn't make theological sense to either of them. When Little Sister insisted, "I'm sorry, Sister Anne, but my accepting this as the only truth is about as likely as Sister Farm learning how to cook. It just won't happen." She never went into detail about the precise issue, but she did say that Sister Anne responded with a grateful sigh. "Well then, why don't we set the Bull Cantate Domino of Pope Eugene IV aside and return to it if ever we feel it merits another visitation?"

What have I written to you of Little Sister? I keep expecting that you are familiar with all the Sisters, but perhaps you would like to know that Little Sister is the tiniest nun I've ever seen (for some reason, the religious life seems full up with pint-sized Sisters). She's cook and baker, both. Her baked goods are sold under the company name Bings Monastery Bakery, and they sell locally to cafes and restaurants: layered cookies, pastries, and specialty breads. She also teaches the occasional baking and pastry arts course at Johnson & Wales, a food school in Rhode Island. And though our Sister is unusually immaterial when it comes to the body, when she is in the kitchen or in front of a class, she looks like Stuart Little but presents like the apostle Paul, who became the roaring voice of the early church.

Most late mornings, who knows if it's the baking or preparing lunch, but Little Sister is fed up with anyone who might cross the threshold into the kitchen/bakery. "Out. Now," she'll say with a very convincing tone for one so small. And anyone who might be there or passing through, shuffles respectfully, and a little fearfully, out. Or if someone in the kitchen is talking and going on about something, she'll say, "Oh, blah, blah, blah," which effectively lets anyone know she has little use for conversations of any length. (Usually me, I'm afraid.)

And as we are speaking of the smaller of our friends, I will close on a bird note. An orchard oriole was discovered near the garden and all Sisterly eyes have been following him along the tops of the fruit trees, along one of our three trails to the water. A treat, Miriam, for your day. And I, in turn, am wondering what sorts of bird-creatures are visiting your various feeders, as you watch them from the oak table of a July morning.

Hellos to Franklin. Tell him all the Sisters give a good Catholic wave his direction. And Little Sister (don't tell him this) has planned to send a package of her macaroons to your house for him, since you mentioned his sweet tooth. She will insist that he not share (but I think it might be worth a snitch on your part).

Yours, Sr. A.—

(3 August 2003)

This letter grows as I add dates and additional lines.

Lunch is our silent meal, for spiritual reading and for prayer. But to evening meals in the refectory I sometimes bring your letters, to read portions (the bird news, which Sister Bird insists upon, and health updates, which all ask to know). All are concerned to pray for you and Franklin and your children, who must feel that sense of fear and distance that cancer brings. I can imagine, as you write, that with Brendan, in his summer college program, the distance seems horrible. And your daughter, Emily, trying to find her place in the world, just when she is trying to appeal to independence, feeling torn to push off from the shore, and trying to come close, but only in stealth, as though to come too close would be to fail in something.

Thinking about your children, and your note about feeling old: I have witnessed Sister Anne's coming into old age, though never known her to seem old in spirit. And myself witnessing these odd seventy years (hush now, don't even think what you are thinking, Miriam—that I am in the elderly way myself). I recall that at 20, thirty seemed old, at 40, fifty seemed old. Then at seventy, only 110 seems at all old.

Still, these days, worn down at 85 years—the same amount of years, she reminds me, that the Red Sox have not won a World Series—"Who wouldn't be a little worn?" she asks. "I was born into a world of hope: three months after the Sox won the World Series in 1918. Who wouldn't live with a lot of hope when they won in '15 and '16 too? Every year they have my hopes. But this one could be the year. The season has two determinative months yet."

Miriam, of all the Sisters I would like for you to meet in person, our Sister Anne is the one who would speak to your kind heart. To see her advance from her cell in the cloister to the monastery is to observe a three-sheets-to-the-wind way about her. Mother Lourdes has insisted lately that Sister Anne hasten down hallways using a rolling walker, which she only agreed to since she felt she wouldn't need me as much, but I am always one ear toward the sounds of the walker banging into walls (better her walker than her), watching out for her.

Other than the Red Sox, her passionate work is prayer up the hall and prayer down the hall. Prayer for Miriam and Franklin, prayer for our Father Martinez, for each of the Sisters. Prayer for the news of the world and the news and people of our hometown. Even though she starts with the sports section, she always finds some little story that bends her heart in sorrow, and will pray for some stranger lost in the world, in some extreme circumstance. I sometimes wonder if the clunking down the hallway, the little run-ins with walls, are her way of trying to rush up God for response. As though God were the hallway walls she were walking between, as though each hit to the walls sufficed as a kick in the divine shins.

Almost forgetting: Birdwatch. Today the egret has claimed the marsh grasses and only seems to share with the starlings. Usually at low tide, the egret shows a great fondness for fishing in and around the edges where mud meets water and the brave shoots of marsh grass climb higher as summer progresses.

Sister Bird piles up her field guides 4-high on one of our 5 benches/ tables/observation points near the bay. Keeps her years-old red plaid coffee thermos with red plastic cup-top at the ready. You may be too young to remember these old thermos bottles, but I've always had great fondness for them (and not only because they hold that divine liquid). They are reminiscent of our family outings to the Boston city beaches, picnics in the early mornings, or oh, just anywhere.

Sister Bird keeps vigil. Wool square over her knees even in summer. In cold weather, gloves with fingers cut off. Like a hunter at a salt lick, she waits. Her Bausch and Lomb binoculars (*binos,* she calls them) have been with her since the seventies. Her journal and watercolors marking the birds, coloring, numbers, habits. And her daily field card for Massachusetts.

Our Sister Bird consults with both the Cornell Lab of Ornithology and the Mass Audubon and sanctuaries. She's a keen observer, but a wash when it comes to watercolor sketches. Still, she keeps accurate count—like umpires at baseball games—clicking off the number of herring gulls or redwing blackbirds, catbirds or grackles sighted on the wing. But her counter is her rosary: immediate, nearby, handy for quick counts.

Miriam, you will be glad to know the mandated 3 week silence between Sister Farm and Sister Patrick Gertrude is over. There's little to report, as what could I have reported: a cold shoulder? a disapproving glare? all manner of twistings of the human frame to show distinct disregard. Still, it's more cheerful to have their words sounded out once again. Little Sister made a celebratory meal, with a heavy accent on cream sauces and desserts, petit fours and a 3-chocolate mousse, whose smell covered all other smells to everyone's satisfaction. She has a surprising path to conciliation, that, employed, always brings a contentment to community life. We don't often indulge in the sweets she bakes, but when we do, a kind of hum pervades—ah, the mysterious gifts of the cocoa bean and the bakery.

Sister Bird, along with counting the northern mockingbird or the chipping sparrows, has taken to using her rosary to also keep track of in-house strikes & outs in the game of Sister Farm and Sister Patrick Gertrude. Her own system of managing to keep tabs on this game: a thin stare in the choir, between breath and chant and kneeling, that Sister Patrick Gertrude directed toward Sister Farm; there next to her, the perceptible click of the rosary, which was not Sister Bird's way of keeping track of the verses of psalms. Maybe a nervous habit she brings in from the bay. Without anything to count, she creates something.

Well, Miriam, on to other things, shall we? Yesterday: a flick of starlings in the marsh grasses whipped up as I walked along—though I can't believe I walk fast enough to scatter or surprise any creature, still, they put on a show with their thin yellow and black bills and their shiny-flecked bodies, as though there were some metal or night sky to them.

Then, too, the usual herring gulls doing not much of anything. They strike me as being mostly on break. Double crested cormorants.

Nearer the monastery, on land side, in the sparse pines, are our warblers. We also invite horned larks, who disappear in winter, but family together come summer in their quiet, private way. And down in the marsh toward the bay, the swamp sparrow. Then, toward the monastery and the drier land, the song sparrow. And, right here, in my line of view, chipping sparrows congregate with a respectable nest and cheery call notes.

Miriam, I have been in a habit of dispensing your bird news to Sister Bird, who asks me if you saw pine siskins this past winter, and who lives near the life of your feeder: purple finches, common redpolls—even evening grosbeaks? That would be a treat, she says, looking a little like football players. According to my Ken Kaufmann *Birds of North America*, a birder has a good start if she loves birding. So, in my mind, both you and I are "in." And we have the happy company of Sister Bird, who fills in the blanks.

But I frustrate Sister Bird, as I like coming to a conclusion myself, rather than asking her for birding wisdom or migratory patterns or local fauna and seasons matching with specific species. Of course, this stubbornness translates to faith & religious community, too. Coming to a conclusion by oneself isn't the preferred monastic wisdom. It may be the key to good birding, but turns troublesome when it translates to an approach to faith or to one's unique professional work. Oh, this is my struggle of great proportion—to know the work that I am called to, and to know the spiritual life without a constant spiritual itch to test the nature of the spiritual life. These itches—none enough to gather up my habit and run, though my age would prevent any running—but they confuse and test me. And when one in a community struggles with central understandings, the ones around us do, too. Mother Lourdes not least for those who joy and sorrow in this obfuscation.

But here's another mystery. On the bay for weeks. A lone visitor. A small white heron, or egret, with yellow long bill. She comes and goes, and I take great comfort in the surprise of presence and even in the absence—because I maintain a certain hope for her return.

Perhaps a snowy egret, but with a black bill and its neck almost always long and outstretched. Too small for a great egret, too far north and too small to be a great white heron.

Well, there you have it, Miriam, questions and mysteries, all of which is to say, our lives.

Wishing you joy, friend, engaging as you do in essential questions of faith and relationships and illness and health and birds and seasons.

Yours,
Sr. A—

(next day)

Miriam, as I neglected to mention in my writing yesterday, the poem you sent me last week spoke exactly to the interior struggle of questioning and humility that I have pondered so often. These lines from Linda Gregg:

> . . . a hunger for order,
> but a thirst against.

I suppose our little cosmology here is the living, breathing version of those lines of the poem.

Our noon meal—often a light meat like chicken in herbs, boiled potatoes, and a salad of assorted colors and greens and tastes—is eaten in silence. During this time, we have a Table Reading, when one of the Sisters, now Sister Patrick Gertrude, reads to us from a set of short spiritual biographies. Today, it is about the life of Brother Lawrence, who wrote the thin classic *The Practice of the Presence of God.* Do you know it? Might I recommend it as a worthy addition to the knapsack of the spiritual journey? The book packs light and has simple key ideas toward spiritual contentment. Lesser things can be said about other books. This one attains to things important on looking for life lived in God during the daily rounds of pots & pans, of the quotidian chores. But if physical work is not also the spiritual life, then it's a narrow faith we keep. As Sister Anne said to me once, "Knowing God in each moment simply raises that moment."

There's something to hearing words about living faith read aloud to the clicks of forks and spoons, the sound of pouring water that makes me see the words as practical and true, as though my heart were enlarged to it, so quiet and profound it seems, punctuated by the sounds of living in earnest.

15 August 2003

Miriam, dear—

I reread your letter. How brave even your anger looks, and righteous. And how large the task of living daily between work and tiredness and the touch-and-go of children pulling away for independence and drawing near unexpectedly. It's as though motherhood and family life were a tide, isn't it? Your Emily standing on the corner, at the edge of the crowd of schoolgirls, the struggle to be within her place, while being without.

And your Franklin, your note about his reading late into the night about breast cancer, books and online, there in the living room, and when you asked him, his saying, "If I study, if I understand, it's as though I could do something for you. It's my one way into the place you are. I don't want you to be alone." And your response: "Franklin, let me count the ways you have made me not alone."

"Now, don't think all mushy and cry," he said. "But"—I love your note here, —"I did anyway. And why not? If I can be angry and brave, I have the right to go mushy too."

And then you wrote:

> *How odd to have my depression of a few months ago lifted by of all things, cancer, but now to be crying all*

the time. I am mush, poor Franklin. He has this helpless calm to him, a sort of stiff upper lip that seems both unshakeable and sometimes as though he wants to swing me around, bury his face in my belly and cry. And we are that close to both of us losing it, and then he'll make me angry or I'll make him angry and we've both preserved something like distance. We've gotten close. It's this dance where we're intimate, but then we'll both do shuffle steps away. We're ridiculous most of the time, then add kids who want to be with us while pretending they want to be away and it begins to sound like a high school band. And sometimes I'm glad to go to work and be around people who are helped and those who function, like me. I am thinking about your note about sacred work, but sometimes I just like working, having it be not like anything, not connected to the spirit, just away from everything. So it's not the time for Brother Lawrence yet, but I keep meaning to ask you about how you came to be a nun, the history there, and I wish you'd write me a bit more of that, and more about the others. Franklin sometimes will sit with me, after a night shift, have coffee together, though sometimes we don't say anything, and we don't seem to remember what there is to say. But if there's a letter from you, he'll say, "So, how are your old girls?"

So, Miriam, tell your Franklin as long as he plies you with your morning coffee, there will be letters to read alongside the morning, a note with news of the "old girls." So I will write as you asked about my coming to the monastery, and that is a question I haven't even considered in years. As though it were a question one stops asking. Here, coming to a monastery, you often have a sense of laying aside your story, as the religious life becomes *the* story, as though one were rewriting history using another starting point. At first, of course, you tell your story of your calling to the director of Novices, at the initial visits and into postulancy, testing your calling. But then, from the novitiate, temporary vows, and then, final vows, the stories get quieter and quieter. A Sister walks into this new story, and the old personal mythologies and family lore shift off into another sphere.

But I myself revisit past moments, the smells of rural New England, the view from the flat nearby pasture of the whole night sky lit up with stars so clear. I think of those nights often, you could smell the clarity of them, mixed with nearby white pines, and the eternal laundry on the line, then my college days and love of books and people, conversations that carry on their meanings still, even though I shared them long years ago.

I grew up with the genesis of so many: mixed blood Scottish, French, Austrian and, I was told, a little strain of Roma. My grandparents saved money from laundry work and a small greengrocer in New York City, brought their city money and family to rural New England. Behind our house was a little caravan, those sorts of things that traveling salesmen used who sold potions and snake oil. "Doctor Pete's Proprietor and Detailer of Medicines and Cures" (you can imagine what fun we had as children looking at the letters in faded reds and peeling yellows on this oversized moveable covered cart).

Yes, beginnings are often rough. I remember clearly coming here, the novitiate days, the leading toward solemn vows. In many ways I felt busy in the learning—Latin, Greek, church history, doctrine—and the dailiness did not seem that daily, but new.

Then a day came. Late winter. Gray. The sort of day that is not a harbinger of good news. We were chanting the psalms on the Feastday of St. Alexis Falconieri, and then I realized, *Here I am; this is the life I am leading.* And for some dreadful moments and days it seemed so paralyzingly limiting and limited. The habit constricting, the endless sound of prayer quickly losing meaning. My cell so small and contained. The way that an entire earth can be—as Julian of Norwich noted—contained, a microcosm of the universe in a small thing such as a hazelnut. Now, here, it seemed that the small place was simply a small place that I had entered, a place drained of life, a few voices—never enough to feel full, like a chorus.

In a way, perhaps I met up with the way something would be—anything: work, leisure—without the heart of meaning. If I took the aspect of faith—of living, trembling, troubled, confused, daring faith—if I took it away, then there was only the dark cave.

Miriam, I know you have written, too, about those times, the sudden removal of meaning from a scene. Your marriage, and work as a nurse, your children, home tasks—without entering into it as something holy, it can feel like a weight. Mere duty, at least that's how it felt for me.

What agony those moments are, those deadening hints of something taken away. And not knowing how to restore joy. I know you have hinted at that same pain, Miriam, when your letters first began. What my father called the black panther: that swift quiet paw of seeing no hope in the middle of what looks like such full life everyone else is living.

After forty-seven years of monastic life and an insatiable desire for it to be different, I'm discovering there are no secrets to the life of faith. No short cuts. One time Sister Anne told me, "My dear, looking for short cuts to spiritual meaning cheapens the life of the religious." She looked at me, a curious look. "You don't want to hear it, I can see," she said, "but there it is." And over the years, the bewildering shift, from daily rhythm seeming meaningless to daily prayer and work being a way we climb back toward meaning. I suppose I was hoping for something a little more miraculous sounding than daily life. But I am leaning into the hard work of the spiritual life. It doesn't sound compelling or fancy, and I'd sort of hoped for something more divine sounding, a constant high plane, but in the words of Sister Farm, and another Loose Rule I've collected (this one is #7), *Ups have downs.* And for some reason, that came as a comfort to me, those years.

Speaking of Sister Farm, she has her heart set on a little donkey to fill in that last little stall in our small barnyard cacophony—our ecumenical creaturely community. With Advent and Christmas coming in months, Sister Farm insists that a donkey would speak to the world of the barnyard creatures providing a presence for the king, explaining that the donkey would further double-usage for the days of Lent, to double as the young colt carrying Jesus down the dusty roads of Jerusalem. She contends hosting a live crèche Nativity would highlight the work of our community and creatures of the farm ("not to mention," cough, "the coming of Jesus," Little Sister adds).

But as you can imagine, Sister Farm's genius for filling the stalls does not go over with Sister Patrick Gertrude, who sees each new creature as an olfactory attack of spiritual dimension, rather than, as Sister Farm sees it, the earthen representatives of spiritual milestones in the life of Jesus. It can be argued both ways. And is.

So our blessed Lord just may not have a little donkey to keep attendance or to ride this year over the fresh green palm fronds, even as Sister Farm has her sights set on a Poitou jenny donkey, with Roman nose and scrubby coat, and discusses her plans with Tom, who cleverly can seem to agree without expressing an opinion either way. Miriam, you would have met Tom from the Feed & Seed, where you bought Sister Bird's book. What a small world it is.

Oh, we all take sides, really, in all these things, feuds and rilings. Sister Patrick Gertrude insists that the farm is gaining all the traits of something closer to a petting zoo than a functional farm, and if you count the pennies, she's got a point; but really only neighborhood children come, and Sr. Farm would never charge for a little time with the Buff Orpingtons or the Jerseys.

Sister Anne, alone, seems to rise above the opinions, praying every day for what is at stake in the spiritual sphere, and Mother Lourdes exhausts herself in trying to ease some path between them. Between discipline, encouragement, correction, and a constant offering of a fullness of communion.

Miriam, dear, your Sister friends are petty sometimes. Luminous sometimes. If this sounds like your family's life, then we share a certain place of faith and devotion and community. Isn't that beautiful? And I pray for you in your calling, just as surely as I know you pray for me in mine.

I must close the (now long!) letter, as the Sext prayer hour is near and I must gather Sister Anne toward the chapel. But one note, which you will find amusing. I went for a walk down River Street, on the land side of the monastery, in the neighborhood, as sometimes it's easier to walk on the sidewalk, rather than the uneven paths here. A woman came from one of the side streets and asked me, "Are you a Catholic?"

"Yes, does that bother you?" I answered.

"No, but there are so many of them around here."

What could I say, but that the Boston area is full of them, it's true. And with that little tidbit of conversation, Miriam, I close.

Blessings ever,
Sr. Athanasius

20 August 2003

Well, Miriam,

You have perceived cleverly and correctly that I somehow bypassed the in-between years, skipping from the growing-up years to the days as a novice testing my vocation. And, as you wrote, *but not a word about the* how *and* why *you came. I like knowing a person's route if it's not prying to ask, that is. Maybe it's my own questions about my life, have got me all curious for how others made a go of major things like faith and direction, after all.*

And, no, Miriam, it's not prying. I suppose I left a large chasm there, which I sometimes visit interiorly, but haven't out loud or on paper made sense of it. You will find me curious, but I would like to test it out for myself, see how it sounds, so awkward a time it was, and abrupt, and maybe in the way that novices are testing vocation, I now would like to revisit that place and hear, in the inner ear, how the vocation has stood in me, and where my feet have landed, and as you say, *how* and *why*. And with time, I will write to you again and let my pen say these things.

Meantime, let me shove off into another realm, with something more easily answered. A recent note of yours suggested that the distinctive work we all do—or "jobs" as it were—and how we support the cast of characters was a bit thin on explanation. I suppose that this is in part because it is thin for us as well. We are not bubbling over in income, piecing together funds as we can.

Our land is owned outright, given to us by a generous and devout couple. She was a nun for years and never made her peace with leaving. Perhaps this was one way she felt she could offer something with love—and it has been wonderful, the land here offers such variety: ocean bay, low dunes, a tidal edge, rough grasses, marsh, meadow (which the sheep love), garden, groves of various trees from sumac to pines—all to make an ornithologist's heart glad. And a farmer's, and the others of us who wonder at the wealth of the variety in so small a spit of land.

We make do, financially, from royalties of Sister Bird's books (decent), to the bakery income (less small), to farm income (pitifully small), to donations from individuals and organizations for our community (almost the largest of our total community's financial support).

And as to special work each of us does:

* Sacristan (preparing the chapel for prayer: flowers, trimming candles, cleaning), Laundry & Housekeeping & Bookkeeping—Sister Patrick Gertrude
* Kitchen & Bakery—Little Sister
* Pots & Pans and Spiritual Counselor—Sister Anne
* Farm & Garden: (this includes slug detail and an overabundance of tomatoes grown in rounds of old rubber tires, so that when it's winter, the garden looks like a large square with many black rings)—All Sister Farm's domain. Her domain also includes tool upkeep, chickens, cows, sheep, bees, stalls, and all things farmerly (along with the constant search for the elusive shaggy donkey).
* Prioress and Visitation of the Sick & Elderly—Mother Lourdes
* All things Ornithological—Sister Bird. This includes notebooks, clicking rosary beads, binos, watercolors, thermos, camera. All-weather ventures. She has her postal worker's share of the elements.
* General care over the elderly of our community (Sister Anne). Secretary to the Prioress—your very own Sister Athanasius. Though, Miriam, my deep personal vexation is that while our monastery and our Order focus on "especial work"—professional trade for all the Sisters—my profession has always felt "thin" to me. Never have others said anything. Ever. But I feel it within myself.

That said, we all have our skills and special work and believe it is all God's work. No one's work is fancier or better than another's. Still, one can safely say that some Sisters get more recognition than others by those outside the monastery. Tom from the Feed & Seed thinks that Sister Farm's work is most important; the elderly visited by Mother Lourdes know that work to be most important. And this is good: that all the work that is done is seen as essential to a community. And those to whom Sr. Anne offers wise spiritual counsel know that to be the most important work.

Then, there is the work that we all share, which sometimes looks a lot like sitting. Or staring. Or sweating. Or pacing. Or the counting, clicking, knocking, and seeking of rosary beads. This work is our hardest and best work. And it is for the mercy of those who have lost their way in the world. And for those who don't know to ask for prayer. And for those who do. And this is work that we all do, giving ourselves, as Saint Thérèse of Lisieux wrote about the saints, which we hold in such high regard as to this work: "'Give me a lever and a fulcrum on which to rest it,' wrote Archimedes, 'and I will lift the world.' What the scientist could not obtain ... the saints have obtained in all its fullness. God has given them a fulcrum to lean upon himself alone, and for a lever the prayer which inflames with the fire of love. Thus, they have uplifted the world, and on earth will continue to raise it until the end of time."

And if one were giving degrees of importance to work, collectively, we would be glad to be counted in the number who lift up the world in love and reverence, to God, whose name we say in reverence, is also Love.

Yours,
Sr. A—

22 August 2003

Dear Miriam,

August 22 and a late summer birding report: sanderlings (2), greater yellowlegs (12), Baltimore orioles (3), Caspian terns (3), ruddy turnstone (surprise visitor).

Months of correspondence, now, we have—all beginning with your letter both despondent and looking for hope, the cloud of desperation alongside curiosity about the Sisters at the monastery and the birds that pick along the garden path or those at the shoreline or the several that flutter and wing around the small farm. Your last note mentioned, despite illness, finding a way into work that looks like prayer. Bings, too, have long walked that path. The two are not such vastly different things, both a willingness toward the day and one's task, both a movement of openness toward communion with God.

But, Miriam, you know by now that I am fond of the sound of my pen on paper, and sometimes for wanting to believe something so much, or wanting to offer you something solid and profound. Your letters always speak to looking for clues about the life of the religious, but even more speaking to the life of faith. Perhaps I am not so much nearer to filling in any of the gaps you live with, though it's something I would wish to offer. And, as with prayer and work, you already walk the good road.

Just now I was thinking how interesting it is that we share a common state with the very long name, Massachusetts. You near Quabbin, we in Weymouth on the South Shore. Do you know that our spit of land used to be a munitions bunker? Now it is heeding nature's call to move back to its original form, with sumac bushes, meadow grasses, pines that claim proper place near the shore, as though as soon as it could, the land reverted itself from a sword to a plowshare.

Today we are off to visit a parish church in Boston, St. Alphonsos. Sometimes we will go there for a special Mass and always for the blessing of the animals on the feast day of Saint Francis (Sister Farm's insistence). And Mother Lourdes is the most involved there, visiting the old, failing. She is called upon at all hours, sitting with the frail and dying, returning here to command the living. And though I don't say it, I often feel that her return here almost carries the heavier weight.

But we all carry our weight, you with illness and the abrupt comings and goings of troubles. Mother Lourdes, in all her weight. And I find it is one of the most silent things of the world that happens, people carrying weight.

With prayers for your days. Know of our share of carrying both the weight and the joy, as we pray so often and openheartedly for you, friend.

Yours,
Sr. Athanasius

8 September 2003

Dear Miriam—

I am sorry not to have written to you in these two weeks. Sister Anne has been ill, miserable with flu-like symptoms. Each day, there can be a hush of time when I think she might be getting better, but a new host of symptoms arrive. It is not as though, having one long list of struggles, a person might become exempt of the others. As though arthritis would, then, gallantly bow out.

I think Little Sister misses Sister Anne in the kitchen. Little Sister created what she calls *the filling station*: a corner at the end of the long stainless table for Sister Anne with coffeemaker, a sturdy stool, either *Baseball News* or the *Boston Globe,* with the Sports section out and ready for reading, and Sister Anne's Red Sox mug. Sometimes, when the season is right, if there's a game on or running commentaries by Dale Arnold, she'll keep the big kitchen radio on WEEI. "The filling station is my way," Little Sister says, "to keep an eye on her. You never know what mischief she could get in." Everyone watches out for Sister Anne.

Having not heard from me, Miriam, you were kind to call and inquire. (I am glad, Miriam, that you have our number, and feel free to call.) Mother Lourdes told me along the hallway to Vespers late last week. And then your letter came in a rush of consolation for Sister Anne (and, too, for me. I am fond of a good word from you, along with what I have come to expect from a Miriam letter: a line or two of a poem, Emily Dickinson, Denise Levertov, Lucille Clifton, Richard Wilbur).

The task has fallen to me to read to Sister Anne, as her eyes have, she says, "gone south, O, disobedient green eyes." And so I read to her, with my reading glasses peering over your letter. Two things came to mind, Miriam, as I read your letter to Sister Anne: Your generous kindness of heart, suffering alongside her. And an understanding that you have for Sister Anne's doggedness toward life. It was a letter written in love and listened to in love. And few things equal the kingdom of God like those two.

Sister Anne has carried that letter in her habit pocket, "both material and spiritual comfort. And you tell that Miriam that I am grateful for it. And now, you should assure her that I am doing somewhat better, keeping close to my more faithful companion, the aches in my joints. And I have been grateful for Miriam's prayers and intentions on my behalf."

More later, Miriam, but so grateful for your call and the letter,

Sr. Athanasius

(2 days later)

About *doubt*. Miriam, as you gently and cunningly inquired (as though a mention about the appearance of doubt in the life of the religious could be slipped into a letter without apparent notice). I will tell you: I have a pair of bedfellows. When I am alone in my cell, doubt remains as constantly with me as faith. They have learned to get on quite well, though in the middle, I am sometimes roughed up. The pairing strikes me as apt during this long liturgical season where Ordinary Time meets the long day's light lessening, and the last of the flowering sea rockets marking the tide line.

At first, doubt magnifies faith—as though the friction between them were creating a newer, shinier thing. I sometimes wonder when I look at how Sister Farm dutifully dirties the track between the small barn and her cell, and the way Sister Patrick Gertrude tries to redo that very path, that these two extremes make way for something true. Even when it seems both have dug heels into their various versions of faith.

Our Lord's grace makes a changeling of our doubts and failures and even crude versions of righteousness, rinsing them in a clear true light. Then, it can become less about faith or doubt and more about that clear light. And Blessed Julian of Norwich's tryst with this hope comes out in clarity: "And all shall be well and all manner of things shall be well."

Among the things that the religious life offers—is a learning to wait. Waiting. And working out the details of waiting as God skips in between the lines of our doubt and faith. At that place, something, amazingly, can be transformed and has come into all manner of being well. Not fixed, but well.

With those like Sister Anne, there is an eternal patience toward that wellness. She is like those who bide the struggle in time and trust in a rich undercurrent of the Holy Spirit at work.

Sister Anne once said it to me: "Grace will not be rushed or smashed into the forms we'd like it to acquire." Today is not the day for Sister Farm and Sister MPG to swing the gates wide to each other. It is not the day that accepts with calm dignity an illness that, by turns, debilitates Sister Anne, nor a squeeze that loosens for a few moments, nor the illness in your own body.

It is not the day, unless God intervenes, when your daughter, Emily, with amazing softness says in fond voice that she has watched your desperate love for her and knows it, truly, to be love.

Today, no.

Tomorrow, perhaps.

In eternity, in all certainty, yes, yes, yes.

Fondly,
Sr. Athanasius

PS: Birdwatch for the week: off the marsh grasses, into those estuaries throughout the bay's inlets these September days: Bonaparte's gull, black-bellied plovers, double-crested cormorants, some sort of tern (don't tell Sister Bird I can't identify it, but it is certainly not the common nor arctic), and the great blue heron—that still and tall friend of saints and sinners.

PPS: Sister Farm keeps her sights now set precisely on the Poitou donkey. The donkey, she reminds us, the animal God spoke through to Balaam, but also the chosen beast on which our Blessed Lord rode into Jerusalem through a praising crowd.

17 September 2003
Feastday, Bd. Hildegard of Bingen

You have caught me at my old tricks, Miriam. (You see I have refrained from writing *Miriam, dear* in opening the letter—for who appreciates being caught at her own game?)

And you were so gentle in your questioning, so quiet and thoughtful—a bit like the heron who in gentleness stands among the saltwater marshgrass, the tarsus in water, the body in the salt air, standing stately and quiet, until, in a swift and deliberate moment, it spears an unsuspecting fish and commences lunch.

And I am the wriggling, startled fish—yes, on this account: I wrote of faith and doubt as so abstract as they sometimes feel to me, almost beautifully unreal. But here, Miriam, is my service of truth-telling rendered with more clarity.

I don't doubt my calling, but sometimes I look around at my companions in the religious life, earnest, a river of blue habits, a crucifix around the neck, a thick leather belt with long end hanging down to the knee, all these women have a fervent desire to live this calling. And I wonder where I am. But this world moves onward, and my questions don't seem to have weight. We chant the psalms, this chant a form originated in the early church, then taken up in the Middle Ages. Before Vatican II, all our chant was in Latin, stark, beautiful, a logic to the language, and grace, but hardly an outsider would understand. They wouldn't doubt our sincerity, but may wonder at the reasons for using a dead language for a living faith. Now, less graceful, but more immediate, we chant in English.

And, Miriam, between doubt and faith, another Loose Rule I've spent time with, Loose Rule #27: *Do not disregard small things*: faith may find refuge from doubt among words, textures, or coffee. That is to say, sometimes earnestness and work gear blue and Little Sister's Ode to Cinnamon in the bakery speak to faith and faithfulness. And doubt loses its thick grip.

But a missing piece in this, my story of faith and doubt, is also tied together with those missing years before my novitiate—that I wish at some point to write to you. To tell one part needs the telling of other parts, and then others. Miriam, bear with me, to tell the story of this all is, as T. S. Eliot says, "to arrive at the beginning, and to know it for the first time." My own beginnings toward faith spark from a host of questions, most of which I have stopped asking years ago. Questions that I will ask again, I promise. And I am beginning to revisit them, seeing how they sound—doubt & faith—in the deepest chambers of my heart, which resides in the body which wears the habit, upon which a simple crucifix speaks to a life opening up and also sacrificed.

I often think spiritual gifts come as a sort of alchemy: large quantities of faith mixed with a clot of darkness, and sometimes doubt. My Aunt Lorie, of whom I spoke in an earlier letter and for whose spiritual eternal rest I pray daily, had a prophetic gift, divining upcoming events, whether joyous or tragic. But who—even for the glory of our Lord?—would give a person fateful news early? It came as wisdom for her simply to bear down under the weight of this knowledge only through prayer, praying for those who would be soon afflicted by accident, illness, pain or loss. In that way, she carried them to Jesus.

I know of a man, an iconographer, who, over his sink, keeps a photograph of Saint Thérèse washing laundry. Underneath it in simple handwriting are her words, "As for ecstasy, I prefer the monotony of daily sacrifices." And I think that my Aunt, and also Sister Patrick Gertrude, tortured (and impassioned) by each smell that presents itself, might agree. And there are the saints and stigmatists, with a constant oozing of thickened blood from hands, forehead, side, feet. It is a gift for the faith of others, more than for the one with the sign. Those who see him, maybe come with curiosity, but leave with a sense of the presence of a God who touches, here and there, the world, making it bleed. A mystery, is all, this God, these ecstasies, this hope and faith and a troubling sense that these gifts come with a cost: either doubt or a weight.

I will end this letter, for now, and conversations to continue —assuredly.

Yours,
Sr. Athanasius

PS Lark bunting discovered, these mid-September days near the bay. It is always a wonder to Sister Bird that somehow we get strays from such diverse patches as Europe, Canada, Iceland, but this handsome fellow took a wrong turn and we've enjoyed our curious traveler from the Southwest.

[Postcard, postmark September 21]

Miriam, what do you make of this?

A quote from Teresa of Avila: "The feeling remains that God is on the journey, too."

Interesting, isn't it? Delighting. I will be ripest of old age before I understand what it means. So it is with real life, a real faith.

Sr. A—

PS Sister Bird discovered early autumn nest-building by the American goldfinches, just above a burl in the old maple near the garden. A bright, busy, and welcome neighbor.

25 September 2003

Miriamest,

The day, my dear, has quickened itself through and now I'm writing at night, with Compline, our evening's last office and known as the "tender hour," having hours since been prayed.

I write from my cell, my room, a white board room with equally white wainscoting, and a simple olivewood crucifix on the wall above my bed. A chair. A small desk such as college students have—with side drawers so that my little papers and musings and mess can be easily tucked away, small scraps with quotes on them, poems, verses, titles of books, lines, sayings of the Desert Mothers and Fathers, and such tidbits from the saints and mystics. On top of the desk, rocks from landscapes of significance to me, a wren's nest.

You always treat me with stories, a line from a Mary Oliver poem, a psalm, an insightful story about Franklin or Emily, your mornings, the finches at the feeders. Though I am wondering about your health, your tiredness, and the news the doctors give you. Please do let us know, as our prayers continue with you.

I know I often respond to your letters with ponderous and philosophical notes, which makes me not the best letter answerer, as I get so involved in the process of the letter itself, I forget to respond to some of your direct questions and notes. But I did think that Franklin's fury to clean the garage, when it all of a sudden seems like something *one can do,* speaks so much to all of our desire to do something when we feel lost: to clean or organize or do some task that seems logical and fixable. Perhaps that is how we all learn to pray, for the feeling that we are in a life bigger than we are, and once we have done what we can to fix or do, to then open up our hands and offer what we can't possibly do over to God.

And speaking of what one can do, as you inquired about Sister Farm and Sister Patrick Gertrude, the latter is in all manner of the spirit of doing and has found uses for bands of twine, settling herself in the hallway, affixing twine to the mudroom doorway with the elaborate tying of one door to the other, creating some system (akin to a teenage boy's at camp) so that when Sister Farm enters the building, the string pulls pulleys to have room deodorizer fill the hallway. But the amount coming out of the can is too much in the other extreme, making us all rather factious. Sister Anne doesn't seem to mind, and says, "If I can smell something with my old nose well past prime, then I am grateful." For the others of us, in our humanness a bit more thickly, they do not provoke friendly thought.

And in other news from the monastery, Sister Bird is working on a book she calls "A Determination Guide." Of course, without the name Sister Bird in the title or without the repetition of the words *Bird, birdwatch* or *Birder,* it hardly seems like a book she'd write.

But I'm curious to find out what a *determination book* means, though it sounds like a book on the spiritual life or religious callings—perhaps about God's call, *determining* us toward a certain work and professional skills? Of course, if that's the case, then this is entirely the book for me.

We all want to know, but are hesitant to ask Sister Bird about a project: between her enthusiasms for the details and the enthusiasms for the enthusiasms, we fear for the delivery of a tome, as though the more we ask about it, the more will be written to explain it.

Little Sister suggested we ask her about it during one of our silent meals, in which we use small hand signals and a whole array of little motions to communicate, if needed—"She'd have to run out of sign vocabulary at some point, wouldn't she?" Little Sister said.

Finally, it was Sister Farm who had the nerve to ask and then say, "but keep it short and sweet there, no trailing off." And so our Sister Farm has discerned the height, breadth & depth of Sister Bird's Determination Book. In Sister Farm's words, "It goes like this. You want to determine bird kind? Say it is a big bird. Go to page 5. Does the big bird have long legs? Page 18. Short legs, page 34. Does it have a yellow beak? Page 52. By 10 flips of a page you've found your bird. *Determined* your bird," she said, "and Sister Anne, the bet you had going with Sister Athanasius that it would be a 3-hour response, well, Sister Athanasius can drain her monies—not that the Sisters of Saint Athanasius gamble or anything." And that was when Sister Farm went to the barn and started the first day of the week with a new cigar (one per week) after telling us that she suggested the following title: *Sister Bird's Bird Guide for Determining Bird Types: Another Bird Book for Basic Birders.*

And that is how I lost my bet with Sister Anne, who wanted, rather than cash on the barrelhead, to be paid in a baseball card, a 1986 Oil Can Boyd Topps card, from the World Series playing team that year. "That was a good year for baseball, and close enough pennant race and series to make me giddy with all of it," she said.

8 October 2003

Miriam, dear one,

Sister Anne, whose life is washing dishes, prayer, and waiting, now is waiting to win the World Series. There is no Red Sox fan like our Sister Anne. Sometimes, Miriam, being a Sox fan is like grief.

We are now, as you may know, in the play-offs with the Yankees. How does Little Sister simply bake her cheese brioches, just steadily filling the pans with yeasty dough? "Don't you, at least, know they're heading into the 1st ACLS game?" Sister Anne asks. As though it were some spiritual insight of Sister Anne's.

And no matter if it's all baseball talk on WEEI, with a pennant race, when later morning comes, even Sister Anne gets the boot while Little Sister prepares the noon meal, and finishes off the bakery orders for local stores.

Miriam, you have mentioned the Red Sox in some letters and I wonder, are you and Franklin old fans?

The workings in Sister Anne's universe are mostly all God, often the dishes, and through spring training and the regular season there's a quiet Sox hum in the background, but if it's October and playoffs, it's the Sox, Sox, Sox.

But Sister Anne has lived a life of the Red Sox, with family connections, having gone to many games, knowing old managers, still getting Christmas cards from old bullpen coaches and players, with a distinct weakness for pitchers and designated hitters.

She has companions come baseball season: Sister Farm and I. I'm usually just along for the ride. But the truth of the matter is, we can't watch TV after 9:30, and there's a night game tomorrow at Yankee Stadium. But see the game or not, Sister Anne won't even get a peep of sleep until she reads the scores in the next morning's paper. Some say April is the cruelest month, but Red Sox fans think October's the crueler month.

Miriam, you are kind to let me go on and on. And whether it is your kindness to encourage "all sorts of notes about the Sisters, all of which I love to read, odd and not odd, random or peaceful, I like reading all of it," you wrote. And you see I do.

Sr. A—

11 October 2003
Game 3 of the ACLS
[currently part of our liturgical season]

Oh, Miriam, what a wonderful and dreadful gift—a little transistor radio. I've never seen one so small, like a flat egg, just fitting for the pocket of a habit. And, what did you call it in your note—an earbud? One could almost be a Sox fan imperceptibly, except that you'd have to keep returning to Max & Papa Jim's Mini Mart & Bait for batteries.

As you may know, all gifts must be approved by our Superior. And the gift was approved for news and classical music; so, in a way you could say the Red Sox are current news and we hope the current news will extend for the month of October.

Well, you now have 3 friends who have an "interpretive understanding" of transistor radio usage. Though Sister Anne could not be persuaded to listen to games much after Compline. So here's what we came up with: after Compline, TV till 9:00 or if we can push it, 9:30, then return to our cells.

Felicitously I have a room next door to Sister Anne, so—thank *God* she's not deaf or this wouldn't work at all—we've created a system of knocking on the wall. Sister Farm is on the other side of Sister Anne, so you can see how handy the entire system is. Sister Farm came up with it, though it seems the kind of clever thing one might learn in prison. I'm not sure her old gambling habits ever got her that far, though where she's learned such things is anyone's guess. And now we have a Morse code of baseball:

* 4 quick knocks for inning change.
* But 4 quick knocks and one tap means top of the inning.
* 3 quick taps to the wall, strikeout.
* 7 taps to the rhythm of "Take Me Out to the Ball Game" means a run batted in.
* A homer or a grand slam, we can't help it, we yell. If it's Fenway and the ball goes clear over the Green Monster.

You are a bit naughty, and we live neatly in the same domain. Thank God for November, for the confessional, for a return to something so basic as a clean conscience and a good night's sleep.

Thank you, Miriam. Thank you.

It's almost that we love the baseball games for love of Sister Anne. Or love birding for the love of Sister Bird. How love goes wide for those we care for.

And your love has widened for us. Ever grateful for that,

Sr. A—

12 October 2003

Miriam,

Imagine the Red Sox playing the Yankees. Imagine a small woman reading each morning's paper, a small woman with knobby knees, arthritic and groused fingers, hip joints worn and full of spurs. Our Sister Anne.

Add to the imagination late nights, compline at 8:30, bed at 9:30. Transistor till 11:00 p.m., then the bell to rise at 4:30 a.m., and Matins an hour later. Add to that a little crush she has going on Johnny Damon (not unlike most every woman in Red Sox Nation) and Tim Wakefield.

Every time it's the same, just before Compline, a big sports sigh escapes our Sister and we all know what it means: the potential for the World Series mixed with an early curfew (if you will), little TV coverage, no radio (well, the taps from the room next door). For a little old lady, she can be said to rush into the kitchen after Matins for coffee, then rush again after Lauds, by which time the morning paper arrives. She studies that sports section as though somehow she could singlehandedly pray the Sox to a win, oh the way she loves a game.

Every Sox season the same sufferings of soul and spirit happen. And every year, praise God, Sister Anne survives the health crisis that is the Red Sox season (so intense on nerves and heart). And every year we pray the same prayer: *Oh God of every good gift, it has been 85 years since the last big win. Please let us see a beautiful return to glory.*

"No, really, Sister Athanasius," Sr. Anne tells me yet again. "I am serious. I have a good feeling about this year." We have pitched this line wholeheartedly back and forth over the years. There are bad days, she says, when she's not sure she can make the claim. Like in 1966 when the Orioles' Boog Powell played the Sox and cleared the Green Monster 3 times in one game. But then weeks will go by and no one can hit a ball over that wall, and she's back to making The Great Proclamation.

Well, Miriam, on that note, the bad news. You may laugh to hear we've been found out. A paper trail of the sports section, a little transistor radio hidden away with a Sox pendant, and a rosary.

Mother Lourdes has called a meeting: Sister Anne, Sister Farm, myself. If I said it didn't look like a good year for the Red Sox or the Sisters, I know you'd understand.

Mother Lourdes gave the list of offenses (I hate to feed the fire, but) provided in triumph by Sister Patrick Gertrude and a little more sheepishly, Sister Bird, who for the sake of the soul, will faithfully wound the spirit.

Miriam, we didn't look so good, for nuns. But as God's children, as Red Sox fans, Sister Anne said later, "We looked just fine."

"It's that I fear worldly pleasure may be dividing your attentions," Mother Lourdes said to us, not accusing, more like weary. "The other Sisters have noticed the missing sports page and strange tappings on the wall late at night, which they thought, incorrectly, were mice. Then they thought, incorrectly, were very disciplined mice, making similar sounds over and over. Then they thought, correctly, I assume? that a strike equals three short taps and a home run equals a squeal."

Sister Anne listened carefully to the shape and tenor of the complaints, eyes downcast and working decade after decade of her rosary beads.

Finally she stopped and said, "Mother Lourdes—do you feel that my faith in God has really ever become compromised? Or my vows threatened?"

"No."

"Do you feel that the Sox truly represent a *new*—after 80 years—turning of my affections from our Blessed Savior?"

"No."

"You may not believe that the life of faith could be comprised of taking great joy in a perfect game, a curve ball, a bender, a double play—but that does not then make it Satan's domain." She paused, looked up from her beads, "That God is present everywhere means to me that God is present in the baseball scores, in the movement of lovely large men along the baseline and in the bull pen, in the big spits of tobacco"—here Sister Patrick Gertrude coughed—"the loose, sand-colored dirt, the lights."

"I may not have told you this but, before my vows, when we were growing up, my mother was a baseball fan and, maybe it was to keep our family together—three teenagers, my brothers and I. . . ."

Well, Miriam, it turns out that before Sister Anne found God, she found baseball, when she was 15 years old. It was a world she discovered that seemed large enough to contain her—a realm to own, somehow. Fenway Park, her walks up Boylston from the South End, it was a way to participate in the world, to be alone and in community. She called it her opening to the monastic call—a sense of largeness, of a group of people who were as hopeful as you that all would be well. (This, despite the ratings.)

She told us that her mother would slip her money for a bleacher seat, and she'd get there early, those days in the mid-1930s, and watch the world of Billy Werber, Jimmie Foxx, and Ted Williams in his starting year with the Red Sox.

"It became my first understanding of God. And to me, it contains my vow of community and my hope in God."

I suppose, Miriam, you'd have had to be the devil himself to not respond to Sister Anne with great respect and a commendation to go and love and serve the Lord and to go and love baseball. Sister Bird has a look of extreme relief, Sister Patrick Gertrude a respectful nod toward a rightful claim. She may be harsh, but she's uncompromising in her respect for what she calls *points earned and merits noted.*

It is in the nature of God to be aware of the timing of these things, whether or not our sharp prayers regard timing. And God knows there's no transistor, no tapping mice, and the sports page stays in the kitchen, where she can read it, sitting on the stool, sipping her coffee, "If you would like to spend your leisure time in that that way," Mother Lourdes said. "And how many games are left in this competition?" asked Mother Lourdes.

"The whole pennant race is the best of 7 games. We are coming on game five, with the Sox and Yankees tied."

"Well, then, let's keep the TV on in the general room for games 6 through 7. Your game watching will have to wait one game, but I would not have you be stretched unreasonably—or discouraged—as Saint Benedict says in his Rule. I trust I can count on you to maintain all prayer hours?" (As though Sister Anne has any other intention.) At Sister Anne's modest nod, Mother Lourdes continued.

"And, for the Sisters who do not appreciate the sports endeavors of our local team, you may use that time as you wish for leisure or prayer. I prefer that you, in fairness to the Sisters watching TV, not work, sharing in the spirit of games.

"I may, myself, join you if we get into a heated race of games. Sisters," she added. "The blessings of the Lord be with you."

"And also with you," we returned.

And so the night drew to a close and there were no tappings, only the energy of sleepless delight in the cell next to mine, which I did not hear, but nevertheless knew it to be there.

More soon,
Sr. A—

19 October 2003

Miriam, dear,

Yes, you have it exactly right. Sister Anne *is* the one of our monastery who understands such shifts of this life, little excitements that don't seem to put her off balance. She has a great way of leaning into faith, and letting things run their course. In a previous letter you wrote something about her and I've been thinking about it ever since: *She understands the cost of this life, and still spends it anyway.* She spends every resource, uses up every muscle, tendon, pushing past every aching joint's power without any seeming attention to replenishment.

And each morning at Matins her quiet voice chants the psalms with what looks like no energy at all, what looks like an offering to God— who, I note, never seems to tire of it.

Because I am an admirer of the life of abandon to good, to the good of others, to the cheering on of the Red Sox, I pray that energy enough would be sufficient for her days, and a cane or my strong arm would be available as she would need it.

Miriam, you are not unfamiliar with the great inner strength and physical strength it costs someone frail to attend to the day with devotion, affection, care. I applaud both you and Sister Anne for your daily salute to faith and to the care of those around you.

Well, the news has played itself out, hasn't it? From the *Globe* giving us the news of Game 3 in the pennant race and Pedro and Zimmer and all that excitement, to game 4, keeping hope alive. By the 11th inning of game 7, which we all stayed up to watch, our throats rusty and sore, we were both alive and devastated, and I don't know who cried harder at the loss, Wakefield from the field, or Sister Anne for being so close and losing another year's chance. It was a quiet day, following. The rustle of the morning paper, the coffee brewing.

By late morning, everyone exhausted from the late nights and games, along with most New Englanders—you and Franklin, too?—Sister Anne looked up from the paper and said to me and to Little Sister, "Well, I hate to see this drag on, but looks like next year will be the big year for the Sox."

I don't know if it was the loss of hope or the desperate renewal of hope, but Little Sister ordered us both out of the kitchen. "Out," she said. "Too much hope and too little sleep makes no sense. Out."

Oh, let's move on to another topic, something less sore, something not involving baseball, shall we?

So, you looked up Saint Hildegard of Bingen in Butler's *Lives of the Saints* (where does a good Protestant such as yourself find the likes of a Catholic tome? The stirrings of heart and soul and interest are indeed mysterious.) And, yes, you found another connection. Saint Hildegard *did* write a commentary on the Athanasian Creed. So you see, how connected things are.

Saint Hildegard, as I'm sure you read the details, was an extraordinary Mother of the Church. She founded Benedictine convents, though our Order as you know, isn't Benedictine, but it has similarities. As a friend from the Poor Clares says about us, complete with a sigh of disapproval, "the Bings are Benedict Lite."

Our resident theologian, Sister Patrick Gertrude takes offense at this, believing that we are dogmatically sound and creedally faithful. But you would like our Hildegard, Miriam, if not for her thoughtfulness or her musical compositions, perhaps for her knowledge of medicine and healing herbs (which drew Sister Bird to our Order), or her mysticism or intellect. Perhaps, as Sister Farm, you are drawn to Hildegard for her respect and fondness for the earth, its vegetation, its full life. In Hildegard's reading of the Athanasian Creed, she noted an approach to and understanding of aspects of doctrine concerning, say, the person of Jesus. The creed didn't simply say, "We believe in Jesus . . ." but that "we believe Jesus is this, not that. That Jesus has *this* element . . ." Hildegard was taken by the way in which the spiritual life tested understandings of doctrine, sort of wrestled with them. Perhaps the end result is the same in terms of doctrine, but the means toward understanding doctrine or creed was a series of questions, testings. And here is where our Order begins, with questions and testings.

In our tradition, the Holy Rule, as we call Saint Hildegard of Bingen's translated writings of dictums to monastics, covers the basics: a life characterized by balance, by a focused craft or professional work, by community, by a prayer of stillness, of time spent in silent reflection, by meaningful intersection between the monastery and the world. Also, by meaningful reflection on spiritual truths.

In our monastery, a silence for reflections on spiritual truths is practiced 3 times a week, for a half day each, and for 2 meals spent in silence to turn our hearts to God. On other days, the noon meals are spent listening to one of the Sisters read from a spiritual classic. It's always rough going when Sister Farm reads: she has no inflection or any sort of interpretative emotion when she reads, so any spiritual thought that arises comes solely from the text and the Holy Ghost. And as Sister Farm says, "nothing wrong with that." I consider it a great trial and spiritual discipline to keep focus.

When Sister Patrick Gertrude reads, though, she is so inflective and interpretive that one must do the same thing for different reasons: only focus on the words of the text, in order to avoid egregious misinterpretation. Still, she reads so convincingly and passionately, that it is much harder to be spiritually exacting on those noon times.

Also, according to our Rule, the Prioress is responsible in directing the Sisters into spiritual understanding, pointing each Sister through spiritual direction toward the inner counsel of the Holy Ghost. An enforcement of rules without an understanding of the purpose of the Rule will not bring about the spiritual change that is necessary to the spiritual life. Obedience is only partly the Rule. "A sister shall not be forced, but will be counseled in matters of spiritual import, as one walks side by side, until the Sister herself comes into spiritual unity and communion." Without a Sister's conviction that a Rule is compelling, a Rule will never be forced. But this sort of approach requires faith and a dependence on the work and intercession of the Holy Spirit, and a Prioress may be found more in prayer than in counsel, as she hopes to rightly influence a Sister toward a change of heart and life.

The Rule also restates that of sacred writ: that God loves a cheerful giver, but that a heart can be made hardened by forcefulness. The Prioress will not make demands—spiritual or emotional or toward daily work—which may in some way push a Sister away from spiritual engagement. But with clarity of insight and thoughtful compunction the Prioress will strive to build a Sister toward allowing the Holy Ghost to work in the interior spaces and conscience.

Leadership is a tricky thing. In the Bingean tradition, there is a desire for balancing the hard spiritual work without diminishing the person's spiritual joy. It is less about power than about proper attention. For some, the Rule will be harsh, demanding, but that is only as the Prioress sees the Rule will effect a spiritual depth in a Sister. For those who struggle against the rules of a thing, who may rather be open to a principle of spiritual discipline, this is for the Prioress to determine.

Well, that's a lot of fuss and explanation, Miriam. I'm not sure I've captured it well, but there it is. I'm usually more interested in how this looks in practice, and my letters show how it all plays out, from the Prioress to the Sisters, in the life of the community.

(three days later)

For me, the struggle has always been interior rebellion: the constant tidal pool of recessing and advancing in desiring obedient response to the devout life. And yet I am always testing the boundaries of faith within myself.

Different from me would be Sister Patrick Gertrude, who works to tame her interior spirit. Sometimes I think that to Sister Mary Patrick Gertrude, the harsher spiritual disciplines are as ecstasies.

Sister Anne, her soft spot is the gloriousness of the Red Sox: Section D of the *Boston Globe.* (Or, rather, that's the view that some of the Sisters have, that it is her spiritual weakness. To me, it seems to have kinship with faith and community. I don't know how to explain it, quite.)

Our Sister Bird, wholly devoted to prayer and to the particulars of birds: wing coverts, tertials and plumage, colorings, call notes, migratory patterns, the waterbirds, the waders, the sparrows, the grebes, the shorebirds, her herons. The way she contains and can't contain her passion for the particular.

Little Sister's approach to faith, well I don't quite know. Somehow dedicated to her work, somehow fierce and sudden, a bundle of tensions that is hard to tease out. She runs hot and cold, but rarely tepid. When I observe how Mother Lourdes responds to her, seeking ways to engage her spirit, I wonder at Mother Lourdes's patience, her willingness to put forced obedience on hold, to see a greater thing emerge. I once asked her about Little Sister, her privacy, her abruptness. "Oh," she said to me, "Little Sister is a wild flower; she needs a little rocky terrain, and a wilderness space to grow. She is not satisfied to be tamed, but only to grow. We shall see what the Holy Spirit will continue to effect in her." She looked at me, "Be gentle with her. Sister Anne knows that Little Sister is in want of someone who is not a mentor." Because she kept looking at me, I told her I wondered if I should take that as a backward compliment, that I was no mentor. I had noticed, too, I said, the way in which she has the spiritual nature of a leader and didn't want mentoring as much as something to be teased out.

Sister Farm? Perhaps of all the Sisters, she lives so originally in her skin, feeling that work is prayer and community, that scraping off the bumper stickers on the new trailer for the donkey we don't have, she can whistle Ave Maria while scratching at the edges of such stickers as "Save a horse, Ride a Cowgirl." I suppose in that way, she is simple and desires simplicity, not dividing things down and apart in order to sully them as we other Sisters easily might do. As though everything, to her—except for Sister Patrick Gertrude and even then, Sister Farm has a measured patience, and doesn't mind the rivalry, as Patrick Gertrude does—is holy, though the creatures of God, the donkey, the calf, the sow, are the holiest.

Of Mother Lourdes's struggles, one should hardly speak. She was elected to the office of leadership and—to use a baseball image—she went to bat. But it's clear she fatigues of it. Perhaps she identifies with Jesus' role as a leader. She doesn't want that responsibility, but that God called her is enough. She attends to the task. And she prays for the strength to want what she has been given.

Responsibility seems like God's will, but nothing works out for her joy. The weight of the monastery's life: direction, finances, spiritual decisions, small decisions on the various work lives of the Sisters, to attending to the small questions that seem flung toward her: from, "Would it be ok to buy the laundry powder with the extra-scented lavender?" to, "I believe that I need a new set of watercolor pencils for the bird sketches." When she is heading toward the door to go out, if she is on one of her visitations to the elderly, you can witness the change from what I call her shadow look (at 6 feet from the door) to the flushed cheeks look (at 2 feet). And when she returns, she has a mixed weight: lightness of joy at the having come from, mixed with the weight of returning.

And that, Miriam, is the long way around your question as to how we all attend to the spiritual life and what you call "the constraints" of community. And as you live in your own community with your own faith and calling, I will ask the same of you: how is it that you see your own spiritual life in the middle of family life, of illness, of the string of days?

On to you,
Sr. A.—

1 November 2003

Miriam, dear—

Unlike her, Mother Lourdes has instituted a new rule here for the last month. Though every monastery hopes that no rule other than *The Rule of Saint Hildegard of Bingen*, a 70-page missive written for nuns, is needed, our small monastery has seen the need for longer hours of *silence* being instituted, perhaps so that Sister Farm and Sister Patrick Gertrude don't take quick smarting jabs at each other or caution against the noise that came from baseball season. Also instituted, longer work hours, so that our minds, which may otherwise have been tailoring (as I have) a way to find a drink of coffee without having to bathe the confessional with sorrowful presence, are kept busy.

The idea, you see, is to rouse out all of our base plots, deflecting them through steady work, while developing an uncompromised heart.

It's the kind of tough plan that could work. But even at prayer, a little nod toward a little hot water, shot through some dark grounds and a dash of steamed milk come to mind. And deeper thoughts, which one has alone before God, stringier and wilder and fiercer that form a spiritual struggle.

And it didn't fare well for our poor Farm and Patrick Gertrude. In order to steel her heart within the will of the community, Sister Patrick Gertrude has begun giving herself music lessons. In her free time, donning sheet music with a fingering chart, she gets herself up in the prayer garden with our friend Saint Francis—and a little close to the edges of the farm—and *skweeeeks* and whistles and toots and steams out shrill sounds on her soprano recorder.

Between the toots and off-notes, the missed notes—all the clever noises her recorder seems to know how to make— she perhaps has levitated her heart to God, but the gang of us Sisters trying to use our free time for writing or prayer or bird-watching—are devising a campaign to find a way to offer the recorder its own demise.

I know you are Protestant, Miriam, but I hope you will not chide me for my aversion to the newfound musical scores that Sister Patrick Gertrude has discovered. Somewhere, someway, in the attic of the monastery, Sister Patrick Gertrude discovered a little book of notes and chords and words and military-sounding songs otherwise known as the *1934 New Baptist Hymnal for the Saints of God in Christ Jesus.*

I may have been warmer to Protestants as a group once, but we Sisters have grown weary under the weight of "Soldiers of Christ, Arise," "Will You Wait with Me One Hour," and "There Shall Be Showers of Blessing."

And I can say with all assurance that for Mother Lourdes, this isn't quite working out as she thought.

For now, I will sign off, Miriam. Wishing you healing mercies and good hopes in this personal journey. I hope my little notes offer you something for your joy,

Your Sister Athanasius

The Secret of Life

11 November 2003

Yes, Miriam, you are right: I haven't yet attended to your question about vocation, the details of my coming here. Some things touch deeply, and I almost fear the revisiting of them. We may train our memories in a certain direction, making ourselves to be spiritual heroines to our minds. But as you have written in your last letter, *this illness has me at the honestest I've ever been. Just ask Franklin, who might think that an honest look at everything has its down side, for sure. But for me it's like getting a lungful of air after being underwater. How is it, now with cancer in me there's something fierce growing, something completely alive? I want to look at everything like this.*

Your struggle with cancer has gotten me desiring to revisit the painful notes within the mixture of the treasured ones, for doesn't that imitate life? Over a plate of too-browned bear claws (which Little Sister didn't feel she could sell in such a state, which Sister Anne alerted me to, making me tea and not making herself a coffee, which goes to show the kind of character she has, when the rule for bear claws is Always an Accompanying Coffee), I told Sister Anne about your letter, and my own interest in developing a little fortitude in desiring honesty within myself. She took a bite of the bear claw and gave me a wink, saying: "The secret of life is honesty and fair dealing. If you can fake that, you've got it made." She gave a little giggle. "That was a Groucho Marx line for you, in case you want to lose your nerve. Either way, you're all right by me," she said as she finished off a bear claw and picked at the remaining crumbs.

Miriam, do you know that my first work here was cleaning bathrooms—alongside the life of prayer—was cleaning linens, washing down the basins. Now bathrooms are a task I'm relieved to say I have not had in years. Still, one knows it's as important a task as any other—but, oh, the thought of the hair plastered down at the drain or those short, private curls of hair sitting in each drain, or bits of chipped nails that never reach the waste basket. All this my imagination looks on with horror. I bless Sister Patrick Gertrude who cleans our obvious messes and does not expect anything other from the human experience of shared bathrooms.

However, the topic of vocation must, herewith, begin, and I will not defer to Groucho Marx. I may have written to you previously about vocation and one's own will—the two necessities for entering religious life. *Vocation,* a calling, comes from God. *Our wills,* then, respond to the extended grace of the calling. These are the dual steps toward the doors of the vowed life.

In order to test both vocation and our wills, the religious life begins with a series of visits to the monastery, then a move to postulancy to the novitiate to temporary vows. In our community, this is a period of roughly five years. This allows a religious community to authentically question the integrity and grist of the young postulant/novice's will.

Oh, Miriam, as though I were presenting a homily, I would like to state my earlier feeling about the importance of the twining of Vocation and Will. And it is what I would wish for you, Miriam dear, if ever that puzzlement of family—husband, children—were ever sorted through to bring you to a sense of place with those you love and sometimes can't abide (as I think back to those early letters from you: how sharp and discouraged and open and loving).

But I came to the convent, and here is the confession: with solely *will*. Not knowing vocation (spiritual or professional), I have willed for so many years, with fervent energies to this effect that I am now a vowed Sister. But the truth to be written is that I came to this monastic life as the result of both great passion and great fear.

When I was 19, my second year at a new Catholic women's university, I felt myself on new ground in this experimental place, opening up, as a young woman interested in new, bold ideas. This was the era of Roosevelt's WPA and FAP. And Jackson Pollock and Georgia O'Keefe exploring the old world in a new visual language. And John Steinbeck and Richard Wright putting pens to the page to mark what no one had quite marked before. And Heidegger and Bakhtin. *Where had I been and what was this new language for the world?* I wondered. I witnessed a change to the world. I read constantly and widely, spending time with people utterly and wondrously unlike myself. I suppose it was expected, the new college experience, the lightness one feels when detached from the source of familial pressure and conventions of religion. In that time I fell into the complication of love. A religion writer, guest lecturing in a class. Typical, isn't it? Quaint, even, these days. Well, during that time many things came clear, none of which I knew how to respond to, surprised as I was by everything.

Twelve years his junior, I flopped into love, my whole self toward two things: my education and this man. The way he wore his watch, loose and silver on his arm, which had fine beautiful and dark hairs against even darker skin—I recall such singular pictures. I have always remembered tiny things, pictures, moments. (Sometimes now I think this kind of memory can be a burden.)

The tragedy was—or perhaps no tragedy at all—was that I understood early on what a great mess romantic love can be—freeing and binding, sensual and greedy, creative and uncontrollable. There was so much heat in my young body that I feared the destruction that I might partake in—or perhaps feared that this also might bring me great joy at someone's expense—perhaps even my own. What a tangle, what a comedy, what an error, what a mess.

Oh, Miriam, you can guess the story—it's so much everyone's story, yet it was my very own: this newness, life afire.

I began slowly to grow impulsive, restless, and found that I had so placed my hopes in the stocky embrace of this writer that I wondered about misdirected longing—was he truly the object of my affection? Or did I have great passion and merely directed it at him, who understood me so well?

You can imagine that for these many years I have pondered these things, wondering if vocation actually was what called me to religious life.

Well, in the writer's study one day, waiting as though a patient at an office as he tapped and zinged at line-ends on his Royal, I came across a book by Hildegard of Bingen in his office, and saw her modern paintings, almost spiritually hallucinogenic and feminine, and her notes about *veriditas*, or divine greening. Something akin to St. Teresa's ecstasy was in it. I don't know if it was that she captured sensual desire and made God the object or if there was something sensual and natural in this greening brought about by God, but at this certain moment in time another kind of importance sounded aloud within me. Daylight was closing down, the writer brought his lovely bulk to me, waiting; I had a book by a medieval mystic in my hands, which elaborated on sensuality and longing and unity—and then, simply, the nearby college's chapel bells rang. And rang. And rang. So eternally long. I grew frightened.

It seemed that the church called to me there, in that small space, with this book in my hands, and I could only respond to the church. I left everything then, and came to this monastery. No goodbyes, just a small packed bag and I left, that's all.

When I came through these gates—5 States and 3 days later—I told myself fiercely, I would redirect my longings. Later I reminded myself of this, thinking: *as Sister Mary Patrick Gertrude devotes herself to faith and ecstatic smells. Just so easily would I.*

Here is the little seed one can call the truth: I came here for all the wrong reasons. With a barely containable impassioned self, and I came with fierce will to make the vowed life *my* life.

So, Miriam dear, you know more directly some of my early turmoil of vocation—who knows what my vocation truly was meant to be? Yet I have found footing here: in the hours of the day, in prayer and work and the company of those, like Sister Anne, who have a heart deep and wide.

I'd like to say at least that there have been spiritual ecstasies. But they elude me. The closest I've come was my being ill with pneumonia, so unmovable and weak that the Sisters had to lift up my bed and carry it to the infirmary, down two hallways. And that, Miriam, has been my only means of levitation.

Romance among humans, and romance with God contain few promises, many risks. And it will always be the way you and I want to live with love, don't you think?

I know in your next letter you will ask me—you try so hard to make connections, figure out motivations—if I have told anyone about my gentleman? Well, Mother Mary Paul (the previous Prioress) refused novices at the hint of misdirected piety. I took no risks, gathering my spiritual skirts and my story to myself. Not the best beginnings in vocation.

Do you wonder, now, that I tell you? As confession, I do. And maybe I have partaken in Groucho Marx's hiddenness of purpose. So I add my story in.

I did make confession to a priest early on, but found it a necessity to tell someone else my heart's failures in later years, my strong will and my weak calling to the vowed life. I told Sister Farm. She, as you have divined through these letters, is no talker, but a hard-staring listener to the core. And Sister Anne, too, knew the story. And they have been faithful to pray for me these many years, there amidst the Buff Orpingtons and our two Jersey bovines: Petunia and Sweetcakes.

The story ever continues. Yours. Mine. Messy or not. Ill or not. Blessings ever as you find a place of rest in your inward spirit, where the spirit of God dwells.

Yours,
Sr. Athanasius

30 November 2003
First Advent

It's quite hard, Miriam, to tolerate a good time when someone else is having it. A string of pennywhistle hymns in the TV room in the waning afternoon light seems to have fouled almost every heart here. (Though there's something about that hymn "Amazing Grace"—no matter that Sister Patrick Gertrude plays only the alto notes (as she hasn't learned the high notes yet)—that hymn shaves down resentments in us—though the "Battle Hymn of the Republic" can undo all those efforts, as fast as the sounds come around the bend.

For Mother Lourdes's part, it's on to another plan, which she has yet to devise. Until then, toots and screeches and the hymn-writer Fanny Crosby from the TV room, and the fear that she'll discover the Birth of Christ section of the Baptist hymnal and ruin a set of our beloved carols.

As for myself, early mornings I am thinking surely sinfully and with abandon about returning visits to the coffee bean.

And Sister Farm, so distracting are the a-musical tones of the

TV room recorder, that she, once again, has set her heart on finding her donkey, her Poitou jenny, for the last barn stall in time if not for Christmas Eve, then Palm Sunday—(I would like to say, on all our parts, that this has been a trying season)—as though Jesus himself, like the Lone Ranger, might ride again. Sister Farm confided in me that she has been reading her *Uncle Henry's Weekly Swap or Sell It Guide* for a possible mention of one such donkey. But the small farm does in fact need a small tractor, so she's looking for that as well.

Miriam, so it goes with our donkeys and shrill recorders.

I suppose my making light of these things tries to cover them, but I don't mean to be glib, about this or about my last letter. I know that we are facing moments of difficulty and all trying our way to attend to the good work of the soul. And I know that your life brings with it, even now, its own set of shrill notes, unbearable, which you even still bear.

Some days it overwhelms me, a sudden gratefulness for our life of prayer, moments through which these things pour over me. In a natural way, as though what came from the heart were simply prayer. And this is the place I bring hopes for you, and Franklin, Emily, Brendan, your minutes and hours and roads and travels. And I am grateful to be for you in this way. And I know that prayer is also the way you bend toward God and others. And what life isn't held slightly more upright when prayer is near?

And you wrote, asking about Sister Anne, who tries to get around without a walker. Arthritis and her diminishing balance put her always in some version of a sway that you think will knock her against the stone walls or floor. But when she takes the proffered arm and we walk along together, she will offer me a succinct line of wisdom. The quotes don't discount complexity, but they do enfold a simplicity.

Within the history of monasticism, the earliest monks and ascetics, the desert fathers and mothers, lived in caves. People visiting them would ask for wisdom, for a simple word, something they could take, ponder, for days or months, or maybe years. Once they had pondered and practiced the word of wisdom and done all to incorporate it in the interior place, they would return for another word.

"Attend to daily things as you daily can," Sister Anne will say to me, in that same spirit, knowing it could be years before I might make that line my own. Still, she is generous with her lines, making her way toward the sink in the kitchen, beginning to disengage the caked-on effects of a meal, cleaning each pot, each pan.

In between those words are her other words, about the Red Sox: the heartbreak over the firing of Grady Little, the manager who took a team from disarray to one of its best seasons; her opinions about keeping Pedro pitching in the last game ("Still the best player for the moment"). When I teasingly ask her where the spiritual teaching is in *those* words, she calmly blinks. "Oh, it's there. You just need to look a little differently for it."

In other news, Sister Farm has gone up to New Hampshire inquiring after 3 of *Uncle Henry's Swaps* and returned with, sigh, a tractor. And with, sigh, no little Poitou donkey for her over-recordered heart.

"I fear trouble" were Mother Lourdes's first words when she heard the news: no Poitou and spirits low and still the recorder notes from the TV room, with "Sweet Hour of Prayer" replaced by "As with Gladness Men of Old," still the alto lines, playing to dreadful monotony. Mother Lourdes added, "I fear that holiness is being misplaced by self-merit, pettiness, and simple indirection."

Sister Anne misheard. "I don't think we're as far as insurrection, Mother Lourdes. Though we don't look like a model community at the moment."

"InDIRection," Little Sister said, heading for the bakery. "And how were the bear claws?"

"Tolerable with coffee. Though I'd need about three more to really be sure on that."

Miriam, we have stuck to them hard, these merits of silence, service and prayer. And maybe it will have to be long since the next plan hasn't hatched in Mother Lourdes's mind yet.

I will keep you apprised, Miriam. And I trust these letters bring you something of the spirit of cheer in Advent days. Even if we are a dour community of religious at the moment, we do have bear claws, and the bright blue skies of December days. And more time for prayer. None of these can be too terribly bad, can they?

Wishing you all directions toward healing that our Lord might grant. You remain in all of our prayers.

Yours,
Sister Athanasius

7 December 2003
Second Advent

Miriam Dear—

As you have told me how your letter routine works: awaiting the quietest moment of the day, slipping to the oak table with a view toward the yard, the birdfeeders (how, by the way, do your bird friends like that nyjer feeder? what sort of bird does it invite these days just before winter?). Then pouring yourself some coffee—the divinity of brown fluid, breathing in the steam, a grand sip, then either your letter to me—the writing process. Or a coffee and steam and when a letter arrives: the reading process. I am so glad you told me that you are, indeed, a coffee drinker. And I respect that teas come the afternoon and evening—teas for the antioxidant properties. Doctors' orders must be followed and cups of tea seem like a fine doctor prescription. Tea offers something, then, special, later in the day, if that is the time of day "for a cupper," as Sister Anne says.

Isn't it grand, the sending and receiving of letters, the attention to small things, the making of a space in your soul for such things as words, ink, alphabets, punctuation marks? I treasure each letter exchange along with you. And even the morning coffee on your part is truly a great joy on mine.

Miriam, in your last letter—how kind you were, responding to my confessional letter, my religion writer. *How hard it would be,* you wrote, *to live in such a community and be dead silent about earlier, important things. It doesn't seem right.*

You are right, a private life—a hidden life—isn't meant to plant feet here. The Bingean Rule #23 speaks to it: of lives surrendered to each other, offering both our strength of spirit and our human fault to be humbled as well as uplifted.

But, Miriam, there are a few ways to approach this life. One is to open up to it—to, in many ways, forsake the hidden life, so that all of us Sisters are working with a commonality, a transparency to each other. This is the ideal in the Bing tradition.

Another way is to nurse one's hidden agenda. Though living in community often makes it unhidden, for even those who hide from themselves often find it hard to hide from each other. That would be Sister Farm's and Sister Patrick Gertrude's approach. They do not pretend that they tolerate each other—all surfaces, out in the open. But the openness to making change, which is also part of the Rule, is not always theirs. With exceptions like Sister Anne, this is where most Sisters here reside. Our inward desires, thoughts, hurts arise like boils on the outside, yet inwardly we protect those boils for some reason. Feeling ourselves righteous in holding on to them. Or, if the Holy Spirit gives conviction, there's that terrible tension inside oneself between nursing an antagonism or presenting the same with open hands to God (I write that as though that were easy, where, from my own letters, you perceive that it is not).

Then there are those who for whatever reason, having been hurt or having a privateness of disposition, reserve the hidden life—the deepest places—for themselves alone—or for themselves and for God.

It's not always clear to me which group a person might reside in, but those groupings exist, don't you think so, Miriam? Of course we like to believe things about ourselves that aren't true, so in that spirit, I'd like to think I'm in a more sanctified version of the third. Though, God only knows where I am.

And you, my dear? Where do you find yourself? I suspect you of openness of heart. In your letters I have been grateful for a clear-eyed hope that offers itself to others so kindly, graciously. As we started this correspondence, Miriam, I had the idea that I might be of some spiritual help to you, but I see that you take a directness in attending to your own spiritual life that calls you to intimacy with God, and that I have been quite in the wrong in my early assumptions. And still you ask me about spiritual matters, and still I know that you have a spiritual stream within yourself, deep and wide.

—

Mother Lourdes asked me into her office yesterday. Often something is amiss. Sometimes she'll ask for my opinion on an aspect of our monastery that is gathered into a conundrum. She'll sometimes ask to meet with the counsel of the older members of the community: Sister Anne, Sister Patrick Gertrude and me for matters that require counsel consent or recommendation.

When it's an issue of personal concern and Mother Lourdes asks to talk about my troubles, it feels like God calling my name on the day of reckoning—that mix of dread (at knowing my failings) and joy (knowing that, failings or not, I am in the presence of God).

Indeed, when called in, I run through the various snags in my conscience, but cannot, this time, find glaring grounds for "a visit."

Mother Lourdes called me in to ask about our letters back and forth. My confession was that these letters, Miriam, are more a delight to me, perhaps rather than the help she might hope for you.

"Miriam's a good soul, isn't she?" Mother Lourdes said, "for you to trust her with your thoughts in these letters? I had hoped these letters would be akin to those from Saint Francis de Sales to Philothea, but," and here she gave a little wink, "but I suspect you of having a little more of honesty and humor and the personality of St. Teresa. I don't know but that the writing might prove itself to be very good. Now, tell me about Miriam, and how she is doing. Do you think we might give her a call, perhaps we could pray with her? And her daughter's name, again? "

"Emily."

"Yes, I have often prayed for her, growing up, coming into her voice and herself. And now so fearful for her mother's helplessness with illness. The one whom we expect should be strong."

And, Miriam, of course we did call, and heard Franklin's voice and yours. And your crying. There is something about Mother Lourdes, when she prays, that crying is the only thing—out of grace and relief and hope—that can be done. And so we met, Miriam, almost in person, and your voice a sort of musical drawl, is how it sounded to me.

And, Miriam, it's true that our letters are a delight for my soul, a way to understand your spirit, and also mine. I am no Francis de Sales. As you well know,

Sr. A—

2 days later

Miriam, dear—

This letter grows long, and I add now bits of news, of inquiry, details of the rhythm in our days. A whole lot of *stuff.* You don't mind, do you? Yesterday, Sister Anne felt weak, so I helped her to the chapel for Matins, then over to the kitchen to her little spot at the long steel table for coffee, the sports page (depending on baseball season, whether she's looking at trades and waivers and contracts or last night's runs, hits and errors), and maybe a leftover sweet bread from the bakery goods on the rack to go to local stores. I sat with her, seeing her from station to station (chapel and meals and prayer and such), and brought a letter that I wanted to start to you. Though started another. Writing, writing away, I was, and she leaned over toward me, coffee in one hand and paper in the other and said, "Now, Sister, don't you forget to put the kitchen sink in there, and my mug, too. Get it all in. And the Red Sox—get Wakefield in there." So here they all are, as most things usually are in letters to you. Everything. The kitchen sink.

Mother Lourdes implemented her latest attempt at quelling the squalls of our little landscape—a little early Advent party. If nothing else, she brings great imagination, if not great problem solving, to our monastery at the edge of the land and the edge of the ocean.

A party. And for a glory minute there was grace in that time apart from the work and silence. Our dear friends, the Brothers from St. Benedict's monastery in Vermont, gave us the last bottles of this year's wine and we, in the spirit in which it was given, took the gift and joyfully imbibed.

Sister Farm, subdued but smiling. Sister Patrick Gertrude, filled with the Spirit, positively left her alone, even came close to Sr. Farm to leave her a little bottle of wine. A genuine passing of the peace.

Mother Lourdes's idea for a party, a splendid one. As you may know, we share some aspects of the Bingean Holy Rule with Saint Benedict's Rule. In Saint Benedict's direction for spiritual leaders, among the things leaders are to take into consideration: "that the strong have ideals to inspire them and the weak may not be frightened away by excessive demands" (chapter 64 of the Rule of Saint Benedict).

Though leadership comes through diligent discipline for her, it is clear that Mother Lourdes holds everyone in esteem. She ponders the faults of each, finding ways to challenge and encourage rather than harshly discipline a fault away. She values discipline only as a means of effecting a change in the heart, not simply the actions of each Sister. She said to me once, "Who couldn't act the part? The real test is if one's heart speaks out the truth." True conversion, to be motivated by what is good, by the God of love—continues to be her goal. And if Mother Lourdes begins with a harsh discipline, she often ends with a party, rejoicing in the life of each Sister and her contribution to the community life.

Even if we were given to thinking crossly of someone, with Bach cantatas in the background, some wine, and the gathering of religious Sisters who live so much in the cycle of days: work, prayer & quiet— it's surprising we all know what to do at a party. As though we were 7 layers lighter. As though Sister Farm could put off her searches (eternal) through *Uncle Henry's Swap Book* for a Poitou jenny. (Though now that I think of it, she may want to swap something—anything—for the soprano recorder.) And since everyone is scrubbed up and clean, Sister Patrick Gertrude was in a feeling of great ease.

Mother Lourdes kept pouring the wine—the last of a full sort of chardonnay. A gift of cheeses (cheddars, and washed rind, and triple cream cheeses) given this Advent from our Sisterhouse in Wisconsin, which has a dairy farm. (As an aside, Miriam, I sometimes wonder if Sister Farm secretly longs to be transferred to that community. But if her longings are in that direction, she does not say so.)

With the shining array of Advent lights against the winter darkened windows, we feasted as though at the Marriage Supper of the Lamb. At 10:00 p.m. (a nun's midnight), cheers and prayers. At 10:30 all were loathe to leave, even Sister Anne who, for such a tiny thing, can tolerate a fair amount of wine; she seemed almost sturdy on her feet. For a thick set of hours in the monastery, we were a community of friends.

And so it is, grace.

And so it is that Mother Lourdes's scheme of charity through parties is the first thing that has provided a few moments of reprieve.

It's now 11:00 a.m. I've wanted to write this while things are fresh in mind; the way a few of us stepped out late in the celebrations, late at night. I gave my arm to Sister Anne, who felt a cane would be inappropriate for such a hopeful evening. Though with the city in the distance it's often hard to see the basic lines of stars and the gathering of light in galaxies—the clear air presented us with both dippers, the Seven Sisters (close to our numbers), a planet—which none of us knew what it was. Jupiter? Do you know, Miriam? And the Hunter with his long stride and crooked belt. And the accompanying vocalizing quickly identified by Sister Bird as an Eastern screech owl. "Oh," Sister Farm said, "is that the whickering owl? What some call the shivering owl?"

"The same," said Sister Bird, "but their song sounds much more whickering during spring and summer," Sister Bird said. "And uncommon here at the edge of winter, so this is a treat."

And so it was, the cold, sharp winter night's gift.

And Miriam, with the whickering owl, I send you the hope of other gifts of winter. Of healing and joy, and fullest hope.

Yours,
Sister Athanasius

(1 day later)

Miriam Dear,

I have discovered a little secret. Perhaps it is wine and a festival that loosens connections that have long been congregating in some minds, but my wonderings about Sister Farm's interests have been revealed: she made appeal to Mother Lourdes about the dairy farm at the Sisterhouse in Wisconsin, complete with 148 cows, 53 sheep, and a shepherd border collie named Eustace. (Though, as yet without a donkey.)

Was it the wine? The quiet sitting near the two Advent candles flickered in reflection against the pane glass windows?

Whatever the case, Sister Farm has requested conference with Mother Lourdes. Perhaps the appreciation for the cheeses—our communal delight in the dairyness of it all, gave Sister Farm a vision of what working with a light spirit might mean.

After the meeting, Mother Lourdes called in Sister Anne, Sister Patrick Gertrude, and me—the oldest in the community. These were among the questions raised.

* Our farm here, despite hard work and efforts to find profit for the community, consistently comes in short in funds for the monastery. Among the incomes brought in by the others (bakery, birding, etc.), it is the smallest amount.
* Despite this, is Sister Farm's desire to be assigned to another farm because she doesn't feel her work here is important? That we impede that work in some way? Is she asking to leave out of fear, anger, frustration and/or the lack of a donkey?
* Is the nature of communal life a calling for the working out of such issues? Or do we accept failure (as Sister Farm sees her work here) as somehow a sign that it would be good for her to move on to a place where her professional gifts would be put to good use?
* Who would take over the farm here? Would we let it go?

The questions went into the long and extreme, so I will not list them all. The one question not raised was the question that finally Sister Patrick Gertrude raised. Though she sat mostly silent, when Mother Lourdes asked, "Would you like to add any thoughts?"

"I wouldn't," she replied. "But I will. No one ever thought the farm would be viable. It shows how ridiculous Sr. Farm is. The one question not yet raised may be the entire reason for her wishing to leave: that is myself. I have opinions on the topic, and none of them will aid a decision. That being the case, may I leave this room to go play the recorder?"

Minutes later, down the hallway the new soprano sounds of the recorder, and I thought it might be "In the Sweet By and By."

To her credit Mother Lourdes listened and held back. This is more than I could ever do when my opinions seem so important and useful on so many issues.

Later we took our leave, after the reasons detailed for staying and for going. And none of us wanted to be in Mother Lourdes's shoes. When a Sister leaves, it means unspeakable loss to holding up the community. But time will tell, and Mother Lourdes will not rush a decision.

Miriam, that is all our news here. The sounds of the whickering owl, ever so far away from this moment.

And you? I trust that your visit with this new doctor means some sort of progress toward health. What a long road for you, each new doctor, each new test. Even that feels like such a wound. I cannot imagine on top of those things, the struggle with cancer, and what you call, *that surreal sense of trying to live within my family's life, as though it could not fall apart for us.*

Miriam, it's a weight I'm sorry you carry. I can imagine that Franklin feels the same, trying to carry things as though the morning coffee together, there watching the winter outside your window, were always going to be the watching of seasons out of the window, the drinking of coffee, essential mornings.

Prayers, always, for God's grace in each day's demands. And God's joy in the morning coffee (it is always my wish, that one).

Yours, Sister A—

PS1 Early Advent Birdwatch: a red-breasted nuthatch munching on birdseed in the garden, a Carolina wren, a very (very) late-seasoned scarlet tanager, and a snowy owl.

PS2 And I *am* mailing this off this morning, handing this letter to our postal worker, finally.

10 December 2003

Miriam, my dear—

Another letter on the heels of the one just sent. Were I not cemented by vows, requested by Mother Lourdes to stay . . . yet so much wanting to be with you now, if only to *feel* that I *could* be of help.

I wonder, sometimes, at having hastened to a life that demands a certain distance from those who form the entire shape of my heart in prayer. Only God knows the mysteries of this.

You'll forgive me, won't you, for reading to the Sisters a small portion of the latest letter from you, received just now? I have let them know of the heavy news of these past weeks—the upcoming surgery. After the hope of a cancer shrinking, now the removal of the breast. Already this Friday's surgery is in our concerns, with special intentions in prayer for you.

Your friend Sister Farm (who often asks about in her abrupt way, "Miriam?" and raises to an arch her right eyebrow, which always pops up in moments of concern) is distraught on your behalf. She has taken to feverish work in the barn. (This is always what she calls her "best kind of prayer" for you.)

Your old friend Sister Anne asked our Prioress, Mother Lourdes, for a special dispensation on Thursday evening, allowing Sister Anne to keep vigil for you in the chapel throughout the night and into Friday. This means, she will make prostrations, keep the candles burning bright, and pray for your safety through this surgical journey.

And, as you know, where Sister Anne goes, I go. But how she makes prostrations is beyond me, entirely a painful process of love and prayer.

You are in all of our prayers. And Mother Lourdes asks that I send all of our best wishes and our deepest prayers,

Sister Athanasius

12 December 2003

Miriam, dear—

This morning you are in surgery. Doctor Wu, the surgeon, has our prayers covering her two hands, her keen insights. We pray for wisdom, exactness, understanding.

Last night, Sister Anne and I were in the chapel. Walking back together to the cloister we heard the same whickering owl declaring its place in the nighttime. She told me that she felt in some way she could carry part of your burden for you, in the hopes of lightening yours.

This morning, the morning of your surgery, we are keeping silence for you, praying with keener, observant attention, our intentions for you. Cheering you on. In this way, Miriam, we share the burdens of the world and participate in them—though we seem removed. How I would like to be a little body at prayer in the waiting room with rosary beads, waiting quietly for good news. Yet I know you have good family and the extended charity of your church friends. All of us, with our place. How grateful I am for the work of God in this world, holding you up.

And, as you are a reader of Emily Dickinson. I end the letter with:

> In the name of the Bee —
> And of the Butterfly —And of the Breeze—Amen!

Sr. A.—

[Postcard, postmark December 16]

"There are many people like many people, but there's no one

like Miriam." That's what I told God today. "Please, gracious Lord, be near her now."

Thinking of you, Sr. A—

18 December 2003

Dear One,

Your own Franklin gave us a call this afternoon. It seems he got our number through Tom. What a small group of friends we are! He was very reserved and polite and thanked us for our prayers. I had him on the phone, so I inquired as to your health especially, but also your children, Emily and Brendan. He let us know that you are feeling better: up & walking, even wanting to go running, which worried him some. He asked me if I might offer a little advice, if you asked. I told him that in your letters you didn't so often mention your health and if so, then in a general sort of way, so I didn't know what I could do. But, Miriam, as Franklin asked and was sweet and concerned, I will ask you to do your part and trust your good sense as a nurse on matters of health and exercise, among all the other things you know so well. So glad, dear, for good days, good news, good hope, and your own kind-hearted Franklin.

We will continue to pray for you. Sister Anne often will stay up late in prayer for you, novenas. I worry about the late nights, her old bones, but she insists that, "a good night in prayer shakes out the cricks and maws."

Oh, Miriam, to hear that the news from Doctor Wu is all of a successful surgery.

The Bings have published a prayer book, along with the Rule of Hildegard (though a shortened version, a sort of Greatest Hits), a pocket edition. I told Sister Farm about your Hildegard research, and she suggested we send one to you. Of course there's always a little deciphering to be done when she makes a suggestion: "Miriam? Prayer book?" Her cut corners rely on intuition on the listener's part to get the job done—and *that* is Sister Farm's delight in any endeavor, to get the job done.

Perhaps as she tinkers in the evening hours on her tractor, a Kioti LK3054, she tells us, or rigging up something new with a hitch bolt and a clevis pin, she tries to sort out a language that is absolutely concise. I don't know. But she is a mix of parts. Do you know this about her, that she smokes a cigar? This is no endearment to our Sister Patrick Gertrude, as you might imagine. By week's end the cigar, which has been cut, licked up and down (to make it burn better, she says), chewed and multiply lit and stubbed, lit and stubbed, looks like a farmyard animal deposit. One cigar lasts one week with her—"for health sake," she says. There's also this, her one bit of vanity, a short and treasured mullet—not quite monastic standard, but as Sister Bird cuts hair here, it's acceptable all-around.

And, as usual, I am digressing. Back to her "Miriam?" and the arched brow: We will indeed send you a prayer book and invite you to pray with us, any hours of the Divine Office that you wish as you recover and gain strength.

Though we live apart from the world, we do not want to live apart from the anxiety and pain you have been living with. Maybe that is where hope has its largest test, in these days where Sister Anne gathers frailty like a billowing garment. Perhaps it makes her the stronger in prayer. And you, with your infusions of chemotherapy, these have also been your daily test of hope.

I do not speak lightly of hope, as though it were merely "the thing with feathers," as your poet friend Emily Dickinson says. I know it is also the very hard work in circumstances that insist that hope has no feathers at all.

One of the psalms we chanted today at Lauds ends, "Take courage, and hope in the Lord"—always reminding me that hope is not facile, but tough and courageous.

And so I end this letter. Take courage, Miriam. Courage,

Sr. A—

Dearest Miriam—

Just received your letter, and adding these notes before I mail this one. Your anxiousness mixes with ours these days as we do not know if we will be losing our Sister Farm. And no one quite knows how we will give her up to the Sisters at the convent in Oconomowoc, Wisconsin.

Sister Farm looks somehow a sort of shrunken version of herself. As though she knows and doesn't know. She wears the suspicion that whatever decision will come, it will be made at some cost to others, not just herself. And she's shoring her wiry body to carry the weight. Still, she's resigned.

Our Sister Patrick Gertrude has quieted down, less precisely verbal in her jabs against the farm and Sister Farm and more melody lines now from the Baptist hymnal. She's one for a corrective, so if she can't affect a change in someone—and someone who might leave in a short period of time—then she'll bide her time.

And that, my dear Miriam, is entire conjecture on my part, but there it is. As we all do at times, I try to fill in the *gaps* that I don't understand, as though some speculative idea regarding motives is somehow a *better* idea than no idea. But I often, maybe you've noticed in my letters, drive conjecture too far. I am not astute about the simplest things.

As Charles Baxter has written, "the point [has been] made that happiness has a quality of invisibility." So, Miriam, we may all be, actually, very very happy. But I've filled in the invisibility gaps in my own little sorrowful way instead. The good news is that within a month or so we'll have something solid—something answerly—to hold onto. In the meantime, I am pondering all over the place and trying to signify everyone's quieted approach to the vowed life.

May I take a turn, asking about your days? Your last letter was short and quiet in tone, except to say that Doctor Wu and the others are positive, after your surgery, that chemo is merely an overly cautious follow-up. And I am wondering if the chemo means it is a challenge to write at all, with the kind of tiredness that I hear pulls like a gravity.

These days I wonder how the sun sets, and if the oak table view of the yard also has the rising or setting sun. And I wonder, in this chill weather, how you manage a return to your work at the hospital. And the notes in your letters, how your daughter Emily is trying to find her voice coming into high school. I think the freshman year of anything can feel like a shadow on a year. When you wrote, *My baby girl—she hates when I call her that—is awkward and brilliant, the way those young girls are. We fight over the things every house fights over: skirts too short, bathing suits too revealing, too much make-up. She says I'm the most conservative mother she knows. I don't mind, unless I'm tired, then I mind everything, even Franklin being kind. I am too tired for even kindness.*

Emily's biggest fear is that she may not be popular enough. 'Distinctive,' she calls it. It's what we all fear at one time or another, didn't you, Sr. A? And then when she goes to college, she'll have—truth!—decided her voice is the most distinctive among the voices. And she'll have a full cry of discovering new and tiny things in the cracks between classes and friends and reading and living. Sr. A, when you wrote about your religion writer and learning, that was exactly how I found it too (the learning part!), my voice growing and interested in this new world. But I'm rushing her ahead to the next stage of her life, hoping that maybe this will be the stage when daughters start liking their mothers again.

Miriam, oh those stages of growth. Each one a lesson speaking into the next lesson. How wonderful it will be to find yourselves, mother & daughter, well past the bathing suit discussion and on to the mutual conversations, where loves are shared—and where you also share coffees. To me, when you have coffee together, it's always a hopeful sign. Ah, coffee. Even writing the word . . .

I write this early morning, and I must be off to help Sister Anne prepare for the day and Matins, and then coffee, of course, so I must rush off to prayer, to tea (oh, sigh), to the division of labors, to the minutiae and beauty that is religious life.

In the meantime, sending love, as always,

Sr. Athanasius

Oh, Miriam—

Yet an addition before this letter is mailed. Our Sister Anne is unwell. I know she's been unwell, but she is somehow, unwell*er* than before. She has begun accepting the cane as her constant companion, though she asked Mother Lourdes if, please, she could defer use of a walker as long as possible.

We are having quieter days. A hush has fallen on us old girls. We all take turns helping Sister Anne to the chapel.

Such a quick note, but more later,

Sr. A—

Donkeys, Trailers, Bumper Stickers, Coffee

21 December 2003

Miriam, dear—

The struggles you mentioned: I think of it as a time of life, the way a person takes a measure, as with sewing, and then makes adjustments in the pattern, and then makes cuts.

Whatever is calling out to us: professional life or relationships, children, marriage, it doesn't seem to matter, our lives seem to shout at these times (if we are listening to our lives) for cutting, sewing, a change in the fabric. I often think back to that first letter you wrote, wondering if that was part of such a measuring place.

Coming into finer focus are the things we may have wanted early on but didn't receive. And now our hearts are ready to effect a change or mourn the loss, or, at least, to create new definition.

In my 40s I saw it as *something* that had been missing for years, now ready to be explored. And we are restless until we find *it*. The capital *IT* may be God. (If a religious doesn't have a theory that the *IT* might be God, then it's a pale sort of nun!) Or something that offers a new look.

It's a beautiful time and a tortured time, isn't it? In reading your letter, I feel I am watching you through a window, wondering what step you will next make and praying, my dear, for you. For God's direction in each magnificent step.

Though, Miriam, with illness I sometimes think the theory doesn't work, since illness itself is such a propelling force toward change, toward hope, toward reevaluation.

I am thinking, with a smile, about your Franklin's comment, when you told him about the surgery. I am shuffling through old letters, since I want to remember your wording. Here it is. You said to him: *"Franklin, it looks like you will be married to an Amazon, with this surgery."*

> *"A warrior race," he said. "Hmm. Now, that could come in handy. Isn't there some legend about Hercules set with the task of procuring a girdle from one of the Amazon warrior women? Hmm. I like this already."*
>
> *And, Sister Athanasius, a line like that can last a good long time with me. When I need good love, he comes around.*

Miriam, you tell Franklin he's a good man, would you?

Oh, and the news here: Sister Farm is both waiting for a new life elsewhere and also attending with real vigor to the old one (I think she's preparing herself either way.)

In the hopes of The Donkey, she has found a small one-horse trailer through *Uncle Henry's Weekly Swap* (aka Sister Farm's Bible)—no idea what she's swapping, but it may be that hymnal and recorder were right up there on the list. But we do have some odd farm machinery, mostly unused: a band-saw that was used about twice, a donation to the monastery from one of those Jesus people from that movement in the 1970s. I don't know if his religious fervor lasted, but this old saw has.

Other things have been donated by others—who, having heard we operated a farm, thought this could actually mean something largescale: a square baler (when of course, we all would prefer a round, though without a donkey, we have little need for hay (except a little for the chicken coop), let alone a baler, now that we have let that acre go to natural meadow. Now Sister Bird has a habitat that attracts killdeer, horned larks, American crows, sparrows, bobolinks (which she is very happy about), the occasional Eastern meadow lark (also a happy visitor). And in boxes up in the rough grasses, tree swallows.

I suspect Sister Farm will hold onto the baler a bit longer, just in case that miracle of mule-flesh comes along. And also because she rents it out to a local farm, come hay season.

We've got a John Deere riding mower, a small thing, which no one wants Sister Farm to swap, it's too perky and bright in the barn. (Not many farm implements really incorporate color or aesthetics, so we all vote it stays.) We do have an old Ford Taurus that's given us 190,000 miles, so that may be tradeable—or lose-able—however you see it. Sister Farm asked me to type up the list of tradeables for Mother Lourdes—"My handwriting won't help my case," she said. But type might give it that kick she's looking for, I guess.

And here's the ad she responded to: *One horse bp trlr used for goats, but good for other. $700, but prefer trade. Call 207.555.0125 and ask for Henry Komaki. Winterport, ME.*

Mother Lourdes watches over any ads Sister Farm writes up, making sure nothing like "will swap all for Poitou donkey" finds its way to *Uncle Henry's Swap.*

Four phone calls later, Sister Farm has worked out a swap deal. Out goes our Schulte horizontal bandsaw (worth a lot, but not to us)—call it $4000 down to about $750. We are also out 1 horse sickle bar mower (won't be missed), an old dump rake, 2 industrial tires and 1 healthy ewe, our own Genevieve, and two nameless lambs.

In turn, we get one small horse trailer and 2 round bales—the hay bales in preparation for the donkey, I suppose, which is in turn preparation for the Triumphal Entry of Jesus on Palm Sunday. It seems all things are preparations for other things.

Sister Farm has asked me to drive up to Winterport, Maine, in Waldo County. Anything with the name Waldo County and involving a road trip is worthwhile travel, in my book.

Well, I'm off to make travel plans. More soon, with road trip stories.

Yours,
Sr. A—

23 December 2003

Dear Miriam,

I am writing at the tail-end of an adventure. As I wrote earlier, Sister Farm asked me to go to Winterport with her, to help her watch the trailer hitch and pour coffee and such. (That this is allowed this late in Advent is an all-out desire to keep Sister Farm in this community.) I love a road trip and don't mind the job of checking the pick-up's rearview mirror for flying trailer parts.

There was talk in the swap, too, of a Suffolk shoat (I don't know what sort of pig that is, but I love things that sound specific and it sounds much fancier than merely *a piglet*). But I think the shoat transpired in call 3 and never returned for call 4.

Do you like a road trip, Miriam? If so, we had all the elements of a good one. We borrowed Sister Bird's plaid thermos with hottest strongest coffee. Though I am not allowed the coffee, who can call herself a traveler without a thermos of coffee? And I like pouring a coffee and smelling it (and those come very close to the entire experience of coffee, don't they?). We also brought blankets, 5 bungee cords, and one shovel thrown into the back of the pickup. "Pays to be prepared," said Sister Farm.

Sister Anne, though unable to make the long ride and hardly able to even climb the large step into the pickup, has insisted on taking part in the trip, somehow. Maybe the sound of a town like Winterport made it exciting to her. Whatever it is, she always cheers us on for adventures, so at 4:00 a.m. she got up to toast some bagels for us, make the coffee, pack a lunch (snuck two of Little Sister's bear claws and two chocolate glazed tarts as well as Sister Farm's favorite, HoHos—who knows where she smuggled those from, but doesn't that make the trip exciting already?).

Who could be disappointed in a road trip after that? And we hadn't even left. We took the Expressway North to the Maine Turnpike, then—my second job—map-reading and negotiating the smaller roads. By Winterport we felt well-traveled. The swap went swimmingly, and Henry Yoshi Komaki helped us hook up the trailer and blinkers once it was clear to him he had the better end of the swap. He had a bandsaw, a set of tires, a ewe and two small ones—all of which fully filled the back of the pickup. The ewe and lambs survived the travels cornered into the edge of the truck, but all made it just fine.

Driving back, to complete the road trip experience, we stopped at Crazy Jane's Diner in that little corner of New Hampshire that I-95 traverses and there we had late night waffles. I don't know why the trip took so long, maybe we stalled every part for the joy of it.

The only problem, Miriam, now looking back at the swap, is that the trailer Mister Henry swapped us looks like a junk-bin. It is made entirely worse by the problem of such bumper stickers as these, which maybe I shouldn't put to pen, but you and Franklin will appreciate the awkwardness:

* Dukakis
* Don't Come Knocking If This Van's Rocking
* Question Authority
* I Do Know Jack Shit
* Where am I and why am I in a handbasket?
* Shut up and drive
* You can have my gun when you pry it from my cold, dead hand

* Don't make me release the flying monkey
* I'd turn back if I were you
* Would somebody poke holes in the top of my jar?
* Honk if you love cleaning up the pieces
* Stop using Jesus as an excuse
* D.A.R.E. to keep cops off donuts
* Happiness is a belt-fed weapon

Henry Komaki. You know he loved hitching that trailer to our pickup, with these bumper stickers glaring.

Our respite at the diner off of I-95 had people coming out of the diner to read the other three sides. And who wouldn't wonder?—between our habits, our late-night ramblings in a pickup truck with a trailer cab, and the depository of all manner of statements—and coming upon Christmas Eve.

In a way, not in a nice way, but in a way, the cab covers everything: the basic issues and struggles related to God, mankind, violence, sex, & politics.

Not that it offers wisdom, exactly, but it does attend to questions we all have, questions that keep nagging at us: What do we believe about ourselves and others? Who do we trust? Will we find love (or sex) somewhere?

But that said, I will not sign up to swap with Henry Komaki again, no matter how fine a trailer or Poitou might come of it.

And, Miriam, you will not wonder that Sister Anne was the most delighted with the whole day—down to the bumper stickers. She asked to see the map, and brought her thick dark glasses up to her eyes to dutifully study. "But where did you say Crazy Jane's was?" And, "What sort of a man was Henry Komaki?" But my favorite comment of hers was, "So many people travel so far for so much less." I am grateful to be part of such a plan that still has no donkey in sight but all the anticipation and hurrah as though a donkey were in *suus via*.

By this point it was late, but Sister Anne, while leaning heavily against the sink, washed out the plaid thermos and cups. ("Start a thing and end a thing, it's the respect you can give a project," she says.) She insisted on being part of the setup and now the cleanup crew. The amount of effort she puts into a day, the weight of every motion is costly. Yet every day she spends herself out, and every night she comes up with more to spend. And she refuses to be overly protected or too kindly handled. "You'd have me forget the feel of hard worked hands. You don't know what you are trying to take away from me," she said to me after the long road trip day and the washing of the thermos.

There you have it, Miriam, a world of mysteries.

I have been chattering on about events here. I hope our adventure has translated into enjoyable reading for you.

As Sister Anne said to me, "You don't even know how important those letters to and from Miriam are, do you. Well, please greet your friend from me. Let her know I pray with the birds, late night with the owls, and early up with the sparrows. She'll like to know that."

And that is how you are cared for here, Miriam: prayers into late nights and early mornings,

Sister A—

5 January 2004

Miriam, dear,

These last weeks have been full and filled and difficult and gracing, and I trust that in your healing days where you are seeking reading and quiet, that this letter will provide at least some of the reading, though perhaps less of the quiet.

We all still wait on the news that no one can bear think about: Sister Farm's future. Sister Farm's newest embraced theology is what she calls farm prayer: attentive farm work. Yesterday was WD-40 prayer, I suppose, because Sister Farm greased every cog, line, edge, and chain, as well as the spring-loaded sheep pen gate, and barn door hinge. Perhaps having the farm in good repair for whatever comes is the goal. Perhaps keeping busy. Perhaps constant prayer.

I think of Simone Weil's suggestion that real spiritual work comes from doing something with attention, which is love. That is, when we focus on something/someone outside ourselves, we have directed ourselves toward something of God. What do you think, Miriam?

Well, as your last letter inquired, the new donkey trailer, which carried us all away with comments for the first week, has now not been so forefront. A vote was taken on which bumper stickers should be the first to go (cold, dead hand), which weren't as immediately offensive (flying monkey) and which might even stay (none really got the vote here).

Still no donkey. That is a reality. And still Sister Patrick Gertrude following trails of boot muck down the hall with Murphy's Oil Soap.

She's taken to quoting verses that sound scriptural, but not found in all Holy Writ. "Who will make a right sacrifice to the Lord? Let it be with sweet-smelling incense." Sister Farm, not the biblical scholar, simply considers it sacred text; she takes a breath as though she's counting to 10.

It's not that it's a losing battle, or a constant battle so much as it is Sister Patrick Gertrude's battle. One she alone fights. Don't pine and lemon, lavender and vanilla, salt air from the bay all sing the joys of the Creator? She, who uses her gifts most, suffers the most for it. Few could attend to a calling when all pushes against it. Yet she does. And Sister Farm does.

Most of us have straightforward calls with our larger vocations: birder, baker, farmer, laundress, hospice care, etc. Professions or vocations which do not seem to be in direct conflict with another's, as though it were complementary to others' work. But Sister Patrick Gertrude lives in a complexity of attempts and defeats.

I have often lingered, longing to be invited in at the doorway of mysticism, hoping for our dear Lord's sweeping hand to bring about spiritual intuitions, prophetic dreams, some charisma. But now I think that most times those gifts come with a grace and also at great cost. If you look at some of the characteristics of the saints, a whole lot of kookiness comes as well—saints are not often friends or lovers or well-balanced. It's rigorous, instead. Harsh making, singular. Do you know that opening line from the novel *Anna Karenina*: "Happy families are all alike;

every unhappy family is unhappy in its own way." The same goes for spiritual gifts and saints: they are all a little strange in their own and different ways.

The lifework I have: secretary to the Prioress and attending to Sister Anne's needs, is indeed a quieter work. Even if sometimes I feel that these are fits by default, rather than a real intentional lifework. And at the turn of each new year, I reconsider this. Unlike Little Sister, whose work is entirely aligned with her gifts.

"I know it's good, but don't fill up on bread," is Little Sister's daily line. Seven years ago, she came to the community, and glad to say, extended her time. The meals are simple and good now, where before they were only simple. The breads, as you might expect, are wondrous: herb breads, pepper breads, cheese breads, cardamom bread. Noon is soup, bread, water, tea, cheeses, usually.

There's something I like about this group, all attending to the vocation of prayer and then to our "littler vocations." Sometimes it's as though we are all gardeners, given a square of land to raise up a crop. We all have our different crops, but we all work hard as though it is the same work we all do, in the field of the Lord.

The generosity of spirit is one that I had not known existed in the religious life—that everyone had a unique work to do. No work is esteemed higher than another, as though we could make a judgment on the importance of a task or the importance of knowing something different or writing something down. For Sister Bird, she takes her "binos" (binoculars) down to the bay, watching the birds who visit the tidal waters. She's an observer.

All of us have a red-cheeked view of work: *ora et labora* (prayer and work). It's the way we live in community and something to offer back to the community and offer up to God.

Here's hoping that in your days of tiredness, these notings give you a little perk.

(later)

Miriam—

Now reading your recent letter. I cannot say, my dear, what you are to do, in these questions that wear into your days, the questions troubling you. A daughter wildly seeking independence while deeply needing you as home base. A husband who has lost his status as your only refuge. One feels, at points, plainly, simply, undeniably alone, unknown, lost. This is the world we share and the world in which I can only pass along my empathy, but no way through, no plan.

The first time I questioned my vows to religious life, this marriage to Christ, I suppose it came, too, the way you describe. It comes unbidden—as though a shudder moves through your body, an unknown thought questions what you surely *have* known. What to do with that shudder? To deny the strength of it would be a counterfeit. To move into the shudder altogether doesn't attend to the vows. This is a tricky spot for any person who desires a *real,* lived, and authentic life.

Loose Rule #18: *To not ask questions is the safest danger.* I also think that to ask the questions without the context of the vows invites another kind of danger. If I leave my calling in the midst of my questioning, simply to find outward peace, it cheapens both the questions and the vows. (Miriam, I realize I am writing this to myself, not you.)

I wrote to you, Miriam, about my own journey into the monastic life, the safe danger of running to the monastery, and now I find myself wanting to tease out that commitment, wanting to look it in its eye. I am not the only one; I feel that Little Sister has somewhat the same look in her eye, an unease, a restlessness that keeps her busy in the bakery, so passionate about macaroons and bear claws that you feel something else is in her, that she avoids or attends to. But whatever it is, she must do the work. Oh, it's easy to look at someone else uneasy in her skin.

Did I ever tell you about my name? It came through a round of uneasiness. Not the prettiest name in the monastery, but I like to think it has poetic meaningfulness. In your last letter you asked about our names—*Does a nun request her name? Are you assigned them? I'd want to choose my own, I think.* We may request names (which will make you glad), though ultimately we are assigned a name by the Prioress on our profession day.

After I entered the religious life, with this feeling of constantly running from myself, from the mess I'd quite created with my writer Dr. Breamer. Oh Doubt. Oh Faith. And Loose Rule #18.

With him, I came across that brilliantness that one feels at various rare and rich moments in life: *Here, this explains it*—this will be enough light to see by—we will offer each other comfort, give each other warmth and the consolation of two bodies linked up between the sheets, and offering each other cantaloupe pieces and coffee in the meantimes. Maybe I idealized being with him, as though I couldn't contain the real thing—to think he may not, in five years, offer the little glass of wine or the water on the nightstand or not be willing to sleep while I read into the night, nervous with energy, tired out with all I'd given and received. And I didn't know how to continue what most would call real life, how to manage daily life with someone, how to, perhaps, risk growing apart or—too—growing closer.

That is all. I was, in short, unable to proceed. Perhaps I knew we created a realm that could not proceed into Blessed Julian of Norwich's idea of wellness without much pain to the deeper spirit. Perhaps I knew I had taken something wrongfully to myself without thought to anything outside the experience of love (had I mentioned he was a married man, though they were living apart?)—perhaps it was that little rub against myself—as though seeing us, seeing myself in the distance and not knowing how this story could end, how difficult this adult life (not in age, I mean, but maturity) around me might seem. Unable to fully attend to my Dr. Breamer, unable to withdraw, I, in one of those evenings of late night reading as he slept with his relaxed soft body turned toward me even as his eyes turned away from my reading light, I came across the Athanasian Creed—oh, I didn't know myself divided then, my faith came alongside wherever I went. Miriam, I wonder how you will read this. But I never felt I turned from God—though from the outside it must have looked like a cutting myself off from the Spirit. Still, I knew I was still surrounded by grace.

But I read that creed, found the complexity of it compelling—that each line spoke of what was, and another spoke *about* what was, and yet another spoke of what was *not*, and it was in this combination of who God is and isn't and does and doesn't that a complexity grew in me, along with a drawing toward something so firmly God and so *other*.

It was that next day, reading in his office, those lines of Saint Hildegard of Bingen's *Book of Divine Works*. Maybe I ran toward what seemed to have more lasting power. I had such mixed motives for staying, or running away, that after all the years I still cannot unveil the motive.

And, now, Miriam, I have written too much, I feel the heat of my own youth and vigorous pride still awake in me. We are not far from our previous selves, our previous years, are we? And this will sort out, too, with God's help, in this life or the next. If you like, somewhere in letters down the road, we can return to this little troubled spot of mine. But forgive me, for now, wanting to move on.

Oh, the Athanasian Creed. It drew me to complexity and to faith and to a fondness for its ugly name, but there it is—in some odd way it saved me. From another point of view, perhaps as someone else might see it, it was an ugly name that I took to cover up my running away from what I couldn't know how to attend to.

And yet, over the years, it's become a wondrous name to me: a mouthful. Wanting in daintiness. Wanting in poetic feeling. Not twinkly or subtle. A bit like Gertrude, Hulga, or Mechthild.

A sort of negation and affirmation.

Oh, Miriam, I see I am in a swamp of thoughts. I will close for today, but not without sending my best wishes to you and my grateful prayers for you, and express my hope that you will finally see the elusive Eastern phoebe or the winter wren, both whom Sister Bird insists have been seen in her recent visits to Worcester County. I extend friendly greetings to your family—dear Franklin, Emily, and Brendan—for whom I grow in warm affection.

Yours in the swamp,
Sr. A.—

(later)

Miriam, dear,

Aging proves itself to be a lesson in the continuous detour. Our Sister Anne is suffering from such a painful bout of rheumatoid arthritis. She is in the hospital, resting under the hum of the fluorescent lights and between blood pressure checks. And so I am sitting here alongside, praying the rosary, attending to her. Though she can barely force herself to ask for help, even here—this may even be more painful to her than her reason for the hospital room. A few days, maybe, some cortisone shots, and she'll be good enough to wobble along the walkways in the monastery.

So in the waiting time, a letter to you.

Though Sister Anne came to the hospital with an ambulance, I followed with a bus and then another bus. Snuck into the Dunkin' Donuts for a cup of tea, but, still, I admit I went in to smell the coffee. After so many years on the wagon, it still doesn't leave off, this coffee heart of mine.

Waiting at Dudley Station for the bus to the New England Medical Center, I was grateful to be there—heading to be with Sister Anne, but also there in the middle of life: of coffees and cigarettes and little children's hands clutching mothers' hands. Of the way people talk or old people wait quietly. For the way people sip their coffee while waiting for modes of transportation.

On the news this morning, sitting by Sister Anne's bed, here, I heard that at the same Dunkin' Donuts, an hour after my wait between buses to the train, there was a shooting. 5 people in front of the Dunkin' Donuts were rushed to the hospital. One has died.

And I wonder, *Why was I there, when I am so rarely in the city?* And the question, too, *Why wasn't it me? Why not me?* It's hard to be grateful when 5 other people were not safe. I am quiet in my thoughts, praying into this tender day, here with Sister Anne. Here with this news. Praying for the dear people at Dudley Station. And grateful our vows call us to the "meaningful intersection with the world," which is these sidewalks and buses and trains and hospitals and the hand pressed over the breaking heart in prayer.

Here I continue the letter. Sister Anne, recovering, "Slow and sure," she says, "the story of my life." Even in this place, this hospital, if you need a little bit of rest and peace, she knows to offer it, quietly, as though she weren't offering anything at all, just making room for you. I have been watching her with the nurses and aides all day, watching how they come in to her in a rush (you know this story, you are a nurse: taking pulses and charts and temperatures and questions and beeps and buzzers and lights and medications) and leave as though they were given something of a quiet heart.

As I sit next to her, I think of other ways she has offered the sign of peace. One day I came into the TV room, the talk on the news about Red Sox players' trades and options and contracts. Sister Anne, in a moment of great willpower, given it was about the Red Sox, clicked off the TV, shifted over on the couch, patted the cushion, and invited me to sit. And we sat, quietly, peacefully. Waiting. I don't know for what. But then Little Sister came from the kitchen and Sister Anne slowly shifted her body over, patting the third cushion. Sitting in the middle of both of us, Sister Anne took Little Sister's hand, and mine on the other side. As though the hands held were communion, as though the silence were simply prayer, simply the presence of God.

Then the dinner bell rang and we reluctantly reclaimed our hands and worked our way up from the couch. And Sister Anne said, "Oh dears, thank you. That *was* lovely."

Later, when I asked her about it, she said that early on, in her spiritual life, she thought about joining the Poor Clares, for Clare, who would call Saint Francis to her convent, create a quiet space for him to rest, restore, be fed, renew his human body striving well beyond human limits. "It's tediously wrong," Sister Anne said, "to take on spiritual work without the thought to rest and renewal. That Saint Francis," she added, "would have been more kind to a group of chipping sparrows, making sure he found a little food for them on his way. He took no notice of his own lack of food. This may be what makes a saint, but makes for a sad picture of a human, for by his early forties our friend to all creation—to Brother Sun, Sister Moon and the sparrow in-between—died of malnutrition and exhaustion." It was Clare who offered him what he had offered to others, even to the birds.

And, in that spirit, our Sister Anne offers quiet moments for those who meet up with her, no matter how busy a day may be. Miriam, isn't this a friend to treasure?

And with this, from the hospital room, and in peace, I wish you a heart filling up in hope and in quiet,

Sr. A.—

(later)

My Miriamest Miriam—

Outside it is dark, the snow hard, wet and failing in the warm air from the southwesterly. I have claimed evening for my writing times, time with you. Between Vespers and Compline we are silent save for the turning pages of books, the scratch of Sister Bird's pencil, and the dipping of a brush into water and onto teeny cakes of color. She is, this week, working on the black-capped chickadee that she saw inland, in one of the many bird sanctuaries she visits. Tom said he would make a color photocopy for you, as I know that you have a fondness for this friend who frequents your feeders.

I like the nervous and jittery birds, because they remind me of morning coffee and I never tire of longing for the robust liquid. There's something, too, about a late night cup of joe (or murk, as the Writer used to call it) that I always had a fondness for.

Oh the later part of the day. Compline, the sweet hour, the most personal prayer hour that sinks a restful spirit onto the day's end. The call to make peace and come clean before the hours of sleep. It is in the hour after Compline that the sounds of the day go quiet, and a waft of myrrh-scented candle will declare the day's end from Sister Patrick Gertrude's cell.

The sounds from Sister Farm's cell come evening are, well, farmerly. Things bumped, things moving, the tinkering with a lock, a gear, small farm tools. She's now trying to develop a solution (who knows what it's made of, she uses what's available: kerosene, baking soda, mouthwash gargle, alcohols, both rubbing and ether)—that might take off the last of the bumper stickers on the new donkey trailer that has yet to carry her Poitou. Along with that lengthy list I sent you, are others, which I send for your amusement, including: "Buckle Up! Shit's about to Get Real" and "Life's a Bitch." We had thought we'd keep one or two, just in the spirit of the thing, but it's slim pickings, isn't it? Still, Miriam, would you like to put your vote in?

Someone suggested that Sister Farm use Goo-Gone, but now that we've purchased a trailer, she has used most of her farm budget, so she's looking for other ideas. If you have a *Heloise's Hints* at home, would you look up what household liquids might just remove offensive slogans from trailer bumpers?

Oh late nights, when thoughts get all rambley. As you may have surmised, we are back home, and Sister Anne is doing much better. Your note about Emily's friend and donuts in the church parking lot on a snowy Sunday morning had all of us howling for the fun of it (I hope she didn't get into too much trouble?).

Yours, Sr. A.—

10 January 2004

Miriam, dear—

It is with great pleasure that I announce that you have won

the bumper sticker contest: your two suggestions "Honk if you love" (the partial bumper sticker: as you wrote, *sounds holy and nunlike*) and "Shut up and drive" (*since you have hours of silence and often quite prefer a silence, this might be a good one*).

We are grateful for your thoughtful comments on the contemplative nature of the bumper sticker (or at least its potential for contemplative life) and we, herewith, award you (though I was going to send it anyway) with a prayer book from the community (had I sent you one before?). If you would like to pray along with us, we are on week 2, Saturday. Though, by the time you get this letter, we'll be, probably at beginning Week 3 Tuesday around Sext, is my guess.

One word of monastic caution: there are many prayer hours. Do not feel you need to pray them all. Catholic guilt is the worst of the guilts. Do not succumb! Be strong! Pray as your heart leads, as prayer calls you to it. And we will be glad to pray along with you, our psalms, our prayers, our devotional readings, our canticles.

Wishing you even more winter bird visitation in your snow-dusted yard, under the leafless oak tree,

Sr. A.—

Beehives

(January letter continued)

Miriam, dear,

Well, I failed to fill you in on our Advent and Christmas, but you specifically asked, and I will attend. Our third week of Advent (including the trip to Maine) also had Mother Lourdes in some of her most busy days.

We seek to maintain a spirit of welcoming the stranger among us at Christmastime. Father Martinez, often leading the charge, with nine days of observance of Las Posadas. It is usually Sister Farm who claims some poor soul on his way from one place to another. Sometimes Tom from the Feed & Seed (the farm shop down in Weymouth that first introduced you to us) will have a meal with us. He's not exactly a stranger among us, but he doesn't have family to speak of. He always has an excuse of why he can't come, but always shows up.

Sometimes Mother Lourdes brings what Little Sister calls, one of her *ancients,* for a meal at Christmas, but most of her old ones are too frail for a visit.

This year we had a new Christmas guest: Frankie.

Mother Lourdes, as I have mentioned, sometimes assists local parish churches by visiting those unable to attend Mass. Sometimes Sister Bird goes with her on her visits. During autumn and into Advent, she packs up baskets of clementines, stuffed dates, and baklava, which Little Sister makes and Sister Anne insists on testing for quality control purposes. We then add gifty packages of tissues and soaps. Tiny gifts.

As Prioress all Mother Lourdes's time is stretched and claimed even before she lives in it. To see her skip out for visitations is to observe her relishing the place she doesn't have to be in charge, doesn't have to offer wisdom, make decisions. She offers instead kindness, and says the Our Father, prays the rosary with her old people, and places a sign of the cross on the foreheads of those people who know the worth of such things. While leadership is her duty, visitation is her joy. Perhaps it is her cross to bear, this firm hand of leadership, this calling. I sometimes wonder at God, calling people to roles they desperately could never, ever, amen, want. And I wonder at people, saying yes.

I wonder if we're all a touch loony, we religious, saying yes. We have chosen this life, yes. But some of us seem so adapted to this way, that it fits in its skin. Others don't fit the habit at all—through no fault of their own. They enter the monastery out of obedience and determination. Maybe it is those who are so seemingly ill-fitting who are doing God's greatest work?—What do you think, Miriam?— living a life they would not have chosen for themselves, yet they shoulder the task, attend to prayer hours, to the work of the monastery, cleaning toilets, shoveling the walkway, bringing flowers to the altar, sitting in adoration of the Host.

It's a contemporary fancy that people should do only what

they love and have aptitude for. I find Mother Lourdes noble in her work: conflicted, lonely, weighed down under the details of all these lives in her keeping. I find it sacramental, the way she offers herself up.

Miriam, could there be a longer aside than I just wrote? I was telling you the story of Mother Lourdes's visit during Advent and then got so excited about practical theology and conundrums.

Back to the story of Frankie, shall we?

So Mother Lourdes, snow falling, took Sister Bird and the 5 baskets out in the old Ford Taurus for their first visit, to old Sophie Zagajewski. Don't you love Polish names, Miriam, how they contain so many sounds?—where Sophie lives near Saint Clement's in an attic that she can hardly climb the stairs of, let alone take care of her Down Syndrome boy, Frankie, who is not really a boy, being 51, but so small and bald and always wearing his boyish rainbow suspenders. We all adore him.

I suspect Sister Bird goes along simply to make sure that he gets out and about for a long walk. And even in snowy weather, she makes sure Frankie gets an ice cream at Charlie's Sandwich Shop down in the South End. While Mother Lourdes unpacks the basket, cleans the dishes in the sink, opens up the cans that Sophie can't open with weak hands and bone spurs, to be used in the next day or two.

As Mother Lourdes told it, while she was scraping off the small kitchen table of its sticky lumps, Sophie called her over to the big chair by the window and said, looking out the window at the snow, at Sister Bird and Frankie walking off toward Mass.

Ave. Holding Mother Lourdes's hand she said, "Lourdes, who will pray for Frankie when I'm gone?"

"Sisters," Mother Lourdes told us later, "I'm sorry to say that my first thought was, More to the point, who would *take care* of Frankie? And then I felt a rush of spiritual smallness. To think that hope in God, our most needy prayers offered up, were lesser than what I call practical considerations. God forgive me for such narrow faith.

"Sisters," she went on, "I could not deny the cry of need and the cry of faith." And, Miriam dear, I suspect you know the rest: Mother Lourdes and the Sisters of Saint Hildegard of Bingen in Weymouth will be praying for Frankie. And, "secondarily" as Mother Lourdes puts it, "we'll be taking care of Frankie." And, in fact, he joined Tom in our guest chairs for Advent celebrations. And Frankie will stay on with us, here.

In Mother Lourdes's way, she has found a nursing home for Sophie, no more flights of stairs, no more humid summer heat in that attic, no more cold days of winter. Sophie gave two feeble Polish attempts of protest. But we could see her obvious relief.

Changes like this can be tricky. Sophie now settled at the nursing home. And we are appealing to the Provincial at the Motherhouse. Not all things we believe necessary (that is, Frankie living here, in our guest quarters) are approved. But we will pray and see, and in the meantime Mother Lourdes holds out a beautiful obedience to love.

Frankie even comes to us with a good Christian name in place, so our dear Saint Francis would be pleased. Sister Farm says he's not the sharpest tool in the shed, but she began a mission to develop some farmerly talent in him. Sister Patrick Gertrude said he came to us smelling of filth and sin, and she already has started in on hygiene lessons and a bath schedule. Sister Bird has taken a liking to the short fellow in suspenders and sneaks him ice-cream (despite her own health standards and despite Little Sister's insistence that twice a week is plenty).

Frankie only says a few phrases. He's been with us now a little over two weeks and so far we've gotten the following out of him:

* Peam, peam: ice cream
* Kiss yips: kiss your lips
* Epet EwYoh: Happy New Year (which, thankfully, was recently appropriate, but he says it every 20 minutes)
* Kip it: keep it (which he says when he either wants something or doesn't want something; it can get confusing)
* Bird: Sister Bird (his latest acquisition, since he gained great fondness for her and discovered that she's the only one who will sneak him an extra helping of ice cream)
* Dooogh: dobshe (a Polish word; he mostly says this when we take him to see his mother)

We've all banded around him, even Sister Patrick Gertrude. And Sister Farm wondering if his pudgy hands might be put to use, if he has some farmer in him; and our little empty place at the table is filled. And no word yet about Sister Farm's request to move to Wisconsin and the Nativity celebrated and now gone, with Sister Farm's insistence that in artwork of the Nativity, it's the donkeys and farmer-shepherds who are in attendance.

Sister Farm, for Christmas, often gets the Sisters presents through *Uncle Henry's Swap or Sell It Guide*. "Your 30 Word

(Non-Commercial) Ad Placed at No Cost Using Free Ad Form on Inside Cover, Serving ME, NH, VT, MA, NB, Canada" (and through which we met Mr. Komaki and his trailer).

This year was no different:

For Father Martinez (who comes to hear confessions and say Mass): a Navman Fishfinder, since Father Martinez considers himself an enthusiast, but has no fishermanly gifts whatever.

For Mother Lourdes: an editor's desk lamp with good wiring, to replace Mother Lourdes's lamp that kept shorting out. We feared an electrical fire.

For Little Sister: a large KitchenAid paddle-mixer. (Personally, I think Little Sister has wanted a billiards table. When you put all the old girls together, Miriam, there's some gambling we could do—between sports betting, billiards, and cigars. Though with Sister Farm's propensity in that direction, we've all determined to avoid anything such, to help out, as we can. Life's difficult enough.)

Sister Patrick Gertrude received, in "good, but used' condition, a Leatherman, which will be handy for Sister Farm and can strap right onto the cincture. The gift does not lessen the tensions between the two. Still, I'm sure Sister Patrick Gertrude was glad that the gift wasn't a donkey, so there's something to be said for Sister Farm's restraint.

For Sister Anne: tickets to a September 25, 2004 Red Sox game against the Yankees (this, I believe came through a call-in radio show on WEEI to be the 21st caller for a ticket). She placed a rich 40 or so calls before Sister Anne's ship came in.

For me: a book that must have been extremely on sale, titled *Living It Up at 70: Wild Women Artists, Farmers, Writers, Engineers and Electricians Who Dared Live Up to Their Potential.* I'm trying to assume that this is a book she ordered for herself and that she understands that living-it-up with electricity could be dangerous. She also bought a journal-type book for me, "for your spiritual autobiography," she wrote, "like St. Thérèse of Lisieux."

Many of her purchases swing between extreme focus on the person in need to her own farmer/barn interests. This year we fared a little worse. For Sister Anne, Sister Farm ordered a beehive, complete with Queen, drones, honey boxes, and netting suit. What, in fact, Sister Anne can do with it all in her deflated health is one question. The whole unit is due to arrive when Tom from the Feed & Seed takes a trip up to Vermont, offering to save Sister Farm a trip in the old truck.

You can't say that she hasn't thought about her gifts. Most of us feel as though we have extraordinary ties to Uncle Henry's.

And this year, Christmas cards. Christmas gifts poured in from friends, from various connected religious communities, from those in the local parish churches who know Mother Lourdes.

Miriam, dear one, your card and Franklin's that you sent, despite hospital time and recovery days, was the shiniest of the group on the mantel, and Sister Anne frequently asked me to hand it to her—she so intently studied it, with prayers for you. All of us did, especially during that time, Sister Anne with such persistent devotion. In one of your letters you wrote about your dread of Advent, as *a time when family tensions run high, when Brendan is home and all of us are in an enclosed space.*

Christmas runs a little wild. Your letter said, *Sister Athanasius, it makes for a good series of fights throughout the month of December. Sundays and Advent candles, and Perry Como Christmas. And all I want is nothing fancy: a simple tree, a family visit to a Connecticut farm, looking for a Charlie Brown tree, looking for some Christmas tree no one else could love. But he has high expectations for the season, out of all reason. It doesn't seem at all like the Franklin I know through the year. I'd rather have an argument with him about almost anything else. Oh a mess.*

Franklin said to me yesterday, "Just think of it this way. You're healthy enough to have some good fights with me. This is like other people's healthy lives. And in January you'll start liking me again. I can wait out a stretch of crabbiness."

Well, Miriam, I consider it a special gift, then, to our Advent that you sent a card to us. In turn, we have especially prayed for your Advent, your family, your surgery, your healing, and for the winter yard visitors to continue in this new year, the black-capped chickadees, slate-colored juncos, and the white-throated sparrow.

Wishing you and Franklin the *likings again that come in January,* and a peace and health-filled 2004,

Sr. A.—

18 January 2004

Dear Miriam,

Sister Farm has indeed found a fellow-farmer in Frankie. Unexpectedly, she found he is attuned to the bees. Though they have only a low hum in their winter hives, Frankie spends hours near the hives. He can raise or lower the hum inside by making his own sort of hum. She swears she's uncovered his apiarist talent.

Miriam, this is Grace in its mysterious disguise.

On the other side of grace in mysterious disguise is Sister Bird, who during the winter months takes great fondness in things health-related. Last year, perhaps I failed to report this to you, to the great disappointment of some of the Sisters—she asked to soften Little Sister's duties and make breakfast and dinner, as well as offer menu-planning for the noon hour. This caused all manner of lessening of butter and refined sugars, and all things fried. Sometimes, to aid in digestion, she'll add to a meal fresh carrot and beet juice, "to help us sanctify the temple of God, our bodies, as proper houses for the Holy Spirit."

The great joy of migration seasons and summers is that Sister Bird is off teaching, scrambling to this or that other sanctuary, or out and about with her "binos." But winters come persistent. Last winter she had us in a three-week stretch of no desserts (save fruit), no fresh rolls or butter, even for our potatoes. And all of the goodies we smelled from Little Sister's bakery going directly to market. (Except what Sister Anne snuck out to us, in the mid-mornings.)

Sister Bird also took a sharp turn against coffee, the beloved drink that allows Little Sister and Patrick Gertrude to function amicably. And that gives Sister Anne what she calls "a touch of friendliness" to the day. Mother Lourdes had not a few visits from disappointed Sisters.

And no one was surprised when, a month later (so as to seem unrelated), Little Sister again took over the kitchen cooking duties. The change was imperceptible, seemingly the same diet (to the great disappointment of all except Sister Bird and Sister Anne who prefer a Sox game over a good meal any day), but then a square of butter added to the broccoli, a jigger of cream added to the soup, a dollop of butter, a pinch of refined sugar. Oh, the beauty in subtlety. A full three months after the health disaster we again enjoyed brioches and clotted cream (thanks to the Jerseys) and jam for Sunday breakfasts, with coffee (for most of us) on the side.

By the time Sister Bird noticed to say something, she was also filling her own thermos with coffee and preparing for the late March migratory return of the piping plovers to the coastal regions, as well as the American oystercatcher.

And so Mother Lourdes eased the community back to the appreciation of eating without taking away Sister Bird's dignity and mission. There's something that lingered in the air for a time, a quiet respect for Sister Bird's spiritual vision for our physical bodies. Yet, also a respect for the foods that make the heart merry.

Back to the bees. One mystery uncovers the next. From Frankie's certain hum along with the bees and now, *It's a sign!*—Sister Bird found a book in the giveaway box at the health food store in Weymouth (a place she's only allowed to visit once a month, since her zeal consumes our house). The book she picked up was a 1960s copy of *The Bees: Our Friends: The Health Benefits of Bees: A Book for Bee Keepers, Bee Lovers & Honey Consumers.* The repetition of *bees* and the triple subtitle can only deepen Sister Bird's regard for the book.

Last year it was, in that same giveaway bin that she noodled around to find *Household Health: How to Live Healthy without Expensive Supplements.*

Her first discovery was that a barefoot walk on dew-soaked grass was good for overall health. She would, after morning prayers, gather up Sister Anne for a slow, pink-footed and bunioned walk on the grass on the other side of the garden, nearer to the bay. Near the bay since she read, too, that briny air offers many benefits. But poor Sister Anne, just the time it took her to put her shoes off, pull her socks off, rest from her labors, then walk, then rest, then dutifully pull the socks and shoes on again, was spent by the end of a morning.

She kindly asked Sister Bird if she could be excused from the walks, telling her that the splendid feeling of the cool, wet-soaked grass on feet felt lovely, but that she wasn't sure she was reaping the benefits otherwise. But she did agree to sit outdoors on the sunnier days and breathe deeply three times, shallowly twice, and deeply thrice again of the briny air until she insisted true vigor was hers.

In the same book she discovered the scary (but she insists, nonpoisonous) uses of kerosene for such things as toe fungus for Sister Farm—and surely here you are no longer interested, even though my pen seems to want to keep writing down the details of natural home remedies. She has discovered a bang-up cure for the flu, which can also loosen up a chest cold, a mixture of cayenne pepper, lemon, honey, water, which tastes like the heat of hades, but does the trick.

But now Sister Bird is on "advice *verbot*" by Mother Lourdes, since post-migration through pre-migration, Sister Bird constantly preaches what we must do for optimal health. You can imagine the collective relief when the first migrations begin.

Among those she has cornered:

Sister Anne:

* Tai chi (for balance and joint motion),
* chondroitin for her arthritis,
* and current research into bee venom for arthritic pain.

Sister Farm:

* cigars must go,
* breathing in dung smell in large doses can cause lung problems later in life (this, I believe is unresearched, but Sister Patrick Gertrude applauds the pre-research effort),
* and though you wouldn't know it, according to Sister Bird, Sister Farm is fighting for her very life there amidst the smoke, tractor fumes, and animal defecations.

Frankie was recently introduced to the pre-migration health raids, too. Sister Bird insisted that ice cream be expelled from his diet, causing severe fluctuation in blood sugar the way it does. Still, she wanted to give the impression of ice cream, so gave him stevia-sweetened Tofu Ice Cream Dream. Frankie has been her toughest unwilling customer to date, three times violently throwing the Tofu ICD across the kitchen and saying, "Not nice, Not nice." As you might guess, he's now back on the real ice cream sugars. Sister Bird herself reintroduced the real "peam," as he calls it.

Mother Lourdes: Even Sister Bird knows that health advice given to individuals in leadership and under stress is best left unoffered. Instead she dutifully prays for Mother Lourdes's health, and believes that it's her prayers that keep her strong and vibrant.

Sister Patrick Gertrude was offered a tincture of saltwater, bee propolis, and myrrh to alleviate the effects of strong unpleasant smells. But Sister Patrick Gertrude maintains that after two days on the what she called the smell deafening treatment, our Lord spoke to her and she has given up trying to influence or lessen what spiritual gifts are given.

Sr. A.—

24 January 2004
Feastday of St. Francis de Sales

Miriam, dear—

Another letter on the heels of the earlier one, and greetings on this feastday of Saint Francis de Sales. I have a fondness for de Sales, because he was an ardent letter-writer, and I often return to his letters of spiritual direction, especially his *Introduction to the Devout Life* for paragraphs such as this:

> The first step toward the devout life is the cleansing of your soul. Remove anything that stands in the way of your union with God. This will be a gradual process. It has been compared with sunrise, which brings light in imperceptible steps. Darkness is not driven away immediately. The saying is that a slow cure is best. Sicknesses of the soul are like that of the body. They come galloping in on horseback but depart slowly on foot.

Now bitter weather & winds have come cantering in, with windchills well below zero, looking like it will abide for a stretch. All the Sisters here long-johned themselves against it, having amassed what amounts to Siberian gear under their habits.

This morning I went in to help Sister Anne get herself into the day. I shouldn't have, but I decided to only get her after Matins, the earliest, darkest, coldest prayer hour of the day. I couldn't stand the sight of her bones fighting against the day's bitterness.

I went to her cell, found her shivering and waiting and, though it's more of a whisper than anything, she gave me a lecture on passing her by for the prayer hour. I dutifully expressed sorrow, regret—even remorse—knowing that I would, next severe chill patch, do my best to keep her under blankets for as long as possible.

The religious feel a need to never close up drafts in old buildings or to not turn up heat to what others might consider proper proportion. I know this speaks to ascetical principles: that one's every whim, dislike, or ache shouldn't be responded to. But when I see Sister Anne, I feel differently about ascetical principles.

"I am not the center of the universe," Sister Anne told me. "And my practice of faith shouldn't have to hinge on favorable weather patterns. When it is cold and you wish to pass me by for Matins, please remember that the cold and discomfort also put me in solidarity with most of the world's reality." Miriam, it is only the worst sort of nun who would not be put in her place with words like those. And I think of you, your struggles with illness, the daily strains you have faced. You have said, too, that the one strand that has spoken to you is that you share both in the suffering of Jesus on the cross, as well as *know what it is when I am at work in the hospital, and trying to speak into hope when I know the person I'm talking to is sick under a weight of hopelessness.*

Miriam, I nodded to Sister Anne, but still feel my responsibility for good care outweighs her principles. I may be wrong. I suspect I have, actually, gotten it all wrong. And in my great optimism have a Loose Rule #42 that speaks to this: *Sometimes, by Grace, 3 or 4 wrongs can be the very paths toward right.* I was, at the time, meditating on St. Peter, impulsive and eager, early on as a disciple. When Jesus asks to wash Peter's feet, Peter insists that Jesus should not. And when Jesus invites Peter to walk on the water, Peter looks down into his lack of faith and sinks. And the great voice of the rooster's crow—see how the birds speak to us!—speaking to him in his denial of Jesus. And yet the church looks to him, for his apostolic role in forming the church.

So, if I insist on caring for Sister Anne and she insists on flooding the gates of heaven with her duty to the hours of prayer, I will petition Mother Lourdes to give her warm silk long johns. (Compromise: where neither of us is happy, but both of us get something we want.)

And for the morning, we entirely skipped ablutions, just got her goose-pimpled skin into layers, covered her bunions with the thickest wool socks I could find, and slowly made our way from the cloister to the monastery.

As we walked over toward the monastery, Sister Anne stopped several times to rest and find a balance for her legs. "Sister Athanasius," she said to me, "I know you are of tender heart to me. I didn't mean to scold so about missing Matins." She then changed the topic, wind clipping toward her and into the edges of clothing: up sleeves and down socks.

Sometimes I feel unable to do well the tasks I'm given: to attend, to offer an arm, and when frailer days demand it, to help with bathroom needs. It's odd to know someone so well as that, and still have no understanding for their approach to life, to know that they'd want a cold early morning Matins. While I am old, Sister Anne is elderly. But a wide gap divides the distance between the wisdom I own and the wisdom she possesses.

"Sweetheart," she said to me after a few more rigorous attempts to walk solidly through the cold, getting to the steps of the monastery and another rest for her legs. "Look at the brightness of the moon—only coldest days bring that sort of clarity. Can I tell you why I must go to Matins?"

While I worried that she might be developing chilblains, she said, "'I thank God for my handicaps, for through them I have found myself, my work, and my God.' I read that line by Helen Keller when I was 58, in good health, glad for my vocation, deeply devoted to God. And I thought to myself, Let me keep this line, for future days and for better understanding."

She reached under her coat to the pocket of her habit and handed me a small folded and refolded—almost clothlike—piece of paper with that quote in her handwriting. "I have kept it with me for so long that I am coming into an understanding of it—a living of that intention. I want to pass it along to you, not that I hope you will suffer in life, but that you might know of the immediate and painful way to what might be the largest good you can know.

"I know you fear suffering, child. This is my cold winter's day gift for you." And with that she grabbed my arm tightly and said, "I'll race you to the coffeepot." And Miriam, you will understand that I went thankfully and steadily toward the kitchen (me to my tea), slipped that quote into my own pocket—a new owner of a well-loved thing—and then waited out the day through Compline, the sweet prayer hour, and on return to the cloister and my cell, lit a votive candle, and looked up at Jesus, the crucifix on my wall, and the icon of Mary, beside him, and began to cry for all things I don't know if I will ever understand.

Every one of the Sisters has their way of attending to the cold. Sister Patrick Gertrude patrols the halls, calling out to offenders who come through the front or side door, letting in drafts to rooms and corridors. She, I suspect, is keeping the laundry room working all day for the sake of heat, between her patrols.

Tom came from the Feed & Seed, stopping by to check in on us and wanted to make sure the back-up generator was working, just in case our electricity went. There's something exciting about a winter bite, isn't there, Miriam? A person feels brave just going out. Braver, even, going for a walk in this clear iced air.

We can hear cars almost starting in our neighborhood, just down the road: squeals or a simple 2-turn of an engine, then nothing. I'm sure our Canadian neighbors and our Alaskan friends look with disdain at us at a mere –40°F windchill, but this is New England at its coldest and we don't know how to do it as well, but still we're doing it.

I suspect you are among those brave ones, Miriam, for I know you like a run in the morning no matter the weather. I, from my writing desk in my cell with these feet mysteriously pulling toward the room's sole radiator, applaud you, but I still remember Franklin's caution for your sake, in case you do not.

Sister Farm petitioned Mother Lourdes to spare the barnyard creatures of the extreme cold. She proposed the fragile bees come indoors, at least as far as the mudroom. She fears we could lose the lot of them. Every 2 hours she sends Frankie out with a stethoscope to see if there's a little humming.

"No sow-like creatures, no bees, no chickens, and—even if we did have a donkey—no donkey," Mother Lourdes told her. Everything stays out of the doors of this monastery.

Sister Farm is sulking: which means she's even quieter and even more efficient, coming in from the barn, red cheeks, iced eyebrows, warming up every few minutes in the laundry room, much to Sister Patrick Gertrude's dismay.

When the dryer is off, between loads, we can hear sulky voices, just a couple words piercing around, something about a donkey, a trailer, our Lord. Maybe it's Sister Farm's way of distracting herself from her freezing flock and hives to try to start a fight. Their voices rise and fall. More rising than falling. Except for Mother Lourdes and Sister Anne, we all in our hearts take sides as we listen. Sister Farm has given up the spiritual exercise of removing stickers one by one, given winter chill. Who knows what our neighbors think of us, nice old religious with our questionable trailer.

Once in the middle of one of Sr. Farm's warm-up visits to the laundry room, we heard the sounds of an exchange and then a burst of laughter, both of them howling. Just like that. And then just like that, as quick, Sister Farm was swinging by the kitchen to grab some coffee before entering the cold world of the barn with what looked like a grin on her face.

The Birds: Alas, in weather like this—cold, snowy—there's little to report. I don't know where the birds go for cover, but except for the occasional cry of a black-backed gull, we're all feeling cut off from the rest of the world. Here, snowed in, woman and beast and winged creature. Sister Bird went down to the bay, amidst the drifts, but reported only herring gulls and a Bonaparte's gull, "though piteous looking, there in the biting cold," she said.

Sr. A.—

undated, January 2004

Miriam, dear—

I've been thinking these winter days about monastic life. If we don't know God here, it's not for lack of trying—it's at least one large concerted, relentless effort toward knowing God.

The life of trade, the professional life, though, on most of our parts, has little to show for it. We have a few eggs and are hopeful that the bees will, under Frankie's care, make frequent visits to our flowing plum trees in the spring and bring about the honey. Little Sister has sales from her almond bear claws, specialty breads, and macaroons. Sister Bird, two-bit consultant on things herbal and homeopathic, but her income comes in from her bird books and her work with the various coastal bird sanctuaries: Wellfleet, Plum Island. My own contribution is sketchy, as you know. What income can secretarial work and elder care and correspondence for the community bring? I respond to letters from oblates—those who take a vow to remain in the world, but maintain connection to our community. And, care for Sister Anne. But, Miriam, you have known my struggle with wanting a professional place, a longing to have a named trade, something shiny and short to say to someone. "Oh yes, I am a religious, and along with my vocation, my profession is Novelist. Or Baseball Commentator. Or Scholar of Medieval Illuminated Manuscripts or Agronomist."

Miriam, the work you do, that you do not seem conflicted about, but write of it as though it is your skin, has given me a little itch within myself to say it so purposefully and directly, as you do: Psychiatric Nurse. The way you write about your profession laps at the edge of kindness, faith, attention & good diagnostics. Ably, you bring together someone's life story to their deeper psychological story, and honor and care for both. This is the real witness to faith: a life lived with integrity, kindness, wisdom, gentleness—and a love of Emily Dickinson.

Now, I suppose, is a good time to respond to your note you wrote ages ago about how some of the Sisters came to be here.

Now, *that's* a study, Miriam. Let me tell you about Sister Farm, one of the dear histories to me. And I've made her repeat it down to, as she says, "a labor of details."

Not one of us got a letter one day saying, *This is it. Pack up.* There are roads and crossroads and influences of situation that got any one of us here. And so it was for Sister Farm, growing up in rural Connecticut, the long windy roads, hilly terrain, roads unmarked by white or yellow lines. Her parents, from what I understand, rarely engaged with her or with each other, a sort of clipped life all while she grew up, going to school, feeling like an outsider in any social situation.

It was one day, when she was young—the sort of day where everything that happens within that day seems purposeful, God giving us a call to enter into mercy. She went for a walk, following the boundary lines of a stonewall across fields and near roads in winter, about two miles away from her home: lichen-covered rocks, immense lilac bushes, crumbling stone walls—you know those Connecticut stone walls, don't you, Miriam?

Alone, on a Saturday, her parents gone to Hartford, and Sister Farm—or Sharon, as she was called then—here she felt the small beginning cramps of the entry into womanhood, before her walk sitting on the toilet, wondering at the redness and not knowing what it was (her mother rarely spoke to her, especially about important things), something so bright and harsh coming from her. Here you will laugh. With duct tape (can't you see it Miriam?)—"Well, you just make do, is all," she said—she rigged some mound of paper towels to her and went out into the winter day, followed the Brickyard Road and the parallel lines of the stone walls. As Sharon followed the wall lines, she saw 2 cardinals and one fox with a pale rust-red coat. She knew something was opening up, "something like hope" she called it. A slight shift, a thinness, a wind picking up. Not that she would use those words, but "something almost special," to the reels of the day.

She passed a farm a couple miles down—one of many small Connecticut family farms that are falling down, losing their place in the larger world of corporate farming. A red, red barn and 6 Rhode Island Reds in the yard, so red and bright, she said, "I just stood there, thinking: *Red*."

She stood there so long, a small man with a nubbed cigar came through the barn door, "Mon Dieu," he said, "a guest," and he nodded for her to head with him over to the house. And that, my dear Miriam, began the story. Getting inside, "Mémère," he said to a woman sitting next to a big old dog that sat next to an old wood stove, on which there was coffee, "company we got." Crucifixes on the wall. A picture of the Pope beside it. Chickens in the yard. A red barn. Come summer a tomato garden planted entirely within the fat circles of old tires. A tired old farm she walked to, but the entire day, completely bright red in her memory, she met an open door. As though she met her future—faith & profession and a cigar-loving life.

There you go. "True stories" as an old aunt of mine used to say about anything told of the past that carried meaning.

More later, Sr. A.—

undated, February 2004

Dear Miriam,

I wrote to you last time about Sister Farm, and I have something further to tell you. After many weeks of silence since Sister Farm made her request, we had hoped nothing would come of the Wisconsin direction. But recently Sister Farm asked me to draft a letter to Tom. She said to me, "It needs to read right." So we both went to work on it.

Miriam, dear, I am attaching the letter. When Sister Farm came to talk to me about the letter, wanting to make sure it was right, I said, well, you could call Tom, you know, and go over things. "And you could call Miriam," she said at one point, when I thought that working on a letter with her was a problem with no solution. But as you didn't get a call from us, you can decide if we needed your input.

I do love the form of a letter. There's something about a letter that wants writing: more official, more personal, more attentive than a phone call. So I helped her clean it out and at the end of it she shrugged, as she does when she's pleased. "Pretty letter, isn't it?" she said. And my only response could be, "*Very.*" Herewith, a photocopy of letter one:

[extract]

Tom—

I can't get Petunia to fatten up anywhere near like Sweetcakes. And Lulu, that old hog, only eats all day, the only girth in the barn.

Tom, you save my farm 'bout every three weeks, save

it from collapse. You'd think I'm a farmer, learnt the basics, but you always come through for me.

And still having the same bee problems, poor girls, don't know how they'll make it through the winter. I'm not at all for bees, but they know how to work the seasons: blossom trees come spring, clover come summer, then, come fall they're all about purple loosestrife and a plant Sister Bird calls a pepperbush. Ever heard of it? Well, it will make a good honey, Tom, and I think Frankie will find his way with them, learning to scrape down layers of propolis, cleaning the screens.

I'm worried some, is why I'm writing. Money should be coming out for the work I'm putting in—raw milk sales, some eggs, sheep wool, come shearing time, sheep milk to the Boston health stores. It's all nickels and dimes. I sometimes get to wondering what was Jesus thinking, setting me up here, giving me the joy of farming, with hardly the magic to do something right by it.

You save me every time, Tom. Don't you think I don't know the situation. And don't you go thinking that you're not getting prayed for, either, you old heathen. Every Matins through Compline, you're my extra prayer of thanks in God's ear (and there's always the prayer for a donkey, too.)

Now, I'm just buttering you up, Tom. Got a favor to ask. I need to get up to a farm in Wisconsin, see what I can learn from the Bing girls up there in dairy farming, mostly. I don't want to say it, I might be transferred to a working farm, a big farm, not like this one, a hobby farm, is all this is. A farm where I don't feel like so much depends on me. I'm too scattered to make a dollar, cause I'm too busy making a dime.

God's work—Mother Lourdes tells me—isn't about

money, but about faith and obedience. Still, money besides all that keeps things going. So I'm going to Wisconsin to see if there's some way to work this out.

Also, maybe there are donkeys there. Tom, you'd say, "There's nothing holier about donkey shit than chicken shit," but for me there is.

Would you see to the farm for those 4 weeks or so? I've got a little saved to pay you for the time. Mostly mornings, is when you'd need to come, milking and feeding. And Little Sister can get her own eggs for what she needs in the kitchen. Sister Anne will make sure you have some coffee when you come. They'll take good care of you.

Farm

PS Shame you can't find me good goop to get those bumper stickers down.

[end of extract]

Miriam, I enclose another copy of another letter. This about Frankie. You'll pray with us, won't you, that he be allowed to remain? This is the letter Mother Lourdes wrote to the Motherhouse, an annual letter of update on religious affairs and monastery business.

[extract]

26 February 2004

Dear Sister Mary Luke, Provincial

Sisters of Hildegard of Bingen, Motherhouse

Greetings from the Monastery of the Sisters of Saint Hildegard of Bingen in Weymouth, MA. I trust you are well.

Though I often write an annual letter of update, there are some matters that I wish to address, which have come under my roof to be attended to immediately. We trust in God's grace for the current moment and hope for your wisdom on the long-term arrangement.

The first, as you know, our Sister Burgundofara, who operates our small farm, has added two beehives for honey in order to add to the farm's financial viability. As you know, we do not operate on support from the archdiocese or the Motherhouse (though we have individual donors who have been generous to our monastery), though we have spiritual support from both.

We have trusted the professional skills of the Sisters to supply the monetary needs. We also, as you know, are an Order with a call to the spiritual work of prayer, to meaningful intersection with the world, and to the daily professional work of each Sister (along with vocation), so our endeavors do bring us, annually, what we need, with little excess and sometimes a small debt.

The honeybees are one of the new ventures we hope will expand and help bring additional support, which I hope you will give your blessing upon. We do not go into new business ventures lightly and greatly seek your wisdom and blessing on such matters.

The next matter has some delicacy. But has come to us so unexpectedly and fortuitously that we feel grateful for the help and also desirous of your understanding for our situation, and your blessing: Francis (Frankie) Zagajewski, a man, 51 years of age with Down Syndrome. His mother has passed away, only this last month. His sole support, save our Lord. For the time being, we have taken him in. We have a small sectioned-off guest quarters room that leads to the farm, where he is currently lodging. Sister Burgundofara, in between trying to teach him some basics of the farm, discovered he has a giftedness in the apiary arts. A tenderness and understanding of the honeybees, and intuitively knows much about their care. With this in mind, we may wish to expand the hives into the summer months, as he is able to help us. This will allow him meaningful work, a caring community, and would also help, perhaps, offer the possibility of easing our financial strain, if we can continue to grow by two hives per year.

We are desirous both of your blessing and of your wisdom, as we are in a state of hopefulness for the future.

We also appreciate your thoughtful response regarding Sister Burgundofara and her earlier request.

Yours in continuing faith,
Sr. Lourdes
Monastery of the Sisters of
Saint Hildegard of Bingen

[end extract]

And so I bring my own letter to a close, with these additions,

Sr. A.—

11 March 2004

My Dear Miriam,

Yes, I do think the hope of spring isn't coming a second too soon. Though Sister Bird is entirely one who lives in the weather (scoters and mergansers along the shore these days, by the way), I sometimes feel like I forget about spring here on the edge of spring, as though the Lenten season makes a person forgetful, since everything feels like winter. And then with Easter, it's as though you wake up from a long, dark dream and can speak the word, *hallelujah*.

Lately, I have been thinking about Mother Lourdes's letter and Sister Farm's request to leave that hovers, leaves, hovers. I often find myself pining for their distinct sense of professional direction, skill, and craft. Often, I am struck by the thinness of how I perceived my calling. And, Miriam, you seem to know your own place and call in this world so well. I admire that, the way you write, of how this lives in your skin.

And what of those who feel they have lost their way? I wonder if this could be a way God calls someone, to look over the same landscape again and again, and then finally notice the stirring and quick flight of the yellow warbler? God knows.

I leave you with a letter half started, as I take to pondering these things. Hellos to Franklin, always, and tell him that story you passed along about the tub of butter was very funny. I'd love to hear him tell it sometime. He seemed so awfully proud of that messy turn of events.

Yours, Sr. A.—

18 March 2004

Miriam, dear,

Well, your friend Sister Anne is all joy, now with the *Boston Globe* sports page comes news of the Red Sox in spring training, there in Fort Meyers, Florida. "I predict a good baseball season," she says. "This one, Sisters, is the year." And every year we fall for that old hopefulness trick. Every year.

I'm sure Sister Anne sees it as a sign of our Lord's favor that today we were read the following line from Psalm 37, and in the silence of the noon meal were asked to meditate on the text: "Take delight in the Lord and he will give you the desires of your heart."

I can't say about the Red Sox or about hope, but I do appreciate that our Holy Rule demands patient quietude in reflecting on a morsel from Holy Writ. Our silence is often the best gift of the day—when we eat in silence, which is to say when we listen to each other make little noises with spoons and forks and swallows and coughs. In that space a beautiful thing can happen: a communing—shy and radiant—with God and with others. Though I find I long for longer stretches of silence—don't laugh Miriam, I may be wordy, but I am also silent—I often only settle into the silence of communion about dessert time, which today was naval oranges and tea (Sister Bird's menu, as Little Sister was shopping for ingredients today; otherwise, we should have had scones with clotted cream courtesy of our bovine staff.) And for a briefest space in time, I was internally listening for the breath of God—a little sigh is what I heard today, a little sigh.

And prayer. In baseball terms, that divine starting pitch that sets everything into play. It begins the whole show, big game or little game, I think of prayer as movement of engagement.

All of us here wish that silence was filled with the divine. Some days, the silence is simply silent. Today, though, all through lunch, and before the orange and tea, I thought I heard the sigh of God.

Mother Lourdes has asked me to visit one of the parishioners of a church in Dorchester in her place. Little Sister stayed with Sister Anne for me—set her up comfortably in the corner of the bakery with a coffee, a macaroon, and *Baseball Weekly,* which we bought for her.

Little Sister offered the promise of no late morning angry dismissals of persons. "Though," she said, "next time give me a couple days warning if you don't want me to lose my temper. It takes a lot of work on my part, so it's the least you can do."

I was late in getting there. Rushed to get Sister Anne her bifocals. Missed the #221 bus and the #220 to Quincy T-stop, where I got off at the Andrew Square stop.

Unquiet of mind and heart, I had little grace to extend.

Mrs. Benton Harbly is a very nice woman for 5 minutes, then makes sure you know that you owe her something, she being infirm, and you being so sprightly (at 70-plus, most would not use the term *sprightly*). So I am already peevish at knowing the visit should be a test of my endurance. Her basket of groceries delivered, I am expected to clean not only her stove-top, but her refrigerator, and floor, too.

"Someone came by the other day when I was cleaning my stove," she said to me, "and told me that I shouldn't clean it, I could get a heart attack with the scrubbing," she said, pitifully rubbing her hand across what I took to be a pretend aching heart. Miriam, I thought, *bloody hell, well, why didn't the* other *person clean it for you, then?* But of course I didn't say anything and just cleaned the crusties off. Here I am in a nun's habit—and wearing a ring of blessed devotion to Christ. But in my heart, today I don't believe in the visitation of the elderly or in cleaning refrigerators, nor do I believe in Christian charity (except theoretically, when people *really* want to be grateful for work done on their behalf, or for people who don't try to get out of a task).

I have asked Mother Lourdes twice to be allowed to not go. Twice she said, "You will find it to be a good spiritual discipline. And if you can find it in your heart to remember that our Lord loves a cheerful giver, that will help you through your trial." Today, I returned in time for dinner, eating in quiet resentment, and I don't think you'd call what I did communing with Jesus, but by dessert, again, I did hear the Lord sigh.

And that, Miriam, is all I have for today. A little bitterness, a little sound-making by the Lord.

Yours,
Sr. A.—

26 March 2004
Feast Day of
St. Margaret of Clitherow

Miriam, dear—A short note.

It is nearing Palm Sunday and still no shaggy donkey for our Lord, as Sister Farm had planned. No Poitou, only the donkey trailer parked near the barn, now down to 2 bumper stickers thanks to Sister Farm's dedicated scraping and picking, and, Miriam dear, your Franklin's helpful hint of your homemade goo-gone—you both were fully the hit of the monastery with your contribution.

You can do no wrong in our eyes. And in the eyes of the community, who have endured a long winter of bumper diatribes. Your votes (as you may recall from an earlier letter) were the strongest of the bunch, and we have resolved them down to these two, at your suggestion:

* Shut Up & Drive (as you wrote, "this could be a nod to your silent prayer hours, your contemplation")
* Honk If You Love ("the second part of the sticker would need to go, but Franklin and I think we had a good brainstorm on this—what do you think?")

Miriam, what do we think? We think you both are the smartest people we know in the bumper sticker world and we offer you our grateful thanks. And if ever a donkey comes to ride home in this trailer, she will thank you, too,

Sr. A.—

Migrations

4 April 2004
Palm Sunday

Miriam, dear,

We knew it might come. Sister Farm's leaving our bayside meadow, our herons and mergansers and whickering owls, this small farm, this struggle of a place. Now wide open spaces, long swatches of cleared land, a dairy farm, a hope of a donkey. Miriam, you had the concern too, the sorriness of her leaving. And now it has come.

Sister Farm has left our monastery with shiny new Wellingtons along with a ticket to Wisconsin, via Chicago. There she will pray and work with Sisters. The Prioress there will decide, as our Blessed Lord directs.

Feed & Seed Tom comes morning and early evening to tend to the Icelandics and to our Jerseys. Frankie keeps the bees. Little Sister the Buff Orpingtons, since she gathers the eggs and such anyway.

Tom keeps the barn smells in the barn, works the stalls, pushes the ewes out toward the bay-lined pasture, milks the Jerseys,

Clucky Lucky and & Daisy Lou, lines the stalls with new hay. Drinks his coffee prepared with care by Sister Anne, pulls chunks of cardamom bread from the vast loaves, coughs, shuffles, offers a faint wave, then leaves.

What can we do? We provide Tom a thermos of coffee (the red plaid one, and Sister Bird's donation, friend of many road trips and birding expeditions), and Sister Anne's careful attention, and bread from Little Sister's bakery, and all of our gratefulness.

Of Sister Patrick Gertrude, you will be curious: How does she fare without Sister Farm?

It is both as you imagine and as you might not imagine.

The hallways are now marked with the collaboration of Sister Patrick Gertrude's cleaning scents and Sister Bird's naturopathic enthusiasm for the potential healing properties of aromatherapy. The chicken smells (acrid), the cow smell (thick), and the sheep (lanolin and briny) come to us more and more veiled. And no Sister Farm pounding down the halls with clots of barn drippings falling from coveralls or Wellies. Few reminders of the faithful feud between our Sisters, only the lulling silence of lavender in our cloister (to encourage sleep and peace in prayer), frankincense in the Mainhouse (for clarity of thought and calmness), and a citron mix in the hallways (to enliven the spirit and encourage the heart), as Sisters Patrick Gertrude and Bird assure us it will do.

But there is oddly little triumph in the air, and Sister Patrick Gertrude has waned in her interest in the recorder and the offerings of the New Baptist Hymnal.

No distant sounds of metal tinkerings or throat-clearing from Sister Farm's cell. No cigar fumes following this springtime corner from the barn to the kitchen window and mixing with the yeasty paste of baking bread.

A postcard came yesterday from Oconomowoc, WI. The front, a photo of "3 Sisters with 5 Herefords at the Oconomowoc County Fair" and Sister Farm's note on the back:

> *No donkeys here either. Jesus has no ride come Palm Sunday. Arrived fine. Prayer and work and lots more cows. Same thing. Different monastery (ha ha)*
>
> *—Sister Farm*
>
> *PS Tell Tom there's extra sheep feed behind the hay bales, to the right, if he's looking for it.*
>
> *PPS Sister Patrick Gertrude, admit it, you miss me. And it's not for sure me and my cigars will stay here, just to scare you I might come back.*

and a tiny scrunched PPPS to Sister Anne:

> *Now, don't you sneak out to the barn to feed Daisy Lou celery. She likes it, but she'll get the shits real bad.*
>
> *Don't worry, Tom'll take good care. (Plus, I don't want you sneaking out and slipping there in the barn.)*

In other news, Miriam, Sister Bird has discovered piping plovers at the far edge of the ledge of dune sand, before the grasses, almost imperceptible, colored like the pebbles and sand. A rare bird these days, as you know, nesting along the beach, with its lone whistley sort of bird call. Often they can be found on Plum Island or the other Harbor Islands, along the less trafficked coast. Small, pale, somewhat akin to the wan and fragile saints, these birds nest along the beaches, within a circle of pebbles.

Just as the Red Sox regular season gets underway, the birds in migratory patterns awaken Sister Bird's excitement all of March and April. You can imagine what sort of a change spring is for us. And coming into the end of Lent, Holy Week speaks to moving from relentless darkness to hope. All this, all this life. We are awash with relief and wonder at this new season, even at the same time, with our own sadness, with Sr. Farm gone.

Yours, Sr. A.—

15 April 2004

Miriam, I love this photocopy machine of Mother Lourdes's, all these copies I can make, treats to send along. Noodle around this envelope: Sister Anne sent along a write-up from *Baseball Weekly* on Tim Wakefield's pitching. She's sure you are interested in the news, since this new season promises that the Red Sox will win the pennant and the World Series. What's the life of faith, if not this?

News from Wisconsin, too, Miriam. Our Sister Farm learns a new system. The dairy farm there is lucrative, producing organic milk and cheeses (washed rind & triple cream cheeses), and she sounds busy and satisfied in the new monastery.

Sister Patrick Gertrude has moments of great silence and moments when she rallies, tidying something up or spraying some essential aromatic oil. But with no jabs, no curt comments, no worthy opponent, she's getting rusty.

And as Little Sister was preparing fondant for her coffee tarts that Boston restaurants order, she noticed, she told me later, our own Sister Patrick Gertrude walking into the barn. Somewhere around the addition of the chocolate buttercream garnish, she saw her exit the barn. Called on it, Sister Patrick Gertrude denied any such visit, but Little Sister likes to push just to see if Sister Patrick Gertrude is letting her guard down.

Frankie attends to the bees, though Tom has been trying to explain to him something about reducing brood congestion. He's already been doing some sort of reversing brood chambers, something Tom calls *supering*. "And you better hope Frankie's smarter than me, because they'll start swarming soon if he's not."

In addition to the farm, Tom has made improvements here and there, maybe an attempt to have the barn be welcoming if Sister Farm comes back.

Mother Lourdes pulls ahead dutifully. When one Sister leaves, there's only the noticing of the gap—the missing presence, the missed sound of Sister Farm's voice during chant: cigar-like, low, gritty. The task for Mother Lourdes, bearing the weight of leadership, seems to only gain in challenge and discouragement. It's not only the financial part, but a feeling, she said to Sister Anne, Sister Patrick Gertrude, and me recently in a meeting, "of a slow chipping away at a spiritual community." This, she said, felt like a first stage. "More chipping will come." She held out her tiny hand, palm up and empty and said, "Some communities have back-up plans in place. I wish I took delight in saying that our plan *and* our back-up plan is the mercy of the Lord."

Sister Anne said to her, "You are a good shepherd for your small flock, my dear. Discouragement doesn't always speak to the truth of the work we do, only to what we might feel in the moment." She took Mother Lourdes' hands and filled them with her own and said, "We here are all of us living lives in the grace of God. Don't let discouragement tell you to wish for something different." After she said that, she looked at the watch on her outstretched wrist and asked to be excused: the Red Sox were playing an afternoon game.

And so, Miriam, we learn. And I don't feel the weight of leadership and I don't feel that despair. And small things—how often it is the small things—bring joy. Now it is the piping plovers who have settled along the east side of the point, where the tides and currents have created low dunes. There between the grasses and the tide, they creates crapes, shallow bowls within the sand, around which the ritual of courting and mating meet with the warming winds of the season. Sister Bird is delighted and protective. She won't let anyone go to the edge of the point unless accompanied.

And so it goes, hopes go out, hopes come in,

Sr. A.—

1 May 2004

Miriam, dear—

Father Martinez came to our guesthouse for 2 days. Since everything he reads all the days is spiritual wisdom, biblical studies, critical analysis, or hermeneutics, he goes on retreat with solely his Salmon—Trout—Steelheader magazine, which expands his soul, he says, fish by fish. Oceanwater or freshwater, no matter. He loves to fish.

He has been down to the water (with promises to Sister Bird to stay clear of the east side of the point), slips out after Lauds, goes to the barn where Sister Farm stashes waders and a few snapline poles. He doesn't have the interest or heart to eat fish, just to hook them and "put the fear of God into them," he says with the wicked smile of a priest too long in one parish.

We all gather our spiritual wisdom where we can. You, Miriam, from the movement of the birds, early morning birdsong, from scripture, from life lived with Franklin, your two fledgling children, and a life of health and edges of illness.

Father Martinez brings his spiritual wisdom to the table—though we have silent meals, he always tries to trick one or other of us into a conversational trifle.

Mother Lourdes has been struggling with Sister Farm's move to the Sisters in Oconomowoc. She is missing the New England wisdom, stout and unaffected, that Sister Farm has brought to our monastery. This morning she walked down to the western side of the point to sit with Father Martinez, where two tidal pools meet and dump all sorts of fish at the tidal changes.

Later she told us about the conversation. "Let me tell you something," he said, watching the switching tide and his feed line the whole time. "This is advice that works, because it comes from p. 54 of the *Salmon—Trout—Steelheader* by Robert H. Campbell, 'Columbia and Willamette River Spring Chinook Salmon Rigs.' April 2004: 'It is advisable to lengthen your lead line when faced with this problem.'"

"Father Martinez," she responded. "I suppose that freshwater fishermen sometimes have wisdom, too. I will ponder these things. I don't like it, but then I don't want to shorten the lead line, either."

So, after this shot of fishing wisdom from our dear Father Martinez, it seems that Mother Lourdes pondered that spiritual work of the lengthened lead line. By dinnertime, she let us all know that if Sister Farm's time at the Sisterhouse meant a permanent stay in Wisconsin, then she hoped, at least, she would at last have her donkey. Oh, it's exhausting and wonderful to keep opening our hands, don't you think?

Piping plover report: The piping plovers now have a nest, lined with pebbles and some odd shells and a clutch of four eggs. Sister Bird mothering from afar (binos, notebooks and thermos and threats to any of us who might wander close). She has built a protective fencing around the nest, a simple architecture, but she doesn't know how it will hold. The idea is that a small wire-mesh would form a protective fence around them, offering openings spaced between holding rods for the plover to come into safety, the eggs protected under the mesh.

With this rare and endangered species, Sister Bird is at her guard, wary of the hungry herring gulls, black-backed gulls and the weather, which make any fencing seem less secure.

All of us went down to the southeast edge of this land, where the tides and northeasterlies have worn the land into low dunes and sand. So, to the sandflats this morning, Sister Anne and I slower than the rest, we came. Sister Bird commanded we stay at a safe distance, so we set up camp 20 feet away at one of the benches overlooking the flats: binoculars going from pair of eyes to pair of eyes, grateful, eager to see the plovers.

Little Sister didn't come, but sent along a thermos of coffee and of tea for me, and some pecan rolls. "Maybe this will help your worries some," when Sister Bird told her about the hovering herring gulls. "Maybe you should do something about it," Little Sister said. "Little things always get hurt by big things," she said.

"But what else can I do?" Sister Bird said.

"Well, I'd think of something. Anyway, take your rolls and thermoses and move along."

So we all watched the female plover, nesting in a ring of shells, then within that ring, her eggs in the sand. Roosting on the eggs, now in bright warm midday sun, the nest at the high end of the sandflats, where the sand turns pebbly, 20 feet shy of the beach peas and sea grass.

The plover is a lovely sight. Short orange beak with black tip breaking the color scheme of beach yellows and browns. Black eyes, pure and small. When the female gets up, quick steps, great energy, little grace. And we watched, there, surrounded by bank swallows flying, diving.

We made it back for Sext, which sounded so rich in gratefulness as we chanted into the day. Another of the Loose Rules (#19), Miriam, which needs no commentary, except that of our spiritual lives, and our shared stories: *Every loss is a gain in some form.*

And so it is.

Curious losses, curious joys,

Sr. A.—

5 May 2004

Miriam, dear—

Our beloved Red Sox have gone from a 15-1 winning streak to 15-6, now losing another game to the Indians and one to the Rangers. But they are *our* Sox, our losing Sox—no longer heroes these early days of May, but now like our children we cheer on despite the weakening record, the losing ground.

"In the spiritual life," says Sister Anne, "we seek depth, balance, and a keen evenness of purpose. But in baseball season we are high and low and high and low."

Tonight, rain. Sister Anne says that means another game they will not have to lose tonight, for one night. It's not the best way to be hopeful, but it's one way we know.

Today, tidying up Sister Anne's cell, a growing stash of wrinkled sports sections of the *Boston Globe,* all of the papers folded back to the baseball section. Some with notes in the margins about a game Wakefield pitched: "Good and dependable pitcher, esp. in high humidity and low winds coming toward him."

Her days have two divisions: a cane day or a walker day. Walker days are the most painful days, arthritis gnawing at the bones, and the bones seem to claim new odd shapes daily, bursting against the skin, making shiny whitish knobs on her hands, knees, feet.

Frankie gives Sister Anne bee stings, as Sister Bird insists that the healing possibilities of bee venom are endless. Her hands are helped somewhat, but there's little relief for Sister Anne's knees and hips. She is Sister Bird's experiment, we fear, and if these therapies are a success, we believe she may write another book titled *Sister Bird's Guide to the Bees,* which would be confusing indeed.

During bee sting time (about two times a week) Sister Anne tries to do two things:

1. Not distract Frankie as he opens a jar of bees, uses long tweezers to pull them, one by buzzing one, out of the jar, quickly replacing the lid, and places stings at various spots on her arms, wrists, and knees.

And then, the task that saddens him the most, to then quickly crush the bee that gave her life for this healing work.

It's no small thing to be responsible for the deaths of 10 living creatures on a given day. It must be hard on Frankie. Confusing to him.

2. The second thing Sister Anne tries to do during bee sting time is teach Frankie new words.

It will seem odd to you that someone so capable with bees, stingers, and hive frames is clumsy and inarticulate in other respects. We have tried to encourage articulation of skills in other areas—language, music, etc.—but the apiary arts are the natural arts to him.

I may have mentioned to you the short list of words he came to us with, among them, *Peam, peam, Kiss on ips, Epet EwYoh, Kip it,* and now *hi.* All of which come up in any meeting.

Another area of giftedness—the Frankie hug. Any room he enters, blue pants, white shirt, and suspenders, he gives a round of hugs. Sincere and always accompanied by the fresh, *Kiss on ips.*

Since Sister Bird has become his favorite Sister—which is easily done by sneaking him—against her better judgment, she says—chocolate ice cream or *peam, peam,* his vocabulary has increased to the word *Bird.*

Nothing new on the plovers, but Sister Bird reported a few more gulls nearby, a glaucous gull, and a Bonaparte's gull, and, of course the herring gull—all of which usually bring her joy, but now worry her with the piping plovers near, endangered, and vulnerable. Also a 40+ flock of killdeer following the past cycles of tides. And a tricolored heron.

More soon, Sr. A.—

7 May 2004

Miriam, dear—

We are nearing the end of bird migrating season (with warbler peak left to go), thank the blessed Virgin. One can't get Sister Bird to do anything other than fill notebooks with species, signature markings, delineations, species, numbers, times.

I enclose a copy of a letter from Sister Farm in Oconomowoc, Wisconsin—as she mentions you:

> *The Bing Sisters in Oconomowoc say hi. Busy work on the farm, mostly with calves and at work on the John Deere and 2 Internationals.*
>
> *Sister Anne—sorry that the Sox lost two to the Indians, but this'll humble them some.*
>
> *—Sr. Farm*
>
> *PS Sister Patrick Gertrude: Be glad you only have two Jerseys—this barnful of Herefords are shitters.*
>
> *PPS Sister Athanasius: Please ask Tom to send me the latest* Uncle Henry's Swap. *Nothing like that here, and*

> *I'll never find my donkey without it. Hurry, the Lord has need of it.*
>
> *And hi and thanks to Miriam when you write her. She put her hands on some great Cuban—Monte Cristos—cigars for me. The post office insisted that the package be opened there, for inspection. But all 6'2" of Sister Margaret refusing when she and I went to pick it up, stopped the fuss.*

Miriam, you have become a friend to all of us. Thank you for thoughtful (albeit illegal) gifts.

You asked about Little Sister in your last letter: *Mysteries, mysteries. I am trying to form a picture in my mind of her. I think I like her, but don't know her. Btw, the photo you sent of you all during Advent is lovely. Franklin says your Sister Anne looks like a wisp, that Little Sister looks like dynamite waiting for a match. You in the photo, match the image I've formed of you from your letters. Mother Lourdes, a very-there look to her, but tired. Frankie, you can see the ice cream pudge already starting. Sister Farm, earthy and relaxed. Sister Patrick Gertrude was the surprise to both of us. Franklin said: "There's the real mystery woman. And Sister Bird, she even looks like a bird."*

I wonder why I have written so little about Little Sister. Perhaps she is most unlike me in terms of sensibility, and now that I think of it, I like to write about what I am starting to understand. Writing about Little Sister, I'm at a loss. But a few things: Quick to flare up. Quick to resolve. She keeps her own counsel. And, with others—even if they don't speak of their inner concerns, thoughts—one can observe in their actions and reactions, their word choice, something of the inner self and can reasonably deduce a central personality, the interior person. Little Sister, however, loses this logic. She bakes, and the kinds of pastries and breads she bakes, you would think, here is a passionate person, a sensualist. Yet, I don't think she is passionate about baking, though she *is* dedicated to it. I have been tempted to ask her about these things, but she prefers to talk about things exterior than interior and backs off when a person, as she says, pries.

Will you find this odd, Miriam? But I suppose not, as you mentioned last week in your letter how you and Franklin have developed the ways in which you communicate, as though there are no other doors of communication than those. As though topics are left unattended, thoughts left unspoken, secret desires are left unsaid, even though you might want to find ways to say those things. It becomes quite the chore to keep a relationship flexible, doesn't it? And as you said, we in community, also have the unspoken rule that if one has said or done something 30 times in the same way, it is in effect who you are. It's hard to re-train those around you to see another side.

That's why when Sister Farm would try to clean herself coming from the mudroom into the hallway it might count for nothing, because 827 times she had come in with the muck unscraped from her boots, as though to Sister Patrick Gertrude, Sister Farm were testing her patience, rather than creating a small space for them both to enter in.

If Sister Patrick Gertrude determined to consider the new attempt at cleanliness a slight, then Sister Farm grew weary in trying, and we, again, returned to our basic story between them. The three times Franklin does dishes cannot erase the many times (and the many emotions of those times) in which the dishes were not done.

And so we wear each other down. And so we learn that not to forgive is, perhaps, the easiest form of relationship, though the sliding away is never, as I see it, the better way.

I read, once, the term *unfinalizability,* perhaps from some old Russian literature class I took. Bakhtin described Dostoevsky's treatment of his characters, suggesting that Dostoevsky brought a certain humanness to them, as though Grace were an actuality in the lives of his characters, and that time and circumstance might bring that to light.

It is a sign of a vigorous community and the grace of God if we can avoid condemning each other to the same definitions each day, seeing what this new day holds.

I am far astray from your question about Little Sister. It is as though I know things about her, but not so much about *her.* She is private about her faith, and for someone in the monastic life that might seem odd. She is kind to Sister Anne, I observe. And respects Mother Lourdes. Her humor is dry, a bit like Teresa of Avila's, a bit like your Franklin's.

And her tarts and pastries and cinnamon breads are among the best in the South Shore and the Boston area. And if it doesn't speak to her own passion, it at least speaks to her thoughtfulness, abilities, and willingness to allow her gifts to bring others keen pleasure.

———

I hope you don't mind a long letter. I suppose spring wakes up my pen, the writing simply wishes to continue.

Today Sister Anne insisted on a May's day walk, down back via the farm way, past the meadow and sumacs to the bench near rocky beach. We planned the afternoon around it. Right after Sext, we set out. I gave her too much Aleve to take out the worst of the pain in the old bones, and we set out. We tied a little stool to her walker. For stops along the way. You would have thought we were hiking the White Mountains, the plans we made for a slow walk down a long path to the point.

About halfway, we met up with Sister Bird, binoculars up, her rosary beads as counter. We set Sister Anne on a stool to rest and observed the highbush blueberry, beginning to fruit and pushing toward us in the mix of the briny air at low tide.

Of the birds Sister Bird encountered, there in the sumac bushes: red-wing blackbirds, with their fast wingbeats and patches of bright color on their epaulets; common grackles, cardinals with their loud song, a grey catbird, a solitary Baltimore oriole (with an orange we all agreed was one of the wonders of the earth that our Lord Jesus walked upon), 2 yellow warblers, and a goldfinch.

After the last sighting of a warbler and a good rest, we headed to the shore at low tide to see our new friends, the plovers, surrounded by gulls. Oh the threatening world.

Tom put a picnic table for us near the shore, so we watched, hoping that the imperceptible tide would be made perceptible. Nothing to note, I'm afraid. Imperceptibility.

A great egret by one of the tidal pools, watching us, watching him. All of us, so still in the watching.

Sister Bird met up with us again, watched the egret, too. "Note the spiritual lessons that the ornithological world teaches us yet again," said Sister Bird, "silence and waiting—and I would add, *prayer*—are most natural forms of being."

She pulled out her red plaid thermos, and offered Sister Anne some coffee, which smelled glorious. "Just the thing to give me energy for the long road back."

We sat and watched as long as the egret did, tide coming in, wind picking up, the plovers and the nest still claiming the worries of Sister Bird, who has become nonstop about the gulls and anything with a predatory threat.

Miriam, there, watching the birds, we spoke of you with expansive hearts. Know that you have some good friends here, Miriam, who would rejoice to meet you some fine day,

Sr. A.—

15 May 2004
Feast Day of Saint Isadore

Trouble, Miriam, trouble.

My letters, I know, have been filled with the piping plovers. Sister Bird, as you know, has been lamenting the endangered nests of the plovers and the skullduggery of the gulls, those pirates of the shore. But over the last mornings, there have been gulls washing up to shore. The first day, two gulls. Then three the next day. Little Sister. We have no idea where she discovered that you could poison herring gulls, but there you have it. It has been a brutal moment of revelation between Little Sister and Sister Bird.

In Little Sister's at-it manner, she told Sister Bird, "I won't have those gulls breaking you up, just when we get an endangered nesting bird on our shore. Gulls you have all the time, but we won't get any piping plover again, without doing something. And no one was doing anything, so I called up Tom and asked what would work best. And he said, 'I'd nail 'em.' And he said you'd be 'mad as all hell loose in a firestorm.'"

Sister Bird's been crying for hours. Little Sister has no idea she's done anything of offense. Mother Lourdes, well, what sort of spiritual position do you take on these things? What would you say, Miriam? I have found myself on both sides, switching almost by minute, fifteen gulls so far. Is it a fair trade to save a nest, with a clutch size of four eggs? Four little piping plover chicks who will live pale lives and struggle to keep nests along plundered beaches?

We all have opinions about our bird friends. I guess to equate worlds, it's the difference between the truck driver bird and the ballet dancer bird.

It almost sounds like those lifeboat riddles that those who teach ethics toss out at young minds: Who gets to be saved? Who gets offered to the waves as expendable? Is it worth the loss of commoner life for the special breed?

Well, Miriam, I'm sure things will wind and unwind here regarding our latest travesty of ethics and birds afloat in the incoming tide. Some days it all seems fragile doesn't it? Those eggs the size of an ovalized quarter—and there are none sweeter in the bird kingdom than those orange plover legs holding up a round pudge of body. They are a wonder of creation. More, I'm sure, soon,

Sr. A.—

17 May 2004

Miriam dear, I knew you'd want to know, so am sending another note about the piping plover situation. Sister Bird newly frail-like, her face cluttered with concern for the 20 (to date) lost gulls, washing up to the beach, wings outspread, sometimes, as though they had been swimming through the deep waters and arrived to shore, exhausted by the journey.

Mother Lourdes reminds us to move onward, but as soon as we've come around to finding a solid patch, another herring gull brings its life-lost body to shore.

And Little Sister is shouldering the blame. And Tom, humbly down at the Feed & Seed and making his appearances quickly to chores at the barn and then home again, leaving coffee still in the Thermos, baked good untouched.

If Sister Farm were here, she'd do what any mother creature would do who has been given the care of beasts and birds and then finds a friend has been in some ways hurting them. She'd give Tom a good right hook. I almost wish she were here to do it, if only for his sake, so that he can get up and dust himself off. But now you can tell he doesn't even know how to face everyone.

Little Sister first ran—on schedule—hot, fierce, angry at all of us for having mourned the endangered nature of the piping plovers, and then not rejoicing at their salvation.

"You're all fickle as the devil," she said. "And, you, Sister Bird, especially." Then, after a weak, sad squeak from Sister Bird, she continued, "Don't make dove eyes at me. There's no remorse coming from me today." Then, looking at us—standing there silent, weak—she said, "Now, all of you, out of my kitchen." Right on schedule. 11:30, she kicked us out. Still we all felt that being kicked out on this day at least made more sense.

Sister Bird took her dove eyes upstairs to her cell and you could hear her chair shaking from the emotion of it.

Mother Lourdes tried to rein things in, not rushing us through the tempest of strong emotions, but wanting to avoid a too long time in the soup.

Frankie just kept looking confused and kept saying, "peam, peam," ice cream being his solution for any misery or woe.

Sister Anne, in a grip of arthritis, took the news in her bed and has been in prayer for us all. Finally, she asked Mother Lourdes to call Father Martinez and tell him, please, we've reached a spiritual and communal impasse, would he bring the host for a healing moment in the chapel? And our dear Father Martinez shifted his schedule and brought Delores, one of the Eucharistic ministers, along. Delores, we've discovered, comes with him when he feels that the Host is enough, *yes*, but that woman wisdom from Delores, to use a baseball term, "brings it on home," though Vatican wisdom might not quite agree on this point, theologically speaking.

And so, the body of our Lord. A prayer. Even Tom came. And Delores who ministered with the wine said, "the Blood of our Lord, dear," and to Sister Anne, "the Blood of Our Lord, honey, the Blood of our Lord."

And so I end with the Eucharistic hope,

Sr. A.—

20 May 2004

Miriam dear, your letter came with great delight to us all. You have written your friends the Bings a sympathy letter so kindly framed regarding the loss of the herring gulls, as well as your note about understanding how Little Sister would want to *do something*, having discovered the something to do.

There's an unwritten rule of Mother Lourdes's that with a situation like the piping plovers, a little time and much grace and the presence of the Holy Spirit, a way can open up where it looks like there is no way.

It's among other unwritten rules we don't ever state, but somehow agree upon, alongside the Bingean Rule. Some others are:

#1. Don't give Frankie ice cream. But if you do give him ice cream, clean up the ice cream dishes and leave no trace, minimizing the scoop dents left in the Neopolitan tub.
#2. Listen, always, to Sister Bird's enthusiasms—whether fowl or feathered wonders, or another naturopathic fix for a

health problem. (Whatever you do with the wisdom is your own business, but don't squash her enthusiasm.)

#3. With regard to Sister Athanasius (yes, myself, I've caught on): Allow her all the philosophical inquiries, questions, conundrums. She just needs to sort and stew a while. And *never* ever try to convince her of something. Skeptics never begin to love the Savior for one more rule or reason to love, but for love.

#4. With regard to Sister Anne: Even behind her back, even down at the beach where only the wind can hear you, never, ever speak disrespectfully of someone who hobbles after God.

#5. When Little Sister tells you to leave the kitchen, leave quickly, nearest exit.

#6. Give Tom all the coffee he wants, but when he says he's cutting down, offer to fill it only ½ way, and then pour ¾.

Herring gulls, 27 at last count. Tom has dug a deep hole on the other side of the sumacs. And Father Martinez came to say a blessing for the deceased. Wherever the theological understanding of birds, one hopes there is a paradise for our winged enemies, who now that they have died, we call friends.

And Father Martinez brought Delores again, who has sung the praises of our friends Little Sister and Sister Patrick Gertrude, who know what it means to be faithful to a cause. I don't think Sister Patrick Gertrude was really devoted one way or the other, but she knows the feeling of being alone in a righteous mission, so has buttressed Little Sister's cause fiercely.

As often as Little Sister says, "Leave the kitchen quietly and now" to those she feels are ingrates, Sister Patrick Gertrude will add, "March on out."

But still there's this: We pray the Divine Office together, psalm after psalm, voice with voice. And Mass is the place when we extend the peace—extend the peace begrudged, maybe, but still the peace. Our Lord Jesus, new at giving the long-view plan to the church, spoke of two things needful. He said, "Little flock, love each other." And then he said, "Little flock, live in unity with each other." And here we are spending our days hoping to get it right, even as we daily get it wrong.

Oh, Miriam, it feels like there is no news but this news. Though we do—praise God—have the last of the lilacs lining the edge of the monastery in purples and whites, their fragrant curls a signpost of a summer coming on. Soon, I know, there will be even other things to fill letters. For now, this note, knowing that your heart shares in our soreness,

Sr. A.—

22 May 2004

Miriam, dear—

Along this windy day at the outermost bank, where the sand, worn down by tide, has thrown up a small ridge of dunes, one piping plover has found her home near the beach peas and the sea grass. Within this ring of shells, a clutch of 4 eggs. And a very small bird honors new life by waiting alongside it, hovering over it.

A mascot of the spiritual life: endangered, small, and hopeful in its guileless laying of eggs in a ring of shells along the sand out in the open. Amidst all sort of preying bird. Here, where faith, tiny-ness, pluck, and sea wind meet. Who, I wonder, would not claim this 3-inch creature as the essential-most mascot of the spiritual realm?

Two days later. Miriam, I still haven't mailed this letter to you. I'll add another note before our mailwoman comes to pick up post.

Thanks entirely to the mixed awful blessing of Little Sister's mercenary behavior, we have all of us had a celebration down at the beach yesterday. We have 4 new tiny plover all downy. A full clutch came through, giving their singular high-toned points of light, those bird calls, as they wait for their primaries and secondaries to fill out.

There would be no plover party without the mess and grief.

Oh those bird voices sound like tiny high-pitched drops of water, a sort of soft metal dripping sound. Earnest. Sister Bird, a tortured woman in recent days, now rejoices with the living, plover puffs—almost makes this seem like there's no endangerment of the species, a full four—not eaten, not washed away by storm or tide.

Father Martinez kindly came to the party, for another joyful prayer of Saint Francis's blessing of the birds.

Tom, invited by Mother Lourdes, solemnly declined. "But," he said to Mother Lourdes, at the short end of any conversation with him, "tell Sister Anne, that if the plovers worked out all right—even though we still are waiting for them to fledge, tell her I think the Red Sox might just be able to finish the season off right, too."

Father Martinez even offered to barbeque, though Sister Bird asked him to not use lighter fluid, as it may just poison the air. So with a few remaining early evening plover voices in the distance where the marsh grass meets the pebbly shore, and with a little parade of paper bag lanterns, filled with sand, we all gathered at the shore, baptized our feet ceremonially, and ate with relish, as though at the marriage supper of the Lamb. And Tom sent along some bottles of Connecticut wines, and Little Sister offered a toast to better future rescue operations.

Indeed, Sr. A.—

27 May 2004
Five Days from the
Feastday of St. Rita

Miriam, dear—

The 22nd was the feastday of Saint Rita, patron saint of impossible causes, which is to say, according to Sister Anne, certainly the patron saint of the Red Sox, which is probably why Sister Anne wears a St. Rita's medal.

Quiet evening in May. Peepers peeping. Sun finding fuller light even into dusk. Some evenings simply arrive so quiet and fine, you place a sigh into the air, while you pray bead after bead of the rosary, another sigh, then a little letter to a friend. A wondrous day, and things settling, finding their center again, after early spring's turmoil.

I write this so that you know wonder—starting with minutes, perhaps whole evenings—will return. There will be days (unlike the day you wrote your last letter) when your muffler doesn't fall off, when your radio antenna doesn't get a good shove by the mechanics in the garage who claim to be fixing your muffler, and the antenna is left dangling. And you've mentioned before how your favorite part of the car is the radio. And now, only a silence over the hum of the engine.

Is there no stopping such a day? *Dare I read this note further?* I asked myself. The muffler falling off again, your husband's brush with the garage door opener, in which pieces of your already fragile antenna-less car were strewn and smashed along the garage floor.

And your husband's quiet little line to you as you were in the kitchen—*Dear, I think things actually are worse than they seemed.*

Miriam, my comfort in knowing that that day of yours has ended—knows no bounds. I, in turn, give you an evening falling on a monastery, peepers making their last calls, summer air trying to open up the door from an unrelinquishing spring.

I give you some prayers prayed along a rosary bead. I give you the yellow light from the lamp shining on my paper, my black pen scratching along, and the blessings of our Dear Lord on your next day, and the next.

Wishing you a little reprieve in spring and a radio full volume as you drive down the quiet road with a muffler so attached and quiet that you will know yourself to be in that wishfulest moment I sent your way,

Sr. A.—

1 June 2004

Miriam, dear—

Here, all bird news. First our garden. Birds by turns visiting the dark soil of the garden (Tom's work, though Sister Patrick Gertrude has taken to the dirt—when the cat's away, I suppose—how Sister Farm would be amused at this turn of interests), the nearby bushes, and the feeder. The American robin, the house wren, always visitors. Closer to the water: cedar waxwings and saltmarsh sparrows. And rarer: Northern rough-winged swallows and American redstarts—all sounding out some version of the psalms, but everyone is using different songs and call notes.

And further down the path, toward the water, at the edge of the water. Yes, it's happened. We have had three little celebrations. One for each hatched nestling. One didn't survive, we don't know why but it wasn't due to predators, of that you may be sure. These precocial birds, once the air has dried their down, are already off and wobbling away from the nest. You can imagine, now, that the second round of vigilance, to protect the wanderers, is in place.

How do you fare? Franklin? Your birds? And you tell me your

daughter is changing, claiming adulthood "a little too early and a little too hard." And your son is back from college for the summer. Now is your chance to have the stereo alarm fixed. No more 7:00 a.m. radio waking your entire house on a weekend, with no one who knows which buttons to push.

And what thoughts do you have, Miriam, when day flops over into day, those small quiet unknowns and questions and thoughts. These things, Miriam. I love to read how you see the world, and how the people you love and live with do, too.

Especial hellos to Franklin. Ever since he called here, regarding your surgery, so worried, friendly, and polite, we have warmest affection for him.

And always, affection for you,

Sr. A.—

6 June 2004
Feastday of Marcellin
Joseph Benoit Champagnat

Miriam—

Yes, I should have guessed, a little time, and you'd want to return to the basic questions that I haven't answered—even for myself. You have asked me, as though a different way of phrasing it might bring another answer. Who knows why I left my Writer, why I came to be with the Sisters. Then, I thought I maintained such a spiritual integrity about each decision. But

I remember it as a rush of my own human voice deep within me, to run from the life I had.

No, I will not say that the reasons I came were monastic. But the *pull* was monastic. A sudden quick ideal came over me. I desired a spiritual Order where I could aspire and grow, not be overwhelmed, defeated from the first day there. I was scared of losing my will and spirit, having them be broken when they seemed too fragile. That is why I joined the Order of Hildegard of Bingen. I knew the Order was small, stashed away in 8 convents in Europe, 4 in the United States (including our Sisters in Oconomowoc, where Sister Farm is), 1 in Lebanon, and 2 in Chile.

It was the only place I could think that had something ancient, a worked-through system lived over hundreds of years, an understanding of hours & days & faith. Ultimately, something a person could life-long abide in.

Now as I write, I think, simply, I ran away from some of my biggest challenges in the name of God—relationship, education, profession, vocation. I did it the way people go to Barcelona to find a warm place far away from other known places, where there is sort of soft air, and water, a place that looks more attractive than other places. I recently read a quote somewhere by Freeman Patterson: "If you do not see what is around you every day, what will you see when you go to Tangiers?" Perhaps our then-Prioress saw the draw toward something more, that there or here, I needed a starting place. And perhaps the Novice Mistress knew that my disengagement of place was an attempt at engaging with my own life, but in this community. And that the real story of *why* would take time. And that has come to be precisely true.

My whole life, perhaps, it would take me to sort out the leaving of the liberal arts education I adored: the new voices calling philosophy "the queen of the sciences," like Jacques Maritain. Willem de Kooning's new notes in the arts, confusing and "gestural" paintings. All this as though new definitions arrived into the physical laws, even: physical laws of axis and orbit, volume, speeds of sound and of light.

And of leaving a relationship containing exactly one warm bed, a night table weighed down with almost 40 books of philosophy and the spiritual life, our reading together of Augustine's bawdy life, the shaping together of our own lives, the late-night coffees, sitting on the stoop together, his lines of dispassionate passion. *Dear, if you sit closer you will,* he would grumble in his husky voice, *a) risk the spilling of precious coffee, which I'm sure will distress you; b) risk the avid attentions I might be forced to pay you on the front stoop (which may prove to be an embarrassment to us both, not to mention Mrs. Charkovsky across the street, who has taken a studious binocular to our situation; or c) risk your own enthusiastic gestures toward me, which will intimate that I should carry you upstairs and make wild and wicked love to you, which sounds stellar except for my back which would never recover from the one certainly, but perhaps the both. Shall we have a cigarette instead for the time being?*

Well, if you know me at all, Miriam, you know my choice. I haven't changed too much.

Doctor Breamer, I said, *I want everything—and you, old man, will give it to me. I want to finish my coffee, to play a little snooker with you in bed, but only after we've made a scene, so Mrs. Charkovsky comes outside. And then I want cigarettes resting on all our books, so we later can smoke in bed and burn the house down. Give me a big kiss, now.*

And he did. And his back survived marvelously, the old thing. And I got what I wanted, because the young always want everything.

Miriam, it's odd to revisit him like this—and I realize how many of his patterns, from speech patterns to writing and word usage to ways of love, I picked up from him, kept along with me.

Only with distance can a person say, deep down to themselves, *I knew it wouldn't last.* A writer of fine mind and belly looking for eager love but keeping it at a distance—engaged, but not engaged—while I poured my whole self out to him between cups of coffee and cigarettes and Augustine.

And with that phrase—*cups of coffee*—another thing of my past, these 9 years, 3 months, and 20 days, I will close,

Sr. A.—

(*10 June 2004*)

My dear, what shall I write today? Shall I write of Lauds, joined in the chant by nearby blue jays—taking over our morning song with their beaky insistence.

Shall I tell you that Sister Farm writes again from Oconomowoc that the Sisters there name their chickens but never their cows, a sure sign that Sister Farm has sights on coming back, I think, but I am too hopeful to be an astute judge. I can *no-*

tice a thing—a glance, the way colors shift during the hours of daylight, the driest summer air praising God along with the statuary of saints in our chapel, and swimming all around them. I notice the heavy feet of Sister Anne, a mix of steady and vertigo, her slow pace along the empty hall, the metal click of the cane, her steadying force, her salvific metal.

Those I can notice or describe, but Miriam, isn't it hard to interpret things rightly? Is there anything that the noisome jays *mean* in the morning? Is there something that the male red-winged blackbirds mean, when they offer you a quick glance at their bright shoulder patches. Is there some hidden line of God's that I don't know how to know when I see these things?

And the little blue heron comes knee-deep to the bay in the waning tide, appearing, disappearing, sudden, quiet, gone.

I guess an understanding to bring to a moment is all I'm thinking of, but the thing I bring is looking, and gratefulness. And then if we, chanting the psalms, find a way to God, a little note, that is the thing I will have found, *that* thing.

Tide's coming in, Miriam. It's one of those days like every day, except somehow better. It's as though you feel the air moving more. And with it, you know something clearer about tides, you see a laughing gull white & black against a blue sky.

Little Sister is making bear claws and macaroons in the bakery, and like clockwork, her face goes red, a line up of sweat beads along her forehead. Though most are working, whoever might be near the kitchen still at the tail end of morning break (the coffee drinkers, those still reading the last news of the morning paper) are ordered out. Then, twelve-fifteens, her face is pale

& unflushed, her macaroons made and bear claws soon out of the oven.

Sister Anne, always the first to venture back to the kitchen, to see if any almond paste is left over. I am brave only by complicity, as Sister Anne holds onto my arm as we enter the kitchen. I'm ashamed to say it, as we often are afraid to say the things that are true, but I always figure out a way in which I edge away from the kitchen door while still extending my arm, so that Sister Anne enters first. My shield and my strength.

I help Sister Anne to her stool at the stainless steel table, where Little Sister already has another coffee made and a small bowl of almond paste, and the D section—the Sports section of the *Boston Globe*, informing Sister Anne that Nomar is back to the field, while Schilling's ankle is starting to have some trouble. "Always something," Sister Anne says. "That's the excitement."

Miriam, sometimes writing to you I feel I spill over in writing, writing. Only later realizing what I forgot to ask, to listen for in your letters. Another round of radiation? How can that be? I thought that your last doctor's visit gave the All's Well, the stamp we all hoped would be the All's Well for the Future Too stamp.

And now your letter, your daughter accompanied you to radiation. And in the waiting room, the older couple you have seen before—what an odd community to be formed, but immediately close—Abigail and Edward Leigh, both in tweed, both in their 80s, waiting for her radiation treatment.

The way you write how Emily went with you, though she wouldn't go into the room where radiation is not personal, but a set of coordinates, as though it were algebra. And still Emily came. And this is a promising thing. And you, Miriam, you have a Bingean sensibility, offering a challenge to your daughter, walking with her where you can, letting her wait outside the radiation room when her teenage body would not face the going in. I know it is important to you. And some other important things I know about you: you like quiet places. You like all finches and larks. You like the psalms and the radio in your car and the moment you first turn on your heat in the car, summer changing into the first chill winks of autumn.

Prayers for you, these strangely familiar and frightening days. And you wrote to me once, I never forgot, *Never underestimate the medicinal power of hope.*

And with those words of yours, in the same hope, I end this note,

Sr. A.—

15 June 2004

Miriam, dear—

I think you must be feeling the fierceness of summer storms. Sister Bird worries about the plover chicks, so small there on the shore. So much conspires against them: weather, predators, tides.

That line about the medicinal power of hope stays with me. When I realize how this life of prayer means so much on behalf of others, I am renewed in prayer, this many layered meeting with the mystery of God, with God.

In your letters, you share with me conflicts, observations, wit, wryness, and spiritual notes of hope. Even in the dark tunnel of your illness, you keep writing, noticing small things that gain the weight of so much meaning: a comment by Franklin, his making you coffee in the morning, drinking the coffee at the oak table, watching the finches & nuthatches at your feeder, the same feeder you bought at Tom's Feed & Seed, that brought you to write that first letter of inquiry to us at the Monastery of Saint Hildegard of Bingen.

And now a loud morning cow yawl from Daisy Lou, the noisier of the Jerseys. And the smell of the changing tide. And the smell of beet soup—soup being our usual evening fare—which promises a good dark bread alongside. And the sound of Frankie, generating what we call his bee hum, the sound he makes when he's around bees. Tom helps him with the frames and hive details, but he's got the basics figured out, he knows the timing, follows the hive and details of requeening and extraction. With our clover, some local plum trees, we are hoping for a good September harvest.

Another postcard from Sister Farm, but no real news. Everything that sounds like good news from her, on this end feels to us like disappointment. You don't deny her her joy, but it's something still sore. It's as though it's hard to write about Sister Farm because she's gone. And it's hard to write about Sister Patrick Gertrude, too, because Sister Farm's gone. Not many recorder notes, the chapel and main house tidy and with flower, but she has gotten quieter and may be as surprised as the rest of us are by how much we relied on Sister Farm for a very earthy and wide approach to faith.

Tom still makes his daily morning rounds here. Once the matter of the herring gulls cleared, he's back to himself. Gets his coffee by the kitchen door, double-checks the bees with Frankie, says hello to all the Sisters and sometimes gives a wicked little wink to Sister Patrick Gertrude, as though he knows she needs a Sister Farm reminder. Though he never does traipse the barn smells into the house. Still, a barn next door is a barn next door, there's no getting away from it.

Well, signing off for now. And prayers for strength and courage in these next rounds of treatment.

Keep faith,
Sr. A.—

20 June 2004
Feastday of St. Florentina

Miriam, dear—

I believe Sister Anne is failing. The truth is, I have lost others (my Aunt Lorie, my parents, and my youngest brother). But now, I don't know how to lose this person, who has seen me through every stage of my religious vocation. And she has even given me my work—something I've been grateful for, even as the others so clearly can name their professional work. In losing Sister Anne, this will also be gone.

I watch her life, her slow reckless walk toward daily prayers, and know that not only does she know prayer, and a life lived for others, she is one of God's great friends on earth. As scripture says of Enoch that he walked with God, that is my impression of Sister Anne.

Her frame turns more fragile, her skin more translucent so that you can see the veins and bones and interior colors, as though all her interior were coming through to the surface. The muscles on her arms and legs so small, firm, stringy, and strained, her entire person is like a utensil—only the essential function herself. It's not that I don't know what I will lose. It's that I do.

~

But I make haste to change the tone of my letter and, as you asked in your last note what my cell looks like, I will tell you. My narrow pine (with a cherry stain) writing desk comes complete with old-fashioned blotter. A mug mercilessly stuffed full of pens (a weakness), a spherical wren's nest, now dusty, but a very good effort on the marsh wren's part was a Christmas gift to Sister Anne from Sister Bird, who knows that Sister Anne is fond of the wren family. But, except for baseball memorabilia and her sacred texts, she avoids additional collecting venues ("Who knows where it will go and with what velocity if I begin collecting other things?" she says). It's a nun's primary line of defense to avoid collecting things.

So in my (continual) weakened sinful state, I asked Sister Anne for the nest. Among my collections.

Also on my desk, a line of ten ocean rocks. The first, what South Shore folk call *lucky rocks,* which have a ring of white all the way around their gray bellies. It hasn't yet proved its luckiness, but then I am only 72, so am industriously hopeful on that count. The other 9 sibling rocks were rounded by surf and sand, tidal pulls, and currents: 2 pure white, 2 speckled green, 1 deep blood red (to remind me of what is life giving, the blood that our Eucharist speaks to). Then 1, a purpley blue, for color and for grace. And 3 the plain gray of saturated earth colors carved and released by waves and tides onto our shores here.

The desk is filled with notebooks, papers, and 7 sets of stationery (of which you have the full sampling), though sometimes stationary seems a formal thing, and bare white paper sometimes brings things closer, I feel.

And then there are my shelves. Other books may come and go, but these are the ones who stay: three versions of the Bible: Vulgate, Jerusalem, and New English. Thomas Merton's collection of the sayings of the Desert Fathers, *The Cloud of Unknowing, The Way of a Pilgrim,* Gustavo Gutierrez's *A Theology of Liberation* (from Fr. Martinez, who is helping me to think more widely about world), Kaufman's *Birds of North America,* Howard Thurman's *With Head and Heart,* Mary Webb's *Precious Bane,* Franklin's *Poems of Emily Dickinson* (which I keep as a treasure for itself, but also now because I know your fondness for her), Sylvia Shaw Judson's *The Quiet Eye,* the complete works of John Steinbeck, Eliot's *Middlemarch,* Simon Weil's *Waiting for God,* and Brother Lawrence's *The Practice of the Presence of God,* and then the writings of Hildegard of Bingen (I especially like her writing about *veriditas,* or spiritual greening), and St. John of the Cross. That is all. Or too much, according to Sister Patrick Gertrude, who feels every book is an addition to the cloister's dust collection.

A bed along the wall, with a prie-dieu facing a plain wooden crucifix on the wall above the head of the bed.

And between the bed and the desk, a window, that looks toward the water, but with so many trees in the way, only the salt air promises the ocean. But I watch the sky, listen to the birds here.

And this is a large part of my world, this cell in the cloister. Here I pray, sleep, and dream. I write letters and keep a journal. The white walls faithfully follow the quality of light through a day, coming bright into my window in the morning, and following the edges of the cloister to the other side, at which time the day is ending and my walls darken to gray.

Your recent letter about Mr. and Mrs. Leigh. How they come to radiation, her old body, his old self, driving every day to the hospital for hope. And the way you describe the scene: Oh, you should see us. I come at the same time with the Leighs. We have our own seats at the back of the waiting room, which we mutually discovered is close to the tea, closer to the basket of Saltines and graham crackers. And those little things lift us up. The Leighs always ask about my beautiful Emily, since she came with me once. And always about Franklin. And sitting with them I wonder how we will ever get through this. I pray for them and for me, sometimes angry and sometimes resigned. But when I'm here, I have a little community, like you do, Sister Athanasius. And we are waiting together for something to bring healing. You would like us. You are one of our number. We always, greedily, sit far at the back, away from the front of the waiting room, where the people sit who like noise, who have given up, who talk and talk and talk about what they are going through, who wear head covers and itchy wigs, who have gray circles around their eyes. The Leighs and I only want to be near each other and quiet together. And it looks like I will be wearing a wig soon, too, but I won't give over to it.

Miriam, in your letter where you wrote about the art of war and not giving in to cancer, I thought that's exactly what not giving into it is: the art of war.

And then you asked me about "my art of faith," you called it, the things that I hold onto. My dear, your art of war surpasses me for essential wisdom, for the place you are in pares things down between yourself and God, and gives you an understanding of what to hold onto, what to let go of. Sometimes I feel like I know these things theoretically, but you *know* them.

But as you asked—I will respond. I read Scripture—especially the psalms and gospels—to meet with God. Every day we chant the psalms. Every day I come for only that one reason.

You already know some of my Loose Rules. Maybe they are silly to you. But they come from my faith meeting my struggles and so would be different from others' Loose Rules. Or as Sister Patrick Gertrude calls them, "Fast and loose rules," since she insists I am playing fast and loose with basic theological teachings of the church. Still, God, midway in conversations with humans, God's yesses shift to nos, or an officious thundering response comes into the quiet question asked. Who can know God? And still, all of who I am wants to know.

Loose Rule #1 (and not a word breathed to Mother Lourdes) is: *It's a better yes, if you say no first.* I love that first fiery heat of refusal, because then all the options of faith—of a big yes, of an early agreeable mistake you can't back (or don't dare back) down from—are not there. A flat no. *No* is a place you can build from. A no can slowly build, in the quiet plane of one's soul to an *ok, it's a no, but I'll think about it.* It's a slow conversion that happens. The blanket *no* turns into a silence. The silence turns into a persistent question inside you. The persistent question turns into a wondering. The wondering turns into a *what if,* the what if turns into an *I wonder.* The *I wonder* turns into a *what might yes mean.* The yes question turns and turns and has lovely alchemy with the spirit. Then a hope and the early response that you abruptly retorted to God eases into a place wherein the lesson of the *no* might be the start of the *yes.*

It's the place where healing happens, the place we shake out our fear and hatred or dread or stain-ridden selves and enter into a new sort of space, as wide as a *no,* but without all the work of closing door after door after door. *It's a better yes, if you say no first.*

On weekends, we open part of the point (the west side, where there are no plovers) for those in the neighborhood who want to swim. There are plenty of neighborhood places, so they don't often come; still we do offer it. From my desk I see a line of them walking along the path toward the water. Miriam, the funny thing about aging, about being in summer heat, is that while the world is dressed in bikinis and flip-flops, you, the old one, wear layer upon wooly layer under the habit, along with thick winter socks even on summer days.

Now, well into June, at cusp of spring and commencement of summer, while sparrows, plovers (their young growing), and the stray sanderling ruffle feathers up to get a spray of cool air under the downy layers, I am positively Siberian in my approach, down to flannel underwear. And I am remembering college days swimming in the buff, along an early summer evening, with the company of Dr. Breamer and the moonglow blue across everything: ocean, sand, skin, hair, the entire universe.

I have thought recently that once more—that sort of once more before I cross over to the far shore—I'd like a summer evening like that, the August-warmed ocean, and the shining blue world again, swimming entirely buck naked in my old old skin.

Signing off for now, the dinner bell rings,

Sr. A.—

27 June 2004
Feast Day of St. Emma

Dear Miriam—

As Sister Farm would say, "Oh, Sister, you're on a roll." I have continued thinking about Loose Rule #1 this whole week.

Did you know that Sister Anne, though she rarely speaks of it, was for two years a member of the Convent of St. Romuald, a strict religious community in northwest Iowa? The Rule there turned viciously inflexible, no longer serving the life of the community, but the religious, rather, served the Rule.

And you will find it also curious, perhaps, that Sister Patrick Gertrude did not enter one of the stricter Orders, such as the Trappistines. Some time ago she told me, as she brought in fresh-cut lilacs from the yard, filling the entire room with their May-like scent: "When I realized my vocation, I knew two things. The first was that I could be severe, exacting. The other thing followed, that if I chose a strict Order that further fed a personality trait like mine, my brother who once told me, 'You'll end up harsher than when you went in,'" would be right.

"I struggle with life here, surrounded by Sisters who smell, who take pleasure in rebellion, who favor shaky theology in the name of grace. This is my cross," she said. And then she added, "And my brother also told me when he heard I was joining the Bings, 'You might just find it a great salvation.'" Then she left me and the lilacs there to wonder at this revelation, this moment, when there were thousands of other moments for saying such a thing.

Sister Anne told me about the two years at St. Romuald. When she petitioned to leave, according to the Prioress's letter, she was denounced and considered ". . . disobedient. A rebel and a heretic. Not inclined toward the spiritual life at all."

When Sister Anne petitioned to join the Bings, back in 1944, our then Prioress, Mother Luke, read the letter from the Prioress of the Convent of St. Romuald and said with a nod: "Well, Sister Anne, I can only say that you will be in good company, here. We are teeming with spiritual slackness and with rebels. Perhaps your training at St. Romuald's will come to our aid."

And so she began as a novice here in the Monastery of the Sisters of Hildegard of Bingen.

There are Rules and Orders that focus on balance, on charity, on Mary, on adoration of the Blessed Sacrament, on the Trinity, on silence, on contemplation, on being cloistered, on poverty, and on hospitality. And no Order can fulfill your truest calling: to lovingly surrender your will to a loving God.

Miriam, with a Loose Rule #1 (*better yes if no first*), you can see the struggle I have with this surrender, though I usually come around.

With Sister Anne, however, there's a great ease in her faith. It's uncrowded, uncluttered. She is in her entire being simply *toward God.* And a little toward baseball, which (according to her) may not be one and the same, "but they *are* close."

Miriam, do you know that Scripture that says sacrifice or suffering is nothing in comparison with knowing the Christ of God, our Lord Jesus? Sister Anne offers herself, her weariness, her sleep, her entire self in a day for God.

I sit at Adoration before the Blessed Sacrament and wave upon wave of my own fears overtake me. I am usually yes, with a lot of no in getting there. There will never be an end to my questioning myself or God. And yet, at the exposition of the Blessed Sacrament, I am in the presence of Jesus. That is all, a resting soul waiting for what God wishes to give, *who* God wishes to be for me, with me. That is all. How utterly, astoundingly simple.

One day Sister Farm said to me, "Your mind is way busy. It must be exhausting being you."

It is indeed. Let's pick up with Sister Anne, who has had a rough week, with the news of the Red Sox, as you can imagine (injury, losses, errors). But at least she has a coffee in the kitchen, the paper, her stool, her outpost.

Miriam, I am glad to know that even in the radiation, you have your outpost, there near the tea and Saltines, with Mr. and Mrs. Leigh and their concern for you.

All best,
Sr. A.—

4 July 2004
Feast Day of
St. Elizabeth of Portugal

Miriam, dear, here's good news to cheer you: Flying! Our plovers have fledged, taken to the air streams. Sister Bird has exhausted herself for watching out for them. And Little Sister takes credit for saving them, though she won't say it out loud, but she believes it's true.

Hope is a curious thing, isn't it? You mentioned it yourself about hope in the oncology department of UMass Worcester, where those waiting for radiation sit in johnnies and drink green tea and eat graham crackers and compare notes and dare to live their lives further down the line. The place where you live is hope. And the place your daughter Emily is, is hope, and Franklin and Brendan. And we, too, live in hope for you.

Miriam, I think you half laugh at me when you asked for my "Loose Rules," and I replied so seriously. Don't deny it, dear. But I know you have your own version, too. And Franklin and Emily and Brendan and our friends the birds, and each of the Sisters. To take myself too seriously over them might be a tragedy, but

I do so like passing them on here and there, so if you'll humor me, another:

Loose Rule #12: *Old maps bring you home too.* I learned this from Sister Anne, now about 15 years ago. She was given the line by her mother as she prepared to drive a 1939 Chevy station wagon—the Woody— out from Boston to Iowa City, to test her vocation at St. Romuald's.

As Sister Anne tells it, she had her earthly possessions down to a pope-blessed rosary, a prayer book, a small stash of Red Sox memorabilia, among them a bottle of dirt from Duffy's Cliff, before Tom Yawkey flattened left field at Fenway Park, and a Jimmie Foxx signed baseball.

After she packed the car, Sister Anne—then Grace Emilia Plásent—said goodbye. "My mama and the three smallest standing at the curb in front of our three-decker on Avenue A. And I had a sturdy car, my rosary beads, and a wallet of bills to get me there, largely donated by my mama and Petey. And I realized I didn't know how in hades to get to Route 20—this was before the interstate highway system—let alone find my way to Iowa."

"And my mama went into the house and came out with an old 1932 map with rips in it. 'But it's so old,' I said to her, 'I should probably get a new one.' And she said, 'Old maps bring you home, too.' And it did. That map brought me to Iowa and then brought me back east, and gave me a few side roads and back routes too."

And, Miriam, it's a line I've taken for myself, when I want to find some shortcut, a spiritual trick to get me through. I remember old guides are often faithful ones. And with that old story about old things, I close.

Your friend,
Sr. A.—

9 July 2004
Feastday of
St. Veronica Giuliani

Miriam, dear—

Here you are, your celebratory letter, recording the end to the radiation and the long end to the round before that, of chemo. One letter of yours named the chemo Gabriel—the angel who brings fear, storm, and healing. We celebrate this day with you. And we pray always for your continued healing.

Sister Bird looks over my shoulder, as I am in the library, and asks me to remind you: green tea, green tea, green tea. And blueberries. Keep those antioxidants in your system. She gave me a whole list, which I enclose in this letter, of cleansing teas and foods and herbs. She also asked me to tell you about French Mark, who has a hog farm and some sort of cleverness with healing dandelion root for cancers: a recipe given to him in a dream by God. Another rabbit trail by Sister Bird, probably. I told her we Sisters are used to stories of God speaking in dreams and pouring forth revelation, but as none of these usually involve dandelion root, I am loathe to pass it along. I'm a nun who likes a back-up plan.

But all of us pass along love, prayer, and intentions for your continued healing. And hopes that your hair would grow back and your energy return. How good that Brendan could be with you to drive you to the hospital for the last of your radiation treatments.

I am thinking back to those letters you have sent about the radiation, about the waiting room and your friends, the elderly Leighs. About the shared time, tea together. About the waiting room at UMass Worcester, the basket of graham crackers and Saltines passed out by the kind short lady in a perpetual pink outfit who has a circulatory problem with her legs. And your favorite, the doorman, Mac, who prays for each cancer patient that God would be with them. What grace even there.

Your friends, the Bings, have witnessed your anger, patience, joy, hope, reason, un-reason, ill-reason, frustration, and hairlessness in your letters. From Sister Farm (in her letter from Oconomowoc) is an offer to cut off her mullet if you'd like her hair. I wrote back, telling her that I thought you had brown-blond hair and that the brunette mullet look might not fit. But she directed me to write you saying, "Sister Farm's hair is Miriam's if she wants." So I have written it down and will let her know and she will be happy.

And here we have just an ordinary summer day, Miriam. Sometimes isn't it delicious, coming at the news of being done with treatments and being declared cancer free? The motion of air wrinkling at cut roses—fully opened—out on the refectory table. The smell of coffee and vanilla rushing through the July air from the kitchen. Little Sister mastering both cinnamon and almond paste within the confines of her bakery walls—and the monastery smells with the genius of it.

Sister Anne, at her stool next to the counter, her Red Sox mug warming her knotted hands, the sports page warming her beating heart as the Sox have made small change of the Oakland A's—after yet another lost skirmish with the Yankees. But who can fault a game that goes to 11 innings? Even losing, there are some fine, fine games.

And as I write this, plovers flying along the dunes and over water, old and young. And as I went to watch them in their flight, witness that they are living their every day, I think, some days there are only the daily things—after long stretches of illness and hope and fledglings and extraordinary days. Then there are days when there are no extraordinary stories, no new word of surprise. And still every psalm from Matins to Compline calls out the name of God. And every hour we chant it. This, Miriam, is a rich day on a revolving earth.

Miriam, your last letter to me, I read with that growing awareness that you, especially recently, know of your important place in the world. Not only in the world, but within yourself, have entered into the inner doors of, as Saint Teresa of Avila calls it, your own Interior Castle, to find that place where prayer and meditation take you deep inside to the rich presence of God.

We haven't much written about it, but you wrote last week about "*what's at stake*" with your life. That the cost of holding to a false crutch when things around you feel like they are diminishing is "*awfully way too steep.*" I have watched you, from months of a marriage feeling like it might hit bottom and you dare to look very evenly, carefully, fully at the sacrament you have created with Franklin. And your bravery to be both willing to save something and, too, willing to lose it. I don't mean it in a sense that you take sacraments lightly, but that the sacrament, given *by God* and meant *toward* God, is *simply God's*.

All there is to do, I suppose, is to live in God's love. What else is there to fall back on, to fall into? I think, too, of your months of surgery and waiting and chemo and then radiation—and your chemo, Gabriel, the angel who always sought to make you better, but often in the process made you afraid and weak and sick.

Miriam, I pray daily, that you'll need never re-enter that place again. Never. Who knows God's mind in this? I'm so rarely in agreement with God that I constantly amaze that God regards our prayers. But, dear, this is one prayer that Sister Anne prays too, and her heart and God's are quite akin on most matters, save the matter of the Sox winning the ALCS and the World Series, with her double prayer that the win would involve a good trumping of the Yankees. Her beloved Sox prayers? Well, that's another matter.

—

Some days you can just let go of, knowing that God will, somehow, be in the day that you yourself are somehow forcing yourself to be in, to endure. Miriam, I think you sent me a Mary Oliver poem last June, and the lines: "the world offers itself to your imagination, / . . . harsh and exciting— / . . . announcing your place / in the family of things."

Sometimes you feel as active and full as the turning earth—you've found an axis around which to revolve, your feet planted on the earth, strong feet carrying your strong determined body.

It's those days of weak feet, the shuffling feet, that all you are called to do is enter "your place in the family of things." Not even to do what you can, but to enter into, simply, each prayer hour as it enters your day. Shuffle if you must, or even if you like.

For now, let God redeem the world, which has been turning so long and in such motion with its own axis and in simple rings around the surrounding bands of planets, all in acknowledgment to the sun. Isn't it enough, some days, to know this?

Sr. A—

15 July 2004
Feastday of St. Bonaventure

When enough years go by, Miriam, history keeps calling your name. This is what I am learning. After spending so many years trying to understand the things of my history, I remain muddled, knowing that my idea of vocation comes from some of those places I don't understand.

My three-year relationship with Dr. Breamer: I came into the monastery as though it didn't exist—as though we hadn't written a shared history. As though he hadn't read Dante's *Inferno* or Donne's *Holy Sonnets* to me, as though I hadn't found the changing shape of myself with him, as though our roots didn't crag and bend and reach down to the same water source.

Coming into each new year, and in some of these letters to you I see how I might have lied to myself, as though when I made this decision to become a religious, I believed it might be as facile as looking at a map and deciding upon a new place to live.

But when I look now at the map, at Weymouth, it's only a name of a place we give ourselves, when always, we are still connected to the old histories of self on those other places on other maps.

Miriam, you have persisted in asking me how my past choices shaped my present, and how they might affect my future. Some letters ago, in your not subtle way, you suggest that I am *a package of unresigned places and conflicts and hopes.* And how can I respond, except by saying it is true. But as Sister Anne said to me recently, as I helped put her socks (or woolies as she calls them) and shoes on, "The shape of our lives matter most, not in the way we see them, but in how God sees them: their potential, their place. What you and I think about our lives doesn't really matter, now does it? You like taking your time about things." "Well," I said, "I am seventy-two and slower than some," though saying that to someone who is nearing 86 takes some of my thunder away.

I didn't respond to your notes earlier, since I have been of a mind to think of your radiation, and celebrating with you this last good step, good news, and good hope. But if you like, we can pick up the discussion. Yes, Miriam, perhaps it is indelicate to inquire, as you did. Perhaps, too, it is indelicate to respond. *I meant to ask for a while now,* you wrote, *but then, how do you ask a nun about her sexual life? And I just read* Letters of a Portuguese Nun, *so curious me.*

Hardly anyone trusts a vow of celibacy. I think it is in most people almost a violent curiosity about the sexual lives of monastics, and *Letters of a Portuguese Nun* or the letters between Abelard and Heloïse feed the curiosity.

But I cannot speak for anyone other than myself. I told you a bit about my Writer, but I haven't told you how it was I felt, and how I now feel, about sexual intimacy.

The most tender place of him, the tenderest place of myself, is what we discovered together, as though imprints of each other, his little groans between intense attention, and his well-placed quotes from all places spiritual and not quite so spiritual. He had a lovely sense of humor, a way of disarming me. Such little lines that I remember:

"Quick about it, little woman, catch up, would you, I must to work."

"Oh, the ministrations of little fingers."

"This, my dear, is the closest you will ever be to another person. I am aspiring to give you everything, but you wickedly withhold from me." "See, I have risen and shall do so again. Let's have some joy, shall we?"

An awful lot of teasing he did, me green and deeply serious about love. He, easy in his own skin. "Come, love, kiss me with the kisses of your mouth."

In sleep, I was utterly surrounded by him, his body, his nature. I, a serious student of love. He, a wondrous creature to me, all new, thick-haired, all movements natural, prepared. How many women had he loved in this way? How many of those took love as seriously as I did, a mix of the earnestness of the ant with the hovering passion of the bee. I was nervous in my love, unable to rest. In bed he would say, "If you turn once more, either you or I will be forced to leave this haven for the couch. Don't force me to be a gentleman, I wasn't made for the role."

Oh, I loved love, but was unable to rest in it, in my own self. And found the mix of his sly admonitions made me want to stay, to see how I might fit into this luxurious skin of human love.

My first night with him, he said, "I see I will have to teach you one or two things about love. I challenge you to do the same. But, be forewarned: if you enter as far as my heart, there will be no escape."

Now, of course, with years among the thoughts of him, I have in reserve many pithy retorts. Alas, it is in the quiet of my cell that I return them.

"You are a little slob in the lovemaking field, my dear," he would say. "Curb your enthusiasm and direct your efforts entirely, for the moment, to my mouth and my heart. We'll then see where we go from there."

"Aren't you industrious," he'd say when I worked to find particularly pleasing places to kiss him.

I knew that my place with him was fickle. This was my first place in love, with him, the lovely feeling of the tops of his feet against the bottoms of my own. Weeks? Months? Was I simply another student, a young, teachable toy? For all my earnestness I could only give him earnestness and for all my earnestness, he gave a few lessons learned.

It was among the lines, among the learned things, among the sheets, among my restless thoughts that I knew I had what others take great joy in. And I knew it wasn't enough. I was violently in love. Wakeful. Sincere. Quiet. Studious. I hadn't found my voice yet, but I knew what it was to have a moment in which I was twisting in joy, and then the knowing that it would not be enough pleasure to get me through the longest path of life: it was not, ultimately, an eternal enough moment.

And that's when I began to look for a way toward eternity. But others will call it running away. And I will accept that.

And there are many hours that I have revisited those moments, those lines, the muscles and bulk of his body, and thought I'd want to return. Especially in my forties, when I was training my spiritual body that kept reminding me of my physical, sexual desire.

Who knows how to attend to that? I simply do not. To honor the body, to let something itch and move inside you without thinking that a sexual feeling must only have a sexual fulfilling response. Maybe it is that you see things a little wider. You give yourself grace in your thoughts, and allow the human being inside your skin to be fully a human being. Denying that I was a sexual being would never be the way I wanted to live. And, still, I remain a nun who is a slob for love, the place carved years ago that I revisit, though now less often.

That, Miriam, will probably explain nothing about the sexual lives of nuns. But it is, indeed, the only sexual life I know intimately and can speak of.

I came to the monastery believing that the only decision that would shape my life was the decision toward religious vocation: the initial saying yes. One moment toward God.

But this one yes forgets the grace of a long life, the sheen of grace—that every yes I've said has been a grace (me who—Loose Rule #1—always begins with a no).

There's something to be said for a yes in a good direction. And there's even more to be said for the continual yes toward God's love. More than one night's prostrations in the chapel affords. When we give up trying to prove ourselves, pushing doors open and closed incessantly in the name of God, it's a very exhausted sort of life. I know, because I live it.

I have rambled here. Perhaps I am trying to say something more than has been said. Maybe it is as simple and as complicated as the loving moment in the upper room when the disciple John rested his head on the bosom of Jesus without trying to define Jesus, or himself, or a certain history or even the future.

That's why when I look at Sister Anne, I see a wideness to what might seem from the outside a peculiarly narrow life. It is toward this sort of life that I have aimed my sights. This life.

And see, you have had a long letter in reply to your question.

Blessings,
Sr. A.—

22 July 2006
Feastday of St. Mary Magdelene

Miriam, dear—

We received a short letter from Sister Farm, which we all read, scanning for some hint that she might come back. This card, though, makes it seem final.

[Postmark 18 July]

Sisters—

A large standard jenny donated by the Brothers of the Incandescent Heart of Jesus. Almost 14 hands. Sturdy ride for the Lord—too bad Palm Sunday's long gone.

She's a smelly donkey, Sister Patrick Gertrude. Be glad she's 8 states away.

Other than that, the gears turn fine. Mornings Sister Mary Matthew and I milk 62 cows, fill the tank with raw milk, and see it to truck for the cheeses. Every afternoon, sanitizing the trucks, tanks, hoses, coils, and refrigerating leftover milk.

Farm life is good. The new chapel even has a mudroom.

Lots of land for a tractor to tame. Lots of time to tame the land. Glad to be part of something that works. Not as lucrative as gambling, but more respectable.

Heard the Sox lost to Anaheim, one major stomping. Only Cubs fans here. Pray for me, Sr. Anne, all this enthusiasm for the Cubs wearing me down. Pax, Sr. Farm

If Sister Patrick Gertrude read the part about the donkey, she didn't say. She did say, though, after reading the part about gambling, "That woman has more vices than Satan himself: smoking, drinking, and gambling and whatnot."

Miriam, the card contained a PS.

PS: Miriam?

Clever old girl. How boiled down language can be, conveying full meaning. So, you know me, I fill her in with details of your letters, and told her, too, about Franklin's knee, along with your story about the nuthatch and the cat, in which you proved yourself, again, protector of fragile creatures. One nuthatch life spared.

Sister Bird may have a suggestion for Franklin's knee. Every time Sister Bird would make a suggestion, Sister Farm used to say, "*Suggestion* is another word for snake oil." And Little Sister would say, "No, *suggestion* is another word for potential hazard." Sister Bird once suggested an herbal ointment to close a wound on Little Sister's knee, only opening up the wound into a veritable swamp of ooze. (As a matter of caution: Unless fairly sure of the curative powers of a suggestion, it's best not to test medically questionable theories on Little Sister). But when Sister Bird's right, she's awfully right, and has helped numerous ill and aching persons. So with the warning label in large print, if Franklin would like the remedy du jour, let me know and Sister Bird will be happy to present the remedies.

Speaking of Little Sister, her kitchen tempers continue while her bake times are longer, which is just as well. For those with culinary gifts, a challenging recipe for gooseberry and boysenberry tarts helps a person face the upcoming day, which might otherwise seem fragile. I don't know that she truly feels fragile, but as Sister Anne said earlier today, "Poor Little Sister, it's as though she were at the bases loaded, and Bellhorn up to bat—and all in her kitchen. You never know what might come of that combination. Never."

Little Sister does have something about her: she is all *stay* with a hint of *go* to her. On a whim, to get a conversation going, I asked Little Sister why she stays, when it looks like obedience comes hard to her, and the certain confines that vowed life demands. "I don't know," she told me, not looking up from her meal-planning lists. "It's not the best theology of sacramental living, but every day I tell myself that I can leave. But so far, every day, I've thought, *Today I'll stay.* If I tell myself, *I* have *to stay,* then I would be gone for sure. Some days, weeks, I forget I need that loophole." Without looking up, she turned it around and asked me why I stay. I said, "Well, I think this is all I ever really wanted."

"Really?" She looked up.

"And Sister Anne's here. And the shore birds. And the chapel. And I know something of God here that I'm not sure I would have learned anywhere else. And I want to know if Sister Farm will come back, if she and Sister Patrick Gertrude figure out a truce. If Frankie trains those bees to successful industry. If Mother Lourdes finds a way to not drain herself."

"And," I said, "I want to keep eating your Sunday breads and your daily soups—especially your barley lime soup. It's rather exciting."

"You are loo-loo," was all she said after my rush of curiosity. Then she picked up her lists and left me and went back to the bakery. "But you're right," she said from the bakery, "that lime soup and my dark rye breads are a good reason to stay. It may be the best of the reasons."

After Little Sister yells or fusses, she then bakes. Sister has her way to address an interior or exterior trouble. I become quiet, mulling things over. Just quiet, as though conversing were exhausting commitment. Sister Anne, when she meets with a spiritual conundrum, goes directly to the chapel, puts her ancient knees on the stone floor and her hands to the rosary. Then she will consult with the blessed Mother for what she calls "woman's wisdom." She once told me it was Mary who taught her what being a woman meant, "*how* being a woman meant."

When I go quiet, Sister Anne's trick is to ask me to go with her through her score cards meticulously kept for any game she watches. Stats for each game: at bats, hits, runs batted in, errors. And copious liner notes: "Wakefield tense, B6 (bottom of the sixth)—change-ups weak." Or "Pedro at 96 pitches—not good for more than 103." Almost every game she'll write, "Oh that Hideki Matsui." Then I become ensconced in batting averages, names, innings, strikes, ground-outs, and double plays. An hour later we are praying the rosary together and I have no idea how I've gotten from ponderousness to baseball to prayer—but, as Sister Anne says, it always shows its spiritual merits in easing a soul through a day.

Miriam, as you asked for another Loose Rule: this is my LR5.

Loose Rule #5: *The longing for that which is holy, is holy.*

I've always heard and cringed hearing the line, "the road to hell is paved with good intentions." I, perhaps not surprisingly, believe it the other way around. It is *heaven* that receives and accepts our best hopes, our longings for what is—or might be—good. Heaven's realm contains a longing toward the divine, a prayer to sustain someone for someone, a hope in a good direction. If our intentions toward what is good were hell's domain, there would be nothing left to heaven, because sometimes it is only a nudge, an itch, a leaning that gets us looking toward God.

Miriam, I write these things as though they are tested ideas for me and new for you. Perhaps it comes from the time that I was the Director of Novices. (That is to say, director of Little Sister and Sister Farm—so now you know what a good job I've done, with one Sister leaving the farm and the other struggling daily to stay.) But I don't mean to be teacherly as I sound. Never feed an old nun's ego by letting her think she can teach. But you, Miriam, are clever, when your letters come to me, they teach without a teacherly tone. And I continue to learn from you, though it's hard to teach an old nun new tricks. You never know, however. If Sister Anne believes the Sox can win after 85 (this would be the 86th) years of losing, then there may still be hope all around for a shifting of an entire spiritual geography of nuns.

Well, I'll finish up my note about LR5. For me, LR5 is a keeper on days when all one can do—and the best one can do—is to long for what is good, and to know that the Divine, in turn, longs back.

Yours,
Sr. A—

27 July 2004
Feastday of St. Ecclesius

Miriam, dear,

A short note to say something terribly sad: Our Sister Anne left her earthly home this morning.

Please would you pray for us?

I will write more tomorrow.

Lost,
Your Sister Athanasius

The Last Inning

1 August 2004
Feastday of St. Mary the Consoler

Oh Miriam. I didn't mean to leave you without a word for these last few days. Sister Anne began her journey at night, when dark fills up even the far corners and open spaces of a room. Mother Lourdes came into my cell, touched my hand. "Sister Anne is nearing her end." Her voice got smaller. "Sister Athanasius, did you hear me?" she whispered it twice, but I did hear. It echoed everywhere.

The one person whom I felt—friend, companion—was the one person on earth I needed to find my own good ending. You don't always voice those sorts of thoughts to yourself, but they come as you walk down the hallway to Sister Anne, knowing that here is the person you looked to, to understand what measure of a life you lived.

We turned the light on, to fill the space, the corners—the crucifix above Sister Anne, Jesus formed by discolored knots of the olivewood, watching her, it seemed, his head hung down over his charge, her face, her body, her woolen night socks, her swollen attempts at dressing herself. The God there in the room with her.

She lay so small in her bed, tiny. Both arthritic hands on top of the covers, the left hand, though: open, limp. Mother Lourdes went to her. "Sister Anne," and louder, "Sister Anne, can you hear me?" and Sister Anne's hand moving like she could almost surface to open her eyes, agitated, restless, to wake to us.

"Sister Anne," Mother Lourdes whispered in her ear, holding onto her right hand, "Sister Anne, I think you've had a stroke. This is Mother Lourdes, and Sister Athanasius is with me." More agitation, restless motions of her right side, the left side of her face, relaxed, seemingly unconnected with the restless right.

"She's going to sit with you. She's your own, good companion. I'm going to ask Father Martinez to come too." Mother Lourdes left after pulling me toward Sister Anne, sitting me on the edge of the narrow bed, placing my hand on top of Sister Anne's.

The night moved so slow, Sister Anne's fingers, her skin, taking on a sheen of thin blue all along the white, white skin.

Miriam, if you could have seen the face of Jesus in the olive-wood, nailed to a cross, as though he were straining to come down to her.

Does having a foot on the far shore make you restless to resist? Or restless to go? I don't know. When Mother Lourdes left, Sister Anne pulled her right hand out from under mine and with the soft knots of her hand, found her place on top of mine. Do you know that children's game, where you keep piling up hands, the bottom hand slipping to the top? Yet hers felt like a parent's hand, slipping over a child's as though my hands were unquiet, the unquiet child I am. Miriam, we don't often hold hands. But now I think monastics should *often* hold hands, know hands the way a person knows a certain terrain. As though Sister Anne had been a hand-holder all her life, she knew this terrain. Her hand becoming so quiet on mine.

Here, being asked to make her hardest journey, dispossessed of bodily strength, she still used her remaining energy to extend her hand in comfort and peace.

I tried to be strong, to pray for her, to put my hand on top of hers, her entire body quieting while her hand would, again, find its way back to the top, a strong hand to my weak child's hand.

"Sister Anne," I said, repeating a verse from the psalms:

> The Lord is a present help in trouble,
> a refuge in a time of need.

Hours went by. And handholding. And psalms. Near morning, before Matins, the other Sisters came in, sitting quietly praying the rosary, praying the psalms.

I asked Little Sister to hand me one of the notebooks with the Red Sox scorecard and stats from Sister Anne's desk. And after I read the 15th chapter of the Gospel of Saint John, about abiding in Christ, I read her stats from one of her favorite games in 1961, with Pumpsie Green. And a September 19, 1999 game, Pedro pitching a one-hitter against the Yankees. But mostly I sat with my hand under hers, her heart all over the room, the broken body of Jesus hovering above us, suffering for the weight of the world.

There's a way you know it's all right, even when you know it's not. And there's a way in which you think, how will I live, tomorrow or the next day, coming into the kitchen to see that Little Sister made a mug of coffee and put it on the stainless steel counter near the opened sports page of the *Globe*? Seeing the empty stool, the missing movement down the hall of Sister Anne's careening body, unbalanced and cumbered by the definitions of old age.

By 7:30, the hour of Lauds, when I prayed the rosary with one hand, the other one resting under Sister Anne's, Father Martinez and Mother Lourdes came in to the cell, starting to smell both holy and a little sour.

Peaceful Father Martinez, quietly gave Sister Anne Last Rites, the seal of oil, the sign of the cross, the prayer for a peaceful death, for heaven and for light everlasting. All the while Jesus brokenly watched us as we watched Sister Anne, breathing evenly, her motions less and less restless, almost soothed. The two times I tried to leave her side, she squeezed my fingers, holding on, so I stayed. And watched her breath work so hard to push her entire rib cage, lungs, in the outward direction, and then release the weight of air.

Whispering to me, Father Martinez said, "God only makes a few like this. It's a losing world we're heading into now, a losing world."

Mother Lourdes motioned for me to stay and I motioned for her that I wasn't going anywhere. I sat through the day breaking and then full morning light, the tiny knob of Sister Anne's hand still over mine in a slow motion, moving back and gently forth.

Between Lauds and Terce, which is the beginning of what is called The Little Hours, her beloved prayer hours, the thing I didn't know if I could say, I now knew I must say. "Sister Anne?" I asked as I put my hand on top of hers. But then she found her way to putting hers on top of mine, a little soft and cool. "I want you to stay with me for a long time more. But if it's time to go, go home to Jesus." My knees banged against the edge of the bed, it was awful, Miriam. "I will be all right."

Then I said—because when we don't know how to speak, sometimes baseball is a worthy language to use—"Now, you know the score. You're up at bat at the bottom of the ninth. Bring it on home, Sister Anne, just bring it on home."

And at the last verse of the last psalm, the morning before David Ortiz did hit a grand slam in Fenway Park, the day a lone blue heron came to stay along the bay and the piping plover young flew further afield, so much prayer directed on their behalf, Sister Anne gave a full long breath and gave her spirit up to God. And then she let go of my hand.

And, Miriam, I'm going to tell you what Sister Anne already knows, that I lied. I don't think I will be all right.

I just don't know how I could.

Though you'd think, having lived this long, that I'd know what language death speaks or what the dying know, I don't—either from never having listened or from an attempt to distance myself from the suffering at hand.

Miriam, you know what I do not know about watching someone die, losing closest friends, confidants.

Doctor Padrin from down the street came and confirmed Sister Anne's death to massive stroke. When he left, Mother Lourdes asked me if I would like to help her wash Sister Anne's body.

"I don't know if I can," I said. "Would you?"

"Then, if you would go downstairs and ask Patrick Gertrude for a scented soap. A scent that Sister Anne liked, and then some warm water and the shallow tin pan and washcloths," she said. "And a nice soft towel."

"Lilies of the Valley," Sister Patrick Gertrude said, matter-of-factly. "She always thought the Garden of Gethsemane had some sort of essence like that, "a lot of beauty and a lot of suffering" is how she put it.

And I realized that Sister Patrick Gertrude knew what scent Sister Anne loved, and this was something I never knew. And then I wondered what the others knew about her that I didn't. And I wanted to call Sister Farm in Wisconsin and ask her what she knew that I didn't, too. So that I would know.

I brought the soap and water and cloths. And stood nearby while Mother Lourdes carefully and slowly washed her face and her throat and her chest, where the one breast was missing, replaced by a scar. I helped Mother Lourdes turn her to her side, to wash her back, and a pungent stomach acid came out of Sister Anne's mouth and dribbled to the floor. Mother Lourdes held out a warm and soapy cloth to me and said, "Would it help you to know that washing Sister Anne's body completes all your services of love?" And, Miriam, I was so ashamed that I had almost let the last reverence go, that I took the cloth and cried big soggy tears at the same time, and began, again, to wash her face, and then her arms, and then the beauty of her craggy hands.

We washed the small, still moveable body of our Sister Anne, the only nun I knew who could spend her life like spare change, and never consider it any cost. And then we dressed her body in her feastday habit, our custom for interment. I've never known such a sad and quiet intimacy. With these old bones she left behind.

So sad,
Sr. A.—

3 August 2004
Feast Day of St. Trea

Miriam, do you ever feel like your life has been like a ride on the back of an old pickup truck, blue paint chipped all over, dull and rusted spots along the wheel rims and cab doors? And someone has always been driving that truck? While you, like a farm hand, sit on the tailgate, pulled down, swing your legs, following the bumps, halfway holding on, halfway not?

I feel like Sister Anne's been driving that rusty old truck. Now, there's the letting go of the wheel, giving me the gearshift, the choke, the brakes, the clutch, the gas. And I am trying to remember the things she said about how to shift and the tender play between the gas and the clutch, what to watch for, how—essentially—to drive this truck, this spiritual life, but somehow I am still waiting for the truck to pull forward.

I've never liked a truck alone. I don't even like the coffee mug resting on the dash alone, the long line of the gearshift with its wide spaces between gears alone, the dusty dashboard, the striped cloth and the vinyl seat alone. Now just me, a coffee mug, a rosary hanging from the rearview mirror, and the rest of the open road, alone.

Sr. A—

7 August 2004
Feastday of St. Cajetan

Miriam, remember that first letter you wrote to me, where you bought a bird feeder for something to do—when you went to Quabbin Reservoir and turned the car on, then off, then on. That sort of desperate and also hopeful feeling—hope being that feeling that you want something, somehow, to step into your despondency, a large strong hand, and pull you safely out? I know it has been many days of struggle for you, days you think you can move into the next day's light fine. Days when you believe the next will be as fully dark as the present day. You at work, talking with doctors who hardly even know a patient's condition, when you know what meds and amounts would work best, you've seen this endlessly before. Or your wondering who Franklin will be in this day, and if this desperate oldness of both of you together, full with disappointment and perhaps the tentative few laughs, watching the old home videos of your son at 7 years, your daughter at 2.

And Miriam, dear friend to me, I have wandered into a wide wood forlorn, with the wondering if the 21 psalms we chant in a day in the gray stone chapel with the crucified Christ and his weeping Mother and the Stations of the Cross will be enough to hold the center, now without my wobbling and true Sister Anne. And I don't know how to walk into these days. And so I write to you, as you wrote to me those many months ago, for a good word in a time of trouble, just one small good word.

Tomorrow I will need another, I'm sure. But today needs its very own word.

Thank you for your friendship,

Sr. A.—

10 August 2004
Feastday of St. Lawrence

Miriam, dear—

Below is a copy of a wire Mother Lourdes, in the old-fashioned way, sent to Sister Farm:

> *Sr. Anne has left us. Sr. Athanasius disconsolate. Pray for us. M. Lourdes*

We haven't heard back. When she got the wire, Sister Farm

didn't call Mother Lourdes or the monastery here. Though she did call Tom. He mentioned it only because Little Sister offered him almond bear claws, but then held the tray away from him, insisting that he tell us if he's heard from Sister Farm this last week. "All of his moral strength," Little Sister said, "lasted the whole of 30 seconds."

"She's called every day since. But I'm not supposed to tell. Um, you mind letting me have a bear claw now?"

Miriam, I have sunk low. From Matins to Compline, there's little solace to the days. None of the shuffled pages, nor the sounds of shifting old bones beside me in the choir stall, no sense of *presence.*

Everyone's giving me a wide berth: I go in, I go out. I sometimes go down to the point and watch the plovers or the blue heron who has been here, now, since Sister Anne has left, as though to say something, but I do not know how to understand it. And the company of terns and mallards here, erasing the lines of the ocean's backdrop. There's something rare, though, sharp: something I can't name about Sister Anne's leaving, about her translucent hand on mine over her last hours of parting.

Your letters, Miriam, that you have sent these days are kind, loving. They are, also, the lovely way you sometimes write about finding steady feet/legs for a life, you are holding so steady, putting out a firm hand.

It has been now two weeks since the valve of suffering has opened. And while the church teaches the beautiful way of the soul's journey, it is the most painful beauty I have experienced. Everyone here continues on. Sister Farm keeps not calling (while calling Tom instead). Tom has asked Father Martinez to help him put the old truck motor on cement blocks to clean it out for an extended life. Little Sister seems a little caught in a pattern of too many macaroons and too few bear claws. Frankie keeps to bees and "peam." Mother Lourdes's shoulders slope lower in the hard pull of leadership.

Sister Bird witnesses the plover young, so fully in flight and piping song, innocent of the travails involved in allowing them safe passage. Innocent of their rareness of species coming into life.

Sometimes it's good not to know the wearying work that goes into fledging life, isn't it? How many principles have costs. A great weight to know that.

Mother Lourdes told me that Sister Anne's great-niece has written to ask to stay in the guesthouse. "And I would like for you to help Sister Patrick Gertrude clean Sister Anne's cell, but also then to be with Lucy Battson Green during her stay. Also," she said, "I would like the baseball cap to go to Sister Farm, I think it would mean a lot to her."

Miriam, you have told me of Franklin's ability to part with all sorts of things: books, pocket watches, heirlooms, crystal, silver, pinstriped shirts, chipped mugs—all with great objectivity, with a sort of rising above emotions and carelessness about—and I love this phrase you used—"the *thingness* of a thing."

I almost want to ask Franklin to come help us look through Sister Anne's short-list of things, but I have attached all of heaven's spiritual meaning to every object. The Sox mug, the baseball cap, the scorebooks, the World series game stubs from 1976, the baseball boxes, the Thomas Boswell books, Branch Rickey's *Little Blue Book*, Paul Dickson's *The Joy of Keeping Score*, "The voice of baseball" Red Barber's *1947, When All Hell Broke Loose in Baseball*, the *Black Writers/Black Baseball* anthology—all gifts she received through the years.

Along with those things, Sister Anne's prayer book, worn and smudged. Flipping through the pages, you can feel the heft of her prayers right between the pages and in between the words, the raspy hum of chant emanating from the psalms. While Sister Patrick Gertrude took down the crucifix to clean the wooden Jesus, I thought that her back turned and Sister Anne's prayer book conspired together to make me a thief. I made free with the book, Miriam. It is now in my cell, with a wink of guilt accompanying it (which I can almost always overcome if I put my mind to it—though if Sister Farm were here, it would have been easier. She's good at meaningful complicity, "as some situations call for it" she would add.)

Back to Sister Anne's cell: Sister Patrick Gertrude has filled it with the scent of Lily of the Valley, and everything looks reverent and hallowed and quiet. In the quiet sits Sister Anne's Jerusalem Bible and a rosary blessed by Pope John Paul II. The crucifix now cleaned and replaced over the bed in deliberateness and love, which Sister Patrick Gertrude cleaned with intensity. I have often thought of her cleaning as an act of obsessiveness, but I wonder if cleaning functions as her highest act toward God.

I would find—today—Franklin a cruel friend as I prepare to meet up with Lucy. And I wonder what it means to be so separated from your relative and know so little of the life she led, either because of the spareness of her spiritual needs or of the few things actually in her possession: her Bible, the Red Sox memorabilia, the rosary and prayer book.

And then strips of paper with quotes or notes in her handwriting. Some freshly scrawled and some in the careful hand of her earlier years without arthritis. About 40 slips of paper in the drawer of her desk.

Every day she carried one in the pocket of her habit. Some very simple: "Faith. Faithfulness. Faithfully." Or others from the desert fathers and mystics such as: "God hides the mysteries that he teaches us / so that he might teach us to search for them in love.—Narsai of Edessa"; or this, "Those who want to be able to listen well to God speaking must enclose themselves in great silence.—Umiltà of Fraenza"; or from one of her favorite books, given to her by a friend in the South End where she grew up, *God's Trombones,*

> O Lord—this morning—
> Bow our hearts beneath our knees,
> And our knees in some lonesome valley.
> We come this morning—
> Like empty pitchers to a full fountain,
> With no merits of our own.
> O Lord—open up a window of heaven,
> And lean out far over the battlements of glory,
> And listen this morning.
>
> —James Weldon Johnson

Her primal cries for each day. Her friends and mentors. I had wondered what Lucy would see of a life, here in these scraps? And then the Sox scorebooks & cards, some sent to her by friends attending games, some few from the annual game she would attend—a gift from the Sisters—games totaling 80, spanning from the mid-1930s to 2003.

But Lucy came into Sister Anne's cell with peace and calm. Out of duty (or kindness) she asked me about every item. Its history, its meaning to Sister Anne's life. She asked me what Sister Anne found important among the scraps and memorabilia.

"There are so few articles in a Sister's possession," I responded, "so each one symbolizes entire spheres, really. What for many people would take 5 churches, two theological libraries, statuary, relics, and some prie-dieu to represent a religious life is encompassed in these abbreviated materials. It's a boiled down life, isn't it? Everything houses another realm."

"I remember the little quotes she had, sometimes her pocket would be stuffed with them," Lucy B said. "And a little book of hours. Is that here, too?"

"It is," I said, more willing to steal than to lie. "I took it to my cell. I didn't want to be without it"—I wanted to explain that articles in a Sister's room are not really owned. That I didn't want to see it lost when the books get sold or get moved to the monastery library. That when Tom sells the memorabilia for us to bring some money in, or when another Sister moves into the cell or clears things away, I didn't want the important things lost to Sister Anne's memory—But I also didn't want to dishonor Sister Anne by justifying the deed or defending it.

"I would have done the same thing," Lucy B said, looking at me with clear green eyes. Then she lowered her voice, "except that I would have taken the '76 Series stub and the *Blue Book*, too."

Between her mix of business-like and personal, I was wracked with relief and gratefulness at her way.

"Please don't feel like I'm changing the topic in order to talk of something else, but, about the *Blue Book*: Mother Lourdes requested I give you that book, as well as any other baseball books from her cell. We'll only keep a few for the library here, and Boswell, too, and the score-books. Would you like that?"

And it wasn't that she cried, but throughout her time here, she just kept talking so evenly even as tears rimmed her eyes. And then the rim would lessen while her speaking voice would not change. A contained person, I suppose you'd say. She looked at the baseball books and talked about Sr. Anne's fondness for all things baseball. "I do remember her fondness for Thomas Boswell's *Why Time Begins on Opening Day,* and her Peterson book about the Negro Leagues, *Only the Ball Was White.*

Auntie Betty—Sister Anne—and the whole family were always big on the Red Sox, it was religion to them—well, religion in a different sense."

"Or maybe not," I said.

"You know," she said, moving the topic further and further from my trespasses, "Sister Patrick Gertrude seems profoundly affected by the passion of our Lord, doesn't she? Before she left the room, she kept looking at the crucifix. There's something about it: peaceful and worn out, I think. Something that makes the Jesus here different."

Sister Patrick Gertrude's dedication to the passion of our Lord: I'd never seen what was so visible. I'd never known that who we are interiorly can be so clear, seen with kind eyes, even despite fleeting meetings.

Miriam, I will sign off. Tired from the day. My Book of Hours: a moment of temptation and degeneration, and then gracious forgiveness. And I will read a psalm, perhaps the 42nd, and then lay my body down to restful sleep, like the forgiven do.

Your,
Sr. A.—

14 August 2004
Feastday of St. Maximilian Kolbe

Miriam, the only story being told in the monastery today is the one about Sister Farm, who found her place on good midwestern soil, who had Jersey cows, 2 old trucks, one devoted border collie, a donkey, and a mudroom that leads right on into the chapel. Well our Sister Farm, knowing what it's like to have a skill and a passion, in the spirit of Mother Lourdes, lay it aside for a small group of religious in New England and was delivered to us yesterday in a truck driven by Tom, who even cleaned up the cab, which goes to show the state of his heart.

"I'm here and I'm staying here," she said, coming in to the monastery. When she put her duffel bag down, she said to us all, circling around her, "I don't know what's better. The Sisters there love me, but don't need me. Here it's hit or miss on love," she shot a look at Sister Patrick Gertrude, "—but it's ripe on need."

After her speech, she went up to Sister Anne's cell and wept like Jesus over Jerusalem. For hours. By Compline, she came to prayer wearing Sister Anne's baseball cap. "You sure it's okay for keepers?" she whispered to Mother Lourdes and to me as we headed into the chapel. "Ok for keepers," Mother Lourdes said while I nodded, "But not ok in the chapel, please."

When she heard of Sister Anne's death, Sister Farm went to her superior, "telling her I was all cut up and heavy about it." The superior asked the Sisters there to pray with Sister Farm for discernment, vocation and direction. "And it brought me right back here."

Miriam, it's now evening. The Red Sox are playing the White Sox. I've left the transistor going in the kitchen, where Little Sister is mixing some stewed fruit compote and listening to the game. This is the first evening with Sister Farm. There's a velvety silence in the cloister. Part of the silence, at least for me, is a grateful wondering what it means to return to a place you meant to leave.

Tomorrow, Sister Farm and Tom and Mother Lourdes meet to decide how best to streamline the farm. I fear our Buff Orpingtons will be the ones to go, but suspect that, since Frankie's beekeeping genius, how he knows the honeybees and their love for flowering plum trees and clover, their hexagonal orderly homes, they'll plan to expand the number of hives. We'll see though. For now, it's just your friend, Sister Athanasius, guessing.

The call of the vowed life urges us toward denying oneself for the greater good. But in my state of unwilling loss, no sharp step of intentional loss sounds like a good decision. Even if

Mother Lourdes wears duty like a badge of courage. Even if Sister Farm will wear the same badge.

Little Sister just slipped a piece of paper under my door: RS won 4-3.

With the score I'll close, wins and losses.

Your friend,
Sr. A.—

20 August 2004
Feast Day of
St. Bernard of Clairvaux

Miriam, dear—

The Sox just lost to the Yankees, 11–1. Even if we do reach the wild card, the series is afar off. I have begun flipping through the Sports page, feeling in some way dutiful to Sister Anne's honor. Though without a coffee alongside, as without real enthusiasm, the effort feels thin.

I write this as nighttime closes the day, this Feast day of Saint Bernard of Clairvaux, who wrote, "If you want to pray, . . . quiet time is best. The deep silence when others are asleep inspires natural prayer. Prayer is a secret thing at night. It is witnessed only by God."

You have asked me what, in the deep roots of my cellar, you might pray for me, and I return this letter to you with little knowing what I need, save a way to turn anew to God. It is I who am lost, I'm sure, but it feels as though God is the one lost.

After Compline now, the prayer hour that marks the day's close, the hour, Sister Anne told me once, "where the prayers said at the end of the day are for the re-creation of the world. The essence of hope, that late night prayer of surrender to the night, to sleep, to death even, a making peace with the soul."

And, Miriam, it may be, then, these late hours that I will come to peace, looking out of my window full of night. And I will wait for the morning returning, and the changing light. Your friendship, dearer to me for my need of it, and your kindness in offering me the story of your American goldfinch, your purple finches, and your yellow warblers.

Here, mornings, with the late summer windows open you can hear the bird choir beginning again, and nearing the chapel for Matins, you can also hear the industry of Frankie's hives.

Frankie occasionally sits on Sister Anne's stool, what Little Sister calls the coffee spot. She will give him the sports page and he rattles it around for a few minutes.

And every day Little Sister, if someone's in the kitchen, they are asked to leave, come later morning. The other day, though, Little Sister asked me to stay, sit on the stool. "Now just be here & read the paper, is all. For company."

Mother Lourdes said to me later, "I noticed your spending time in the kitchen is important to Little Sister." I said that it's hard to tell what's important to Little Sister, other than a well-functioning mixer and a well-stocked larder. "Well, there are a lot of things you aren't noticing these days. But it would honor Sister Anne if you really did read the sports page, and it would honor Little Sister to make yourself as present to her. Can you handle those two vocational calls today?"

"I will try."

"All that is required: a heart engaged toward God and others."

The homily found no room in my heart. For a few moments we just stood there in the hallway, near the laundry room and I looked down at both of our feet. Bunions like elbows pushed against our black shoes. *Old women,* I thought. *We are old women.*

And as I was looking down, she said the thing I didn't want to hear: "Your vocation wasn't Sister Anne. You've never lost your vocation. You just never knew what it was. It was and has always been the way that you are in attendance with people: the letters you write, the simple support you give—and now you have something even better to offer your Sisters here: brokenness. You are not above your other Sisters, not Sister Patrick Gertrude, not Little Sister, not Frankie, not Sister Bird. We invite you to enter into the vocation you've always had—please claim your place."

Miriam, so that was my day. Sometimes a person is ready to hear a word, sometimes a person is not. Today, I am not. But I know that you like a complete story, so I pass the hallway words on to you (complete with bunions) and think that you will know, now, more of what to pray for your stubborn and forlorn friend,

Sr. A.—

22 August 2004
Feastday of St. Sigfrid

Miriam, Sister Anne has gone, the plovers have fully fledged and will leave soon in migration, and the dark space of the chapel contains only a dim unrecognizable light. The psalms, praying the Office, a long test of endurance.

Sister Anne once told me that every ten years or so we redefine our lives. We have to study them and revisit them and then shake them up. And if we don't, she said, not to worry: Illness or loss or fear or something would sneak in there and shake it up for us. And at that point you either say yes, let it shake, or no, I want to keep it this way. "Don't ever," she said, "insist on keeping it the old way if you haven't tried the new one." She was like that. From the outside it looked like she was living the same life of the religious for over 50 years, but she reinvented her life as a person, creatively and intuitively. And I was witness to the renewal.

Yesterday I was in the library reading a book on professional goals and job skills, and Sister Patrick Gertrude came in to bring some flowers to put them on the mantle.

"You know what," Sister Patrick Gertrude said to me, stepping close, smelling of lavender, "You know what your problem is? You are self-absorbed. It's all about *your* Sister Anne, *your* calling, *your* vocation." She gave me a long down and then up. "It's not all about you."

"Who *is* it all about, then?" thinking to at least ask the question she was asking me to ask.

"Jesus. Jesus. That's who, you dummkopf."

"But," I said, "I can't seem to find Jesus just now."

"When you get stuck and lose Jesus, you start cleaning. Work at the things you know. Jesus comes back. That's what I do. You practice faith, until you have faith. We practice all our lives."

But, I thought in response, *we are practicing all the time in this monastery: prayer and work and silence. And I am practiced out.*

Miriam, I know your next letter will have a compassionate response and kind word for Sister Patrick Gertrude, whom you adore—admit to it!—because she acts toward the work of faith, whether or not she has faith in a given moment. Yes, I think that's what you might say. And you might add in your quiet writerly voice, it's not the Emily Dickinson way, but it *is* a worthy way.

For the years that Sister Anne fed me the wisdom of the spiritual life and also put herself under my care, I realize that Sister Anne also filled the gaps of faith, even while I thought it was the God of the psalms and gospels and prophets who filled me up. And I realized that I have gone from my high esteem of Doctor Breamer to the quieter esteems and callings of Sister Anne, and that not until now have I been alone—alone to find the darkness of the world or the delight of a day, which a cup of coffee might help. And now I am writing of my loneliness, my own true fear, of which lacking coffee is the least of these.

Yours, in a swirl,
Sr. A—

24 August 2004
Feastday of St. Nathanael

Miriam, once again, a note from you, writing directly: *The falling of the little sparrow comes under God's eye. And you, Sr. Athanasius, so much more than a sparrow are within God's loving gaze.*

I will return to your letter later, when the words might fill with light. Today, without knowing what to say to Mother Lourdes, even so, with your note encouraging me to face Sister Anne's empty stool in the morning light of the kitchen, the sports page, my vocation, my profession, and to face Mother Lourdes.

But what I said, there, staring at the wainscoting of her office, while she waited to know the reason for the pleasure of the visit, came unexpected: "As of today, 24 August 2004, it has been 9 years, 6 months, and 7 days." Did she really, I asked, think it was of spiritual merit that I continue a coffee abstinence program?

"Honestly?" she said. And I said, yes, honestly. And Mother Lourdes responded, "I was ready to reintroduce you to coffee after Lent that same year, but then you seemed to take the coffee trial so seriously, I thought I'd wait until you mentioned you were ready to come back to it."

"Well, the time is right."

"So it is."

"But I think you could have hinted to my return to coffee earlier. I would have liked to share a cup in the kitchen with Sister Anne before she died." And why I waited until then to cry like I did, I don't know. But Mother Lourdes slid a strong arm under mine and led me to a chair in the refectory, got me a fistful of napkins for my tears, and then went into the kitchen. And that had me crying more, because she left me.

When Mother Lourdes came back to the refectory, around 15 minutes later, she carried that old plaid thermos and a couple of mugs. And I cried again because she came back. And I thought that were Sister Anne watching us from a vantage point in eternity, it wasn't a good show of character on my part. But then Sister Anne extended grace for even a slim show of character, so I mopped up my face.

Mother Lourdes handed me the thermos and gave me a 20-dollar bill and said, "I know you like a road trip to go with your coffee. Why don't you fill the truck with gas, and stop by Tom's, offer him a coffee and buy him a HoHo, which he will love. And thank him, again, for all his work on our behalf. Sister Farm has the keys."

And I'm simply restless, Miriam. I simply keep wanting: Sister Anne or coffee or a change. Something. And I know the spiritual life is not about getting anything. Getting is beside the point. Perhaps we get nothing—or we get less and less all the time, but we feel better and better about it. I simply, downright, wanted coffee. And now I had a truck and a short road trip, too. I went to find Sister Farm. "Oh boy," she said. "I gotta see this. I'm coming too."

I said, "I'm driving."

"I know," she said. "That's what I want to see. You're the worst driver ever."

I handed her the thermos as we neared the pickup. "Get in and no back-seat driving." And we got in and I ground all the gears from Reverse through Fourth between the monastery and Tom's.

Pulling in to Tom's, I got a little too close to a rock that served as an edging at the Feed & Seed. So after Tom re-bent the front right bumper, he said, "Nice to see you girls. I insist on fair payment for work well done," he said, looking at the bumper again. "You can pay me in HoHos." So we ate HoHos and I monopolized the thermos, drinking most of the coffee, which tasted just like I remembered: slick with acids and cream and that singular brownness.

And now it is two in the morning and I am writing you to say that I will not sleep tonight because I remembered the taste of coffee and the look and liquid texture of it, but I forgot its side effect of wakefulness. So here I wait for morning.

And, Miriam, it's not like anything feels *good* these days without Sister Anne. It's just that she would have liked this day, don't you think? Drinking the coffee, driving the truck, putting a dent into it.

Signing off, awake at 2:10 a.m.,
Sr. A.—

26 August 2004
Feastday of St. Teresa
of Jesus Jornet Ibars

Miriam, good timing with your letter, which came on my next meeting with Mother Lourdes (my second attempt to address the questions within). Mother Lourdes asked me to her office, sat me toward the summer light of the window and said, "You like stories, so I'll tell you one," she said.

"I suppose," I said, "it will have some teacherly quality to it. And I'll leave your office having learned some important spiritual lesson?"

"Yes, you will. Even though I suspect you feel no spiritual lesson could make it through to you now. You are treacherously on the brink of despair. Even with caffeine. But we will keep trying."

She told me about growing up in a family of seven kids. "We were all at a park near Candlewood Lake, one day in summer. The kind of day any child wants to extend, by the lake, throwing crab apples at each other, playing baseball in the corner of the large grassy parking lot.

"My father tried to round us all up to go home. He wasn't forceful about it, and we all kept skimming around, playing. Not one of us dutifully gathered. Then my sister, Betsie, came up to me, she went from child to child, and said, 'Pop's crying.' He never cried. We were frightened, especially we smaller kids, not knowing what to do.

"He sat alone at the picnic table, head down on his arms, and walking by you could see sunlight catch big falling pills of salty water as they fell down to the table's edge.

"Betsie sat down next to him. Then me. Then the others squished in, and all of us heaved sobs at this new universe where our god-like figure could just bend a head over a long table and cry for the fruitless work of the world.

"We've always been silent criers. Shoulders might tremble, but no sounds, and only wetness draining down a face. When my father looked up"—here Mother Lourdes looked at me—"he saw us all sitting there with teary faces and we just looked at each other. And he gave a quiet tired smile and got up to go to the car.

"One by one we followed, pulling ourselves into the shiny red 1949 Packard Eight Woody station wagon. I loved that car."

Mother Lourdes stopped. She waited and I didn't know what to say, so I said, "I'm not sure exactly what you are trying to say to me."

Mother Lourdes said, "I think you will find your way with the story. It's a little something to ponder." She came over to me and made a sign of the cross on my forehead and then said, "You can show yourself to the door."

When Mother Lourdes tells a story, she offers a conundrum. All the pieces of the stories don't work, they aren't a parable or stretched metaphor, they don't easily resolve. But they fully are ponderable.

And Miriam, I pass the story along. Perhaps your heart will see something on behalf of your old friend. Or maybe the story is simply meant to do some work, rather than be understood. God and Mother Lourdes know.

Wishing you good stories and a full heart,

Sr. A.—

28 August 2004
Feastday of St. Vivian

Miriam,

Before I mail this letter that grows long (as my recent letters have done), I want to thank you for your letter, which arrived today, perfecting the timing of my thoughts. Especially these days I grow in fondness for Saint John of the Cross. You ask me what I know of Saint John of the Cross? *I ask you because I'm sure of some information.*

I know much less than I ought, but here's what I know: St. John was a Carmelite in the mid-1500s, influenced by the rich work of Saint Teresa of Avila. His own Order disregarded him, betrayed, imprisoned, and removed him from leadership. During this time his great writings about the dark night of the soul emerged. The writings focused on the weight upon the soul when the light of God is withdrawn. The poem you sent (do you know its source? It's new to me), I am writing down, again, in my letter to you, as I find that copying a text brings it closer. And so that you—a lover of letters and of the quote—should have it also in a letter to you:

> *And I saw the river*
> *over which every soul must pass*
> *to reach the kingdom of heaven*
> *and the name of that river was suffering:—*
> *and I saw the boat*
> *which carries souls across the river*
> *and the name of that boat was*
> *love.*

No. No, wisdom on the matter of Mother Lourdes's story, though I revisit it daily, sometimes just to envision all the children walking meekly to the big Woody station wagon, which you are too young to remember and I am too old to forget.

What can I tell you about these days? The world moves on despite me, so that's a mercy and a comfort. As is Sister Farm's constant wearing of the old Red Sox cap of Sister Anne's. She wears it in the barn, in the truck.

Boston just in a series with the Detroit Tigers. And who knows where this season will go. But I am looking more thoughtfully at the *Globe*, the columnists, and the standings. And though Dan Shaughnessy seems to disregard hope as though it were the largest offense, he has said that the Sox this year just might, by grace and good cheer, make it to the series.

An altar of sorts has gathered at the steel table. Sister Anne's coffee mug, a Red Sox placemat of photos of all the major Red

Sox pitchers since Bucky O'Brien. Alongside these things at the altar, there are cracked remains of 2 plover eggs, gathered reverently by Sister Bird. Two keys from previous trucks, and a small can of WD-40 (placed there by Sister Farm). A lily of the valley candle (Sister Patrick Gertrude's addition). And Frankie keeps a spoon there for ice cream and, sometimes when one of his bee girls dies, he'll put the husk there, even though the next minute, Little Sister throws the husk out the kitchen door. And a wrapped Ho-Ho from Tom.

When Sister Farm was in Wisconsin, Mother Lourdes said to him, "Tom, I see how you try to carry the burden of the monastery. An observer might say you were trying to save us all. Perhaps, Tom," Mother Lourdes added, "you, alone, would like to be the savior."

He simply said, "Well, sometimes I think I am."

Mother Lourdes, looking at him, waiting for his brown eyes to meet her blue ones, said, "It is not up to you. We can only move forward, be faithful in the things of this life, and the other concerns are not ours. Not ours and not yours. Our Lord gives stability to any group of religious."

"Well, I hear you, but I'm sorta thinking you *do* need your old friend Tom around." She gave him another good look in the eyes and said, "Well, I never said we didn't. We just don't need a second savior."

Passing along our stories, as I know you appreciate them.

Hellos to Franklin and Brendan (how is his summer work?) and Emily. The photo you sent of you all, there on the screened-in porch, the Sisters insisted should form part of the kitchen shrine, resting between Frankie's spoon and WD-40.

Grateful,
Sr. A.—

[Postcard, 1 September 2004
Feastday of St. Anna
the Prophetess]

Miriam, no more to relate than this news that would have Sister Anne in a tickle. News you and Franklin probably know: Cleveland, underdog baseball friend, beat the Yankees 22–0. What a run. NY has lost no other game by so many. How wicked to rejoice at the demise of the powerful, but goes to show I've not been in top religious form now for months.

More soon, but wanted to send the quick update to you. Any new warblers at the feeders?

Sr. A—

14 September 2004
Feast of the Exultation
of the Holy Cross

Miriam, dear—

Forgive the long delay, after months of letter-following-letter. Today the surprise presence of a little blue heron, a juvenile, shock white along the shore as though the Holy Spirit were coming into the bay for a visit. Sister Bird has been introducing me to the different patches of land, from the small pine grove to the marsh grasses to the tidal sands on the northeast beach, on very local birding tours. I am often thinking about vocation/ calling, the way one *knows* what it is that God is working with us and in us to do, the times we say *yes* (as Mary did) with passion, even though we don't know what thing we've just said yes to.

And I am thinking, too, while among the *yesses*, in the spiritual realm, the *no*s.

Among the things that Sister Anne taught me (along with believing the Sox can win even when they just can't seem to pitch like they believe), Sister Anne had a way of being spiritually minded about a thing without overspiritualizing. She didn't noodle around (the way I do interiorly, thinking, thinking). Perhaps in this resting place, an opening up of Spirit can be found.

Sister Patrick Gertrude said to me the other day, "Can I say, from one old woman to another, that we all have our share of the scaffolding to put up. Your greatest weakness," she said, as though I was eager to hear this, "is trying to figure things out so much that you're a quagmire," she said. "It's not pretty," she added.

Miriam, as though from a distance I see myself, the way I didn't know to respond to Sister Anne's death, the way I withdraw from the Sisters, the way I had no energy, even, to sneak Frankie the late night ice cream while in the kitchen at 2:00 a.m., waiting for a thick plasticky skin to form over the warm milk, sealing the right temperature in. The waiting for sleep, the inability to pray. Even the way I hold tightly to Sister Anne's old Book of Hours, to the popped-lace baseball that Lucy gave me, from a Pumpsie Green's early game with the Red Sox. Sister Anne was there, Lucy told me, that day, his first game in 1959, the sole black player coming to an all-white team. She told me, "There are thrilling games and important games. But that day," she said, "proved to be a very, very important game."

And with that note, I sign off,

Sr. A.—

27 September 2004
Feastday of St. Vincent de Paul

Miriam, dear—

Temperatures, on this September day are subtly dropping, and autumn begins her claim on things, leaf by turning leaf.

Sister Anne's beloved Red Sox beat Tampa Bay, thanks to Johnny Damon and his RBIs. Still, call me lacking in faith, perhaps: Every time I look at the *Globe* sports section, I worry for the next loss (ALCS, the pennant race, the World Series) while faithfully calling out the words, *Maybe this year, Oh Lord,* half with a feeling that, if Sister Anne's prayers could not bring our Sox into a roundabout, then what had I to offer by way of prayer? Though, what is prayer, but to listen and to speak. And so I speak the hope.

As I write here, my desk clogged with notes and nests and rocks and books, I am grateful to be writing you, here amid the swelling gathering of materials, of which I am a scavenger these days. As though more of something, one thing more, will save me.

Miriam, you wrote in your last letter about dusting off some of my Loose Rules, passing them along. We all have our versions. Miriam, it's *your* version, rather than mine, that has been holding the tendrils of the world together. Your last letter, with news of Franklin's new truck (old truck, but new to him), inspired, no doubt, by news of our travels along the road. I am glad he has a beloved truck. Please tell him that if he wants it to last, he should never, Sister Farm warns, never ever let me drive it.

But I am thinking of you these days and I know that the truck means something to you as well, that the things that were so tentatively on hold in the days of both the chemo and the radiation, that you have come to some new footing and together celebrate this next good step of health and this new truck. We celebrate your new truck along with you, knowing that it represents something more, a little exhalation of breath, a new rhythm to the days beyond that simple horrible rhythm of fear.

Today, Sister Bird's affection has run toward two things: Two new visitors on our bay shores, unusual to have red knots here at all, but Sister Bird spotted an albino red knot, who didn't stay too long, but we all tromped shoreward for a view. And then the orchard oriole, unusual, but a welcomed guest. We are, she tells me, in a wonder of a year. This summer, Ross's gull. And now the migratory patterns of birds, pulling along the coast as they head south, where months before they headed north, finding often the same clots of land as stopping points. A little snag of land for birds who hug the coastline, we offer a rest station. "Here," she said, "we save lives so often, this spit of land, that I am compelled to write another book: *Sister Bird's Guide to Migratory and Migrating Birds of the Atlantic Coastal Waters and Shorelands.*"

"Well, that should be a hit," I said, cynic that I am. Still, I'm grateful to be in the presence of someone who embraces changes in life and finds a wonder where I have found a dwelling sadness with Sister Anne's presence gone: the Great Migration. Oh, it's all a grieving, isn't it Miriam? A whole long process. And then I see Sister Bird appreciating the migratory patterns, getting a jizz—the quick observational sketch—of different species as they fly past, and she simply watches them, not needing to hold onto the migrants as they push by. A gift here, then gone, is all.

Little Sister daily pours a cup of coffee, daily puts the sports page on the long counter in the bakery, daily observes vigil for Sister Anne. Perhaps we all have the *horror vacui*, Miriam, that terror of unfilled spaces.

But the filling does come. Someone, every day, will be the one to sit at that chair, to fill the sacred space, to honor Sister Anne and the Red Sox both, by groaning about a score or celebrating a grand slam.

Today, it was Mother Lourdes, there at the counter in the

morning, observing grief on the morning chair, drinking a coffee, saying to Little Sister that Schilling pitched 7 clean innings, talking lightly, watching Little Sister add rows of almond paste and ground hazelnuts and poppy seeds, softened and sweetened, to the centers of sweet rolls, then the quick rolling up of the pastry, the brush of the egg yolk, the radiated heat of the oven, mixing with the chill bursts of inching-in October air.

Miriam, Oh my God, just that scene in the kitchen. Beautiful *vacui.* I realize that I am in love with this life—even alone as I feel—it's as though the amount of light rushing in this morning is filled with Sister Anne, whose presence into eternity is still not an absolute absence here. More like a quieter rendering. And I am struck by the beauty here, the morning light, the morning paper, Mother Lourdes, the smell of ovens filled with sugary dough and poppy seeds.

Thank you for being with me in this day, too, the gift of presence.

Yours,
Sr. A—

29 September 2004
Feastday of St. Michael
the Archangel

Miriam,

Your package came to us today. Filled with carefully detailed gifts.

2 Cuban Montecristo cigars for Sister Farm (illegal, but infinitely appreciated, so please thank your Franklin from Sister Farm).

An additional thermos for Sister Bird (green plaid!), as you wrote, *so that if one of the Sisters needs a thermos, Sister Bird is still assured her very own for autumn days birding along the baywaters.*

Mother Lourdes, a candle for her desk as she works. *Sage green color for wisdom and rest.*

Little Sister, a gift certificate to Baker's Dozen, *the store every baker wants to go to, but those on a budget avoid.*

For myself, a small clear box with a thin cherry wood stand. The box, the size of a pitcher's fist, for Sister Anne's Pumpsie Green baseball, tattered and beautiful.

For Frankie, a polka dotted ice cream bowl. We immediately put *peam, peam* in it for him. His face has not left the smile mode since he saw it.

And for Sister Patrick Gertrude—I'm sorry to say it, dear, but you have just poured about 3 barrels of live petroleum on an already raging, unstoppable fire—your gift of the book *Talking Dirty with the Queen of Clean.* She snapped it up, leaving us to fear that treasured dust bunnies, cigar reekings, and our version of dishevelment will not be spared.

Though you may have made a mixture of enemies and friends among us with these wonderful gifts, we all are grateful to you for remembering us, now these more than 2 months since Sister Anne has found her way home,

Sr. A.—

30 September 2004
Feastday of St. Laurus

Miriam, dear,

Sister Patrick Gertrude, last you heard, swept away in haste, taking your Bad Girls Guide to Good Cleaning (as we are now calling the book) to her cell to commune with Jesus and with the book.

It seems that in prayer she was given a recipe for clearing off layers of furniture wax and polishes on our old and beautiful long-stretching oak refectory table. This is the table around which we share our lives, our silences, and our feasts. Around which we eat, often as one of us does the table reading from a spiritual biography or local history.

At lunch we ate a ginger-peach soup and cheese slices and drank black tea while listening to a biography of Blessed Fra Angelico, the painter. By 9:00 p.m., after Compline, Sister Patrick Gertrude had formulated a plan, to bring back our table to its fullest splendor.

Oh how the joys of hope can be dashed by the hands of reality. Sister Patrick Gertrude, in consulting this book, misinterpreted *vintage mix* as *vinegar mix* when detailing her Plan for Thoroughly Cleaning Dining Table and Wooden Surfaces. And while she often seeks the wisdom of St. Julian the Hospitaller, patron saint of housekeeping, perhaps this time she forged ahead without praying for accompanying wisdom.

Now our refectory table surface runs full of marked and

pocked and filmy and smoky looking effect. Our old good table.

Sister Patrick Gertrude has been inconsolable at the new features of our dining tradition.

Sister Farm, in a courageous debut of empathy, told her, "I hardly notice. But if I do, I like the smoky look to the wood." Upon which the only way Sister Patrick Gertrude could respond was to leave the room. And while we may hear the recorder battle through the Baptist hymnal on any given day in the garden, this day has been strangely quiet.

Mother Lourdes requested that the table remain, for now, blemished. "I find it," Mother Lourdes said, "almost freeing, to have a beautiful table that offers also humble moments. And this, Sisters, is the spiritual life."

So it seems, Miriam, that our table will remain at the heart of the community, full of best intentions and blunder, and liked all the more by Sister Farm as it looks like a cigar's smoky swirls.

And from the silence of a no-recorder afternoon, I write, wishing you a less tempestuous life on the home front,

Sr. A.—

PS Last few games of the regular season, and hoping the Sox make the wild card in this last series with the Orioles. In bird news, an indigo bunting and a lark sparrow. Sister Bird full of joy with the visitors, and the flood of color with the bunting.

3 October 2004
Feastday of St. Widradus

Miriam, dear—

I thought we had cleaned out Sister Anne's cell weeks ago, narrowing the room down to clean lines, hardly a hint of her baseball loves. Now a clean bedspread, a clean desk, a clunky chair, while all the dear things she loved, dispersed.

But I was dusting yesterday—though Sister Patrick Gertrude will, I'm sure, *re*-address the dust issue tomorrow (even though the refectory table problem has sparked a tolerance for others that is heartening).

There, by the desk on the floor, 2 buttons on an old button card, buttons that matched Sister Anne's blue winter coat, which I recall was missing 2 buttons. With her hands too gnarled to sew them on, why hadn't I seen her old coat's need and offered to sew them on for her?

The thought that she, somehow, obtained the buttons to fill in the gap, but would not have been able to sew them, and would not have asked for help, saying, "I don't like to contribute to the burden."

And I saw with those two buttons what I hadn't seen then: a woman who filled in the gap as she could by purchasing the common buttons, while not asking for the needed extra hand to sew them on.

I don't mind telling you, Miriam, that I cried elephant tears at the button card. I cried because as much as I tried to save her, I only see the place I've failed: those 2 large gaps funneling cold air into her blue coat. Now, into eternity, I will never, ever fix that icy cold gap.

This isn't even a letter, but a note from the stage of our ups and downs, knowing that your kindness will know how it's meant and that I send this as an antidote to the wisdom notes, this being my Unwisdom Note #1, of which there are many many more.

Friends, Sr. A—

PS Today, the last game of the regular season. And we're in the third inning (I'm writing with my right eye and left pen, but watching with my left eye) against Baltimore. The Red Sox are in the pennant race as a Wild Card. That's much more exciting, don't you think, than simply Winning Your Division, which sounds so clean and flat? But "Wild Card" has possibilities. Sister Farm wants to take bets among the Sisters on the post season. An idea run down in its entirety by Mother Lourdes. We'll see how Sister Anne's team comes through.

The bunting still nearby.

7 October 04
Feastday of St. Sergius

Miriam, dear—

Autumn now a festival of reds and yellows and chill wind, with every tree saying a different thing, and the ocean re-structuring its waves and motions somehow a little calmer and a little sharper.

Tell me in your next letter, would you, how autumn turns for you, your maples, the last flowering plants calling anything out? And what birds are visiting the feeders now as we shift into colder air? All things I would like to know. I've come from dinner in the refectory at our table of many stains, now cleverly hidden by long tablecloths. Our foods shifting from summer meals of cucumber and brightly colored fruits and vegetables to the pumpkins and potatoes and stews, the colors of our food going to quieter yellows and oranges, the tastes more hefty, the spices more robust. Little Sister follows the seasonal foods around the calendar, while breads and pastries are baked and sold evenly year-round.

Birds on the Wing: The birds are migrating as quickly as Sister Bird can get a jizz and count groupings on her beads, as though they wing past her only to be counted, only to move on. Those coming in for winter: red-necked & horned grebes, brants, common eiders, buffleheads, American coots. And our good friends, the plovers have long left us, and some late migrations of the sandpipers. All the while Sister Bird looking, looking, for avian vagrants, mysterious strangers in the air.

And who among us—bird or human—doesn't want to be named and counted in the motions of our lives?

Sister Bird full of birding travels, too, from World's End (Sarah/Sailor's Island), Plymouth, and down to Wellfleet. She saw a northern wheatear (rare joy!), a Philadelphia vireo, a Lapland longspur, American pipits, a bald eagle, and Caspian and Forster's terns and oystercatchers in number. She's saving up on joys. Come January and February, she will mope (albeit cheerfully) and focus on writing or homeopathic herbs, as our bird guests are fewer.

These days we all have our steps before us. You walk your steps brave and honest, knowing that even on weary days, days when you fear, as you put it, *cancer trying to raise its voice again*. Even then—or is it especially then?—you still put forth into the day.

Now, your son again in college, after some time at home. Does his stereo mysteriously still come on every day at 4:00 p.m.? And if he's fixed it over the summer, do you miss the afternoon voices? How fast your summer scurried along, thinking how can your son change so quickly, his rush of strong opinion and presenting it with firing quickness of impatience mixed with a sort of kindness. And I'm sure I can find a Loose Rule to his hesitation to agree, to say yes. If one can't immediately say yes to it all, as is often the way with me, one can enter the doors of the sanctuary of the Lord, as the psalms say, and be there like a sparrow in the rafters of the high, holy place of the Lord. Entering in. Inhabiting the place.

And Emily, heading into 9th grade, when she feels injustice of not being in college. Is 14 the hardest age? I don't remember. Your letters always bring something important and have the feel of home in them, the stories of Franklin with his new truck and of the morning visitors at the feeder under your maple. Sometimes what I see first is how the letters you form fall together, pen after blue pen row, seeing what place you are writing from, how the Rs and Ks and Bs, all the letters that take three or more strokes are formed. There's so much energy that goes into making words, isn't there? And you make such a good letter, from the look of it, to the meaning of it.

And tell me, what guests visit your nyjer feeder these days, Miriam? What morning calls, chatters, and chirps meet you on the early morning outside your window now that the maple rustles the leaves of color filling the season, a New England autumn.

I am thinking about the note you wrote, how different this season is from last year's autumn, how this feels as though it proved another starting point for your life together with Franklin. Especially autumn to me has that feeling to it, a change toward a different landscape.

I must offer a Division Update: Red Sox have two wins over Anaheim. And if the Sox lose? Well, we simply begin again. As the desert father Abba Sisoes said when a young monk asked, "Abba, what should I do? I fell." The elder answered: "Get up!" The monk said, "I got up, and I fell again." The elder replied: "Get up again!" But the young monk asked, "For how long should I get up when I fall?" "Until your death," answered Abba Sisoes. As we have been beginning—falling, getting up—for 86 years. And one year, as Sister Anne did insist on it, they will win.

Sr. A.—

[Postcard, Postmark 11 October 2004]

Miriam, dear—

Sister Bird asked me to let you know that the snow geese passed over today, like pieces of white porcelain, high up in the sky. Their call notes announcing that they are only passing through. Each year, when she hears them and sees them, is what I think of as Sister Bird's Big Day (maybe she could start a children's line of book titles such as this?), when the snow geese fly overhead with their particular goosey honks. The visit forms our annual adventure, to hear the high and away sound so plain and clear from these windows.

For Sister Bird and from me,
Sr. A.—

20 October 2004

Miriam, dear—

As Dr. Seuss would say, Oh the news. Oh the news, news, news, news. Of course you know it, but I must write it out. Whenever the Red Sox and Yankees meet, there is tension and high heat. This exhausting and invigorating League Championship between the two can be summarized in one word: Epic. A bright red and bloody pitcher's sock, long innings, and a set of games that made David Ortiz a Red Sox hero in an ACLS overturn so dramatic we cheered through the biggest comeback in ACLS history, from 3 games down to 4 up. "A comeback for the ages," one friend of our community remarked later. Whatever the results of the World Series, we have met with a major team breakthrough.

Yours,
Sr. A

28 October 2004

Miriam, dear—

Of course you know, and New England knows, and any baseball fan knows, but I must write it out, as we, along with Sister Anne have been waiting for this day. To me, it's as poetic as a reading from the book of the prophet Isaiah: *In the month of October, in the year that Sister Anne died, we witnessed a lunar eclipse in the full night sky in the creation of a blood red moon. And this same night the Red Sox were lifted up to win the World Series, and all of Boston cried Holy. All of Boston cried Believe.*

Perhaps I never told you that Sister Anne was born in 1918, the last year the Red Sox won a series. She was born before radio broadcast the games, 6 years after Fenway Park was built, before there was a Yawkey Way or a Pesky Pole. Her long wait to see the Red Sox win the World Series lasted her through the spiritual reign of 9 popes, through two world wars, through the clutch and release of Soviet Communism, through the growth and development of atomic bombs and electronic and communication technology.

Since 1918, the year when power of the Code of Canon Law was put into the Pope's hands for the beatification of blesseds and canonization of saints, 643 have been canonized saints. From the first day of spring training on, Sister Anne would read the *Boston Globe* sports page: stats, at-bats, and "ribbies."

On good days, when she felt well or something came easy, she would use baseball terms. Often she'd say, oh this is *a can of corn* or *a tatter* (for an easy day). For the rougher day's journey, it's a *run-down* or *an Uncle Charlie.*

Every year, for the last of the 46 years I've been here, when spring training began in Fort Myers (or in previous decades, in Winter Haven or Sarasota), Sister Anne would announce from within a shock of light from the kitchen window, as she sat majestic and tiny on her stool chair, "This is the year, I feel it." She had many gifts, but prophecy was never one of them. But every year she fell, every year she got up.

She was always quick to add, "—if it be Your will," but somehow that bow to the sovereignty of God never felt as strong as others of her prayers.

What if the good Lord wills it differently? I would ask. "Oh, Jesus knows what an old fool like me needs," she would reply.

And yes, we all watched the series games, even Mother Lourdes and Frankie, who insisted on peam and kept coming around the room to give us hugs between innings. But at around the 5th inning of what would be the final game of the series, Little Sister leaned over and whispered to me, "What about you and me go to the kitchen, make a coffee, sit at the Sister-Anne-spot, and listen to the rest of the show on Miriam's transistor?" So we did, though hardly drank any coffee through the last innings.

After WEEI, the AM radio station, announced the World Series win in St. Louis, after everyone celebrated, cheered, and after the Sisters said a prayer for Sister Anne's celebrating soul, the others went to sleep. By 2:00 a.m. Little Sister went outside to look at the moon, which was no longer red, but a slim darkened line at the edge of the eclipse. When she came back, I made her another cup of coffee, and then she sat on Sister Anne's stool, in this year of our Lord 2004, and cried big soft and sorrowful tears.

More soon, Miriam,
Sr. A.—

Stepping Up to the Plate

4 November 2004
Feastday of St. Charles Borromeo

Miriam, dear—

Autumn day, here, the wind desperately trying to pull the last yellow leaves from the branches—a true fight between the trees and the wind. Let's hope for some victories both ways. A few leaves going, a few leaves staying.

Meanwhile, walking with Sister Bird from the cloister to the monastery with all this wind, the short path that seems endless on a blustery day like today, we both arrived to Sister Patrick Gertrude's announcement, "Comb up, Sisters. You look like a fright."

Down by the bay only the most tenacious birds: either they play with wind currents or fight them, as the herring gulls and black-backed gulls do, burrowing into the knee-high water and windy landscape, facing the wind and waiting it out.

The sometimes good thing about a windy day here is that if we get a big gust of our own cow/farm mix, then the next minute the wind changes, as the large cold burst of briney smell or the simply layered smell of the earth in its change of seasons. The smells of holiness.

You asked about Sister Farm. About a month ago she told Mother Lourdes she's been sleeping poorly, now a few months after she'd come back from Wisconsin. "And I *never* can't sleep," Sister Farm said.

So the next night she made intention and had a prayer vigil in the chapel through the night. And some of the Sisters find their way through a problem, there in the chapel, keeping watch by night, as the shepherds did in the Gospel of St. Luke. The next day, though, showed the keeping watch just meant she was getting less sleep, and she all but did Sister Patrick Gertrude in, deciding that the mud room was now the hallway of the monastery, and little chunklets of sheep dung, cow dust, hay, and cigar ash robbed Sister Patrick Gertrude of every Good Housekeeping victory she'd ever won.

When Sister Patrick Gertrude decided to corner Sister Farm (always a bad choice) near the laundry room, Sister Farm said to her, "Not a word, Sister. I will get violent." In a great show of wisdom, Sister Mary Patrick put her head down, backed up, and quietly moved toward the cleaning closet for a bucket. This allowed Sister Farm to exit back to her cow friends Daisy Lou and Clucky Lucky, who also read her mood correctly and knowingly made hardly a sound.

The next night, after Compline, offering our bodies and souls to God in peace and sleep, Sister Farm held vigil again, through the stinky night, since she hadn't bothered to take off her work habit after her last look-in on the cows.

By Wednesday. whomever she was fighting with in that chapel over the last nights had obviously won. Sister Farm asked if she could talk to Mother Lourdes and to me.

"I think I know what's happening," Mother Lourdes told her, "and I don't think you are going about it the best way."

I, who didn't know what was happening, and *even still* knew it was not the best way, asked, "I do not know what is going on. Should I even be here?" Both of them nodded for me to stay.

Well, Miriam, Sister Farm—unkempt, unshowered, unconsoled—said that anyone who insisted on spending days and several nights alone with God, didn't know what they were up against.

"And what are you implying you are up against?" said Mother Lourdes.

"Compromise," she said. Which is like saying that a mule or a merlin compromises. "This is what we worked out. God gets the donkey. I sell the trailer. I know she has put God up to it"—here she formed a small and tight square with her index fingers to indicate who the *she* was. "But I couldn't come here to stay and a donkey come too. No donkey. But I keep the cigars, smelly or not. Sister Patrick Gertrude takes it on the chin, is all."

"I can't even tell you how many levels of theological incorrectness you have indulged yourself," said Mother Lourdes to Sister Farm. "First, blaming someone for praying for something that might actually bring them peace is not your place. Second, making deals with God comes close to the devil's own temptation of Christ. And thirdly, apart from this conversation, threatening a Sister in the hallway—yes, I know about it—is decidedly unChristian. And, fourthly, even tempting God like that, it doesn't sound like the best compromise God has offered down through the centuries."

"And?"

"And I would like for you to avoid smoking cigars in the monastery. And then I would like for you to get some rest," she said, pointing to the window and to the evening sky. Mother Lourdes also said that she didn't have to do this, but Sister Farm said, "Theology or not, next time you spend 3 nights alone with the Holy Ghost, see if *you* can say no."

Now thinking of it, Miriam, conversations with Mother Lourdes are never long or chatty. They are direct, intentional, and you are then pointed toward the door.

Once we were out of the office, I asked Sister Farm what role she hoped I would play there, since I hadn't contributed anything. "Do what you do best: keep it on record. I want this on the record. And while I'm at it, I want something else on record: Even from my cell I heard Little Sister melt-down after the last Series game."

"I know, I was there."

"Do you know why?"

"Missing Sister Anne, I think. That's why I continue to melt down."

"Doubt it. Little Sister's in some sort of grind. You think I don't talk, but I'm Chat Mama next to her. She should talk to someone. Or someone could spend time with her. Might as well be you."

"You inspire me with your great confidence that I'm the person for the task," I said, but I told her I'd try.

As it does, with quiet whispers and that child-like telephone game that most humans play, the others found out about Sister Farm's decision to give over to God the donkey of God, though to keep the cigars, just to keep the rivalry lively. And Sister Patrick Gertrude knew not to triumph and Sister Farm knew that she had a spiritual stream within herself that made her, if not strong, at least very, very determined.

And, now four weeks into the matter, our lovely donkey trailer (with three bumper stickers!) has disappeared, sold no doubt to some French Canadian up in Maine via *Uncle Henry's Weekly Swap or Sell It Guide*, and I suppose I was also at the meeting because she wanted me to drive the trailer up with her.

And my Loose Rule #1 has proven itself and its poor theology now over this 3-night interchange: *It's a better yes, if you say no first.*

And Sister Farm lately can be found patting a flank of Daisy Lou or Clucky Lucky and sighing, but she then lights up her cigar, gets good and smelly, and enters the house of the Lord for prayers, where her boots and her habit and her entire house of being sits next to Sister Patrick Gertrude and they both pray as the Lord taught them,

Give us this day our daily bread.
Forgive us our debts.
Thy Kingdom come. Thy will be done.

And with this prayer, which we all pray, I will bring this letter to an end.

Yours,
Sr. A.—

8 November 2004
Feastday of St. Martin Tinh
and St. Martin Tho

Miriam dear—

Well, Sister Farm's prescient comment about Little Sister came right, and the hour soon followed when Little Sister asked me to be with her in the kitchen while she baked.

"Stay with me here. Sit at Sister Anne's stool; check out the sports page, who's being traded or sold." When I asked her why, she said, "Just stay with me. And bring your letters to Miriam, you can write them here. You need company, too. No homilies, though, they make me nervous. Just sit. Read. Write. Ok?"

Once she said all that, I thought for sure we'd find a way to a conversation, but I rarely know how to start conversations when I don't know quite what the topic of conversation is.

After I got my two best pens and this stationary, I came back and asked Little Sister if I was going to be kicked out. Today, no, she said. So I told her I could be a very good guest when I put my mind to it, and I started rustling the paper and settling in at the long steel table.

So, Miriam, today on the paint-chipped green stool a letter for you, and I will try to get the smell of the truffle tart experiment into the letter (a successful experiment, I can attest), the smell of it oddly mixes well with the smell of lemon rosemary chicken for our dinner. Let's see if I can fill the pages to waft out this goodness to you as you open this letter.

I didn't really know what to say, Miriam, sitting here in the kitchen wanting to say something to Little Sister. Not a homily, but some way to open a curtain, behind which she lives, from behind which it seems she wishes to speak. But even when I don't know what to speak, I usually always say something anyway, so I said, "Not only am I dedicated to the religious life, I am also very dedicated to your bear claws and truffle tarts. I have now discovered my vocation: I am called to the spiritual life and also to testing fine pastries. I'm glad to bring my gifts to the service of your kitchen."

That didn't elicit much response. So I then asked Little Sister, "What holds you to the religious life? I know you are bound by vows, but seem to be here differently than, say, Sister Anne, who told me that she found the vowed life freeing. Me, I find it compelling, to say the least. But, I've always wondered what you thought about your life here."

Nearing 11:30 a.m. the Time Out hour, me, sitting on the little Sister Anne stool, looking at the paper so as not to be direct, only curious, I suppose.

She didn't answer me for a while, you know how that is, so I thought she didn't hear me. I turned to the sports page with mostly talk still of the World Series and Red Sox Nation, with talk of free agents and possible trades. Then I noticed that the particular sound that wooden spoons make in metal bowls, almost a constant sound here, stopped, the air in the room got cinnamony and quiet. There Little Sister was next to me, eyes red, tears crawling down her face, making her look bruised. No sobs, just every time she blinked, a new rivulet formed down her face.

"Is it your 11:30 hot flashes?" I asked.

"Oh, Jesus," she said. "I have no idea what compels me to stay," she said, tears dripping from her swollen face.

"Please tell me," I said. But she just leaned on the metal table and let silent tears go, breathing in shallow and uneven breaths.

At the time, I thought there couldn't be worse timing when a knock at the kitchen door came, and in walked Sam our post-woman with mail, whistling. Seeing me there, her face flushed and her whistling stopped. She looked confused. She looked at me, then at Little Sister, and then at the little bag of bear claws by the door, where she unloaded the mail in its rubber band.

Miriam, thank God there was a letter from you. Sam dug into the pile, sort of awkward, and came over to hand it to me. "For you," she said. It seemed important to her that I read it right then, so she stood there waiting until I had opened it and began reading—even though you know, Miriam, I often wait until the last of the dusk is faded and the day is over to read it. Your note about the first deep frost and two bird sightings, the boreal chickadee at your feeder, and the winter wren along one of your walks. And your comment, which, if you have created your own version of Loose Rules, I hope you add this one: *Never underestimate the medicinal power of hope.*

When I glanced up from your letter, I noticed that Sam had gone over to Little Sister, put her hand low on Little Sister's back, the way an intimate will touch another: tender and a little casual. It's the sort of touch that you recognize even before your mind catches up and puts it all together: the 11:30 hour, the cleared-out kitchen, the morning surge of irritation, this moment of intimacy.

Oh, Miriam, I didn't feel comfortable leaving the room. Nor did I feel comfortable staying. But your letter called to me again, and I stayed and re-read your letter. What to do, otherwise?

With a little more time the discomfort spread, and Sam said something in a whisper to Little Sister and then nodded to me and left me with the letter in my hands, and left Little Sister looking away, tears still in a parade, as though her chin were crying in neat rows onto her clean kitchen floor.

"Do you want me to go?" I said, feeling that if she wasn't going to kick me out, then I should offer to leave. She grabbed my hand and held it, which I took for a no. And she kept holding my hand and standing there until 11:45 when her chin was finally dry. She let go of my hand, blew her nose and said, "Well, there it is," which I took to mean there was nothing in addition she wanted to say, but then she said, "Go with me early to the chapel?" and so we went, and then soon the other Sisters joined us for prayers and chant, and the psalms echoed along the walls and into the rafters, and I thought this: Every one of us carries a big joy and perhaps a bigger sorrow. And each one of us is looking to find streams of living water.

And so it is with us, and so it is, I know, with you. And with this mix and with this hope, I end the note,

Sr. A.—

10 November 2004
Feastday of St. Tryphaena
& St. Tryphosa

Miriam, dear,

Eiders, grebes, scoters, and guillemots, a full load of locals, and with Tom and Father Martinez we accompanied Sister Bird to the water, drinking coffee (both thermoses, including the one from you!) and watching, with Sister Bird's antediluvian Bausch and Lomb binoculars and, counting with her rosary beads, she numbered them 34, but I can't recall which birds were of that number.

Little Sister made us the coffee, but said she'd stay behind in the kitchen, giving me a meaningful look, though I didn't know what full meaning it held: Stay? Go? But when I offered to stay, she insisted I go, handing me the coffee to accompany the chilly others on shore. As I thought of it later: *Go, stay.* Maybe that meaningful look was about her decision, not my question.

But once I saw the scoters and started getting cold, I came back to the kitchen, and asked Little Sister if she wanted some quiet company. "Or we could talk," I asked.

"I don't know if I want to talk," she said, looking through James Beard's *Beard on Bread,* but she did. "It's not coming clear, and it's not just about my life, but this community, this bakery, Sam, and the entire postal system." I don't know why the entire postal system was connected and I gave a sort of snort, the kind where you try not to laugh, but then you sound more ridiculous trying not to and snorting more. But she snorted too, even more, so that seemed good, to laugh.

But then she sighed and kept on talking. "I'm not romantic enough to believe that one person answers all my needs. If I did, I'd be consumed thinking Sam could. But, practically? No one can do that. It's like James Beard, he's good on bread, really good. But he's not everything on bread, he's not even *bread,* he's just something *about* bread. But then I wonder if God can be everything, either."

She went back to Beard, and I started washing mugs, planning to make another pot of coffee. As soon as I was up as though the conversation ended, she started it again. "And this place is a bunch of dopes. We're ridiculous. And Frankie and Tom are ridiculous. But Frankie gets good honey. And Father Martinez's not ridiculous. But we're all pretty much dopes. —Oh, blah blah blah," she said. "I've had so many conversations in my head. I don't know which ones are the real ones."

All these years of one or two sentences it seems she was just saving it up.

"You know," she went one, "you want to know the thing I know? Prayer. I've never felt so lost and torn, so angry. And what I've gotten is prayer. You don't get prayer any other way. You don't," she said, wiping her nose with a kerchief in constant use these last days, weeks, and possibly years.

"It's like you," she said.

"Me?"

"Well, something is coming clear in you, a person none of us has seen before. It's not like Sister Anne had to die so that you could happen, but you're sad, you pray, you get angry at God, and you keep talking. Then you realize you learned something sweet and dangerous about God just by talking with God. Something real simple and real plain. It's good, Sister Athanasius, you're doing good."

We made another pot of coffee and it felt like we had all day to talk and drink it, thick with cream, and a new oven load of a scone-like bread with almonds and cranberries, and some clotted cream from our faithful Jerseys. A veritable feast on a good birding day.

More later, Miriam. I simply wanted to let you know that the birds are aplenty at the bay and that your friend Little Sister makes a fine bread and that she knows something of prayer, and that I am learning important things as well. Both, as simply as that.

And I am thinking of one note you wrote recently, about how the world seems to be a very different place in November and all hints of summer are gone, and the forced return to, as you wrote, *to the bare bones of things is never the place I want to live, but is always the place I look back to with the most appreciation. Perhaps it was from my early married days, struggling to meet bills, pay for heat, and seeing that the earth itself seemed to be shutting down. But Franklin and I found something good in those days together. A good thing.*

Grateful, always, for your notes, Miriam. Each time a new letter comes, it speaks directly to the seasons of our days here even as it recounts your own days. I can only hope that the blessings with which you bless this monastery are returned in great number from the letters I return with a full heart, and in the care and prayers of this community for you and your dear family.

All best,
Sr. A.—

11 November 2004
Feastday of St. Martin of Tours

Miriam, dear—

You'll humor me, won't you, when I revisit this tired old conversation yet again? Each Sister takes turns hearing me out about my lack of professional craft or skills in coming to the Order, which has not been remedied. As Little Sister says, when I am dipping my feet into loquacity about this: "Blah, blah, blah."

Sister Anne once said to me, "So you feel like a baseball player who can field but has no position of specialty: not short-stop or right field. Well, we all sometimes feel like we live in the dugout, playing as we can."

And then your note from yesterday came (timed perfectly—how did you know?) with a comment about *the dubious nature of profession, anyway,* voicing on my behalf that which may not necessarily be true, but still sometimes we can be buoyed by an untruth until we are ready to be buoyed by the truth. Though even Little Sister's comment about the change toward good in me doesn't seem to speak of me at all, from the view in the dugout.

Perhaps I should tell you that today we were given forms from the Motherhouse, or as Little Sister calls it, the Mother Bing, calling for full compliance in detailing the structure & organization of our monastery as well as requesting a list of the skills and professional work of each Sister, in order to have a clear sense of what each Sister contributes to each monastery and to the Order as a whole.

Sister Bird handed out the forms to everyone after Sext and as she handed mine to me whispered, "Don't kill the messenger."

When I looked it over, I looked at her teeny face and said, "O, help."

"You can always fill in that you are retired," she said quietly. "You know that's an option for anyone over 63, and you're 72, so that's the way to go." But one look at my pathetic face got her to backtrack and feel miserable along with me. "I know I shouldn't have given that form to you. Here," she said, pulling some vial of liquid from the mysterious expanse that is our blue habit, "take some of this."

It was one of her Bach flower essences, Gentian, and the bottle read: "Inspires a positive attitude when you feel discouraged or despondent due to setbacks." I rolled my eyes, though whether it was accuracy of the label or my own sense of sore need, I put some drops in my coffee, (which probably means it won't work) and then I dragged myself to Mother Lourdes's office with the form, empty under Number 5: "Please list your trade or professional calling(s), your areas of expertise, your financial contribution(s) to your monastery of the Sisters of Saint Hildegard of Bingen, as well as your spiritual contribution, as you define it."

When I knocked, the voice of Mother Lourdes came from behind the dark wooden door, the voice of someone awaiting the visitor: "If that's you, Sister Athanasius, coming about the form, has Sister Bird told you that you can be officially retired?"

I nodded.

As if seeing me, she said, "And that's not good enough for you?"

I nodded again.

"Well, please take yourself to the chapel to pray and ask the Holy Spirit for either retirement or clear guidance."

I waited.

"My help is not what you need. Your question is about a spiritual calling to one's work and skills. And you will not be satisfied by a few filled-in blanks. The one who can inform you to your satisfaction is the Holy Spirit. Go to the chapel. God is in the Holy Temple. Let all the earth keep silence. Wisdom will come. We will all wait in sending our forms until you have filled yours in. Now, go, to love and to question and to serve the Lord. —And, Sister Athanasius?" she said, "With openness to Jesus and with patience in your heart, pray. God will meet you there."

So I went, in the manner of Sister Farm of late, whose adversity with God did not cast golden glow on my case. But I sat my bottom down and waited. And listened. And waited. And prayed. And then, near the back corner of the chapel, where Sister Bird has put a small plastic finch at the feet of our small statue of Mary, I lit a candle to our Blessed Mother and prayed for counsel.

Still in prayer and waiting, but a break to the knees to send a note to you, dear, as I know you pray for your old friend and will offer intentions on my behalf.

Your,
Sr. A.—

17 November 2004
Feastday of St. Hugh of Noara

Yes, Miriam, your suspicions have been right, the praying and waiting extended through the days. For hours I sat the first night. And for hours. 5 hours exactly. I sat the second night.

The third night, after compline, I thought the best sign of my inward devotion and humility would be to kneel and disregard Mother Lourdes's injunction to pray sitting rather than kneeling. So 2 hours' savagery to my knees and now I'm limping. After two hours I decided if our blessed Lord didn't care to meet me on my knees, I'd just as well sit.

Gone are the days, Miriam, when my body lay prostrate in the sacred hours of prayer in the chapel, on the chill brown tiles in front of the Host, the cross. I am no Teresa of Avila, no Little Flower, no Sister of Carmel, no discalced, here in my warm woolen socks. Even so, I have learned how to still my soul in the presence of God, and wait.

On the third day of prayer in the chapel, Sister Farm sat in the stall next to me and said in her husky voice, "You are indispensable. If you don't know that about yourself, you don't know jack shit. Now, sit with me in the barn while I have a cigar. It's good praying there too." Of course I went, but then I returned, smellier, to the chapel once more.

An hour passed and Little Sister came to sit with me. "Let's switch prayers for a while. You pray for me and I'll pray for you. It'll be a nice break."

"Sam?" I asked.

"I talked to Mother Lourdes. I think I had forgotten how much I love my vows—when she asked if I planned to leave, I told her, only if she asked me to leave. So if I can live in it all, Sam'll bring the mail. And, Sister Athanasius, you think *I* can be stubborn and angry? She's not going anywhere, she told me, just to see how I live with my decisions. So, maybe nothing's changed except you're here at 11:30 when she is, or Sister Farm is, or it's just me and the kitchen door is open. It's not good. But then it's not, not good, either."

And it was good to pray there, together.

And then again, alone.

And several hours passed, and Sister Patrick Gertrude sat on the other side of me, "I hate to say it, Sister, but this praying all the time does nothing for your complexion, your old eyes. Do you know," she asked, "what you're waiting for?" But she knew that exactly 5 lines were blank on the Vocational Form of the Order of the Sisters of Hildegard of Bingen.

"Well, I am waiting for God to fill in the blanks," I said. "5 blanks. So if you'll excuse me," I said, "I'm off to my stall to indulge in another round of petitionary waiting."

"Hold up," she said, ignoring me while she straightened her scapular. "Why is it that I could fill in the 10 blanks for you, right now. Every one of us Sisters could. You've been living your vocation, now, for 52 years and I've endured 23 years of that." She scraped at something on the armrest. "Not only do you maintain bad theology, you're the worst kind of stubborn," she said, now leaning over and picking at something else. "You're selfish, waiting for God to tell you what *you* already know, what Sister Anne knew, what Mother Lourdes knows, and Sister Farm knows the way she knows when Daisy Lou has something gone wrong in the barn or the feed is bad."

She said, finally hooking her blue eyes on mine, "Quit waiting for Jesus to fill in blanks that were filled in and lived years ago. You're too old to be so dumb."

"Does that mean I can leave the chapel and go to sleep?"

"Exactly what it means," she returned, "Nighty, night."

Miriam, Sister Patrick Gertrude sliced me up, the whole horrible thrill of someone saying just what it looks like to them. The sickening feeling of knowing you wouldn't be sickened if it weren't true. The feeling of going to sleep, thinking, "Dear Lord, this day, I have seen something of myself. In your grace, tomorrow please let me see something of You." I slept the same peaceful sleep as after I made first and full confession, unloading the boat of everything that didn't belong on the voyage.

The morning brought with it a fresh rush of sickness: How do you face yourself, your Sisters with what you now know about yourself? As Sister Anne might have said, well you face them by doing morning ablutions, putting on habit and coat, and walking into the dark chill of morning air and heading to the chapel.

I arrived early. Maybe I thought I could sit there and keep my head bowed until I found a way to lift my eyes level with everyone else's once Matins had begun. But Sister Patrick Gertrude was there, and by the light of the chapel, I supposed she had been there since very early or very late.

"You're here early," I said.

"I never left, not that you'll thank me for the prayers that went into your good night's sleep."

One must always adjust ribbons for the morning Office, for the hymn, the psalms, the readings, so I pulled the prayer book out and marked the pages. When I reached the morning psalms for this day, Psalms 24 and 36, and the Canticle of Zechariah, a piece of paper was stuck into the pages there:

> *Jesus says hello. He's a little disappointed you couldn't figure this out on your own, with all the clues he's given, but that you still seem to need help. So here's #1 & #2: Spiritual Advisor. Philosopher.*

I looked at her, but Sister Patrick Gertrude ignored me, busy repositioning the ribbons in the same of her breviary.

By Terce, I found similar notes from Sister Farm and Sister Bird, one under the door of my cell, the other at the morning counter, near your small radio, Miriam. And in my cell, Sister Patrick Gertrude had placed a small bunch of lilies of the valley, frail and fragrant—from a neighbor's indoor clay pot garden. Another of the miracles of this November day, out of season and bright.

And so the day moved forward in the same fashion. Sam came into the kitchen at 11:30, saying a bold but distant hello to Little Sister. I don't know what that meant, but surmised it to be a reorganization of how one person relates to another. As I suppose it always is, for all of us, a reorganization of relating. She came to me at the steel table, where I sat on the green stool, and handed me a small piece of paper:

> *Vocation: 1. Portress. 2. Greeter. 3. Wise Woman (not a profession, really, but, then, is something like Prophet even a profession? Still, enough to build a whole life around)—Best to you in your many vocations and gifts. Sam.*

Oh, the tears do roll in this monastery. And now it was my turn near the window in kitchen, on Sister Anne's stool, to give the old heaving cry for gratefulness, for shame, for the enlarging heart: Thankful.

Miriam, this afternoon, one day before the deadline, I headed back to Mother Lourdes's office, with the form. I didn't even get the chance to knock. "Sister Athanasius, if that's you, I hope you remembered to add in the following two professions: Writer—and this includes all monastery correspondence—and Caregiver. If you haven't yet, please do so and then bring the form back."

Which I hadn't, so then I did.

I don't know if I feel any different as a professional, skilled worker now, a couple evenings later, with the November wind shifting through the meadow grasses and the pines and the squirrelly bark of the short-eared owl announcing his reign of the night watch. But I do know I like the sounds of night, the scratch of a pen, and a correspondence where two people exchange ideas and understandings of the world, or their worlds. Isn't it grand, Miriam? All you have been through, and still yet the scratchy pen. And all we have lost this year, with Sister Anne gone, and still the scratchy pen. And all your news of healing. And all mine of hope. And still the scratchy pen.

Good night, my dear.

Signed, the writer and philosopher (my two favorites),

Sr. A.—

2 December 2004
Feastday of St. Chromatius

Miriam, dear—

It's still a bit odd to me, to write letters here in the kitchen, rather than the small desk in my cell, where my rocks and nest and the box with the Pumpsie Green baseball keep company. But, now as I think of it, as Sister Anne always read the *Boston Globe* and *Baseball Weekly* here in community, I suppose, as simply as that, I am Sister Anne's replacement. Busily silent with a paper, a pen, glad to sit my old bones down in the middle of the sounds of the paddle mixer and the sound of steely bowls banging.

How noisy baking is, with its machines and whisks and blenders, food processors, and I love, too—which I'm sure Sister Anne did—how angry Little Sister always sounds, banging along, cursing an egg white or a blanched almond batch not quite right, and still looking at the clock starting at 11:00, each sound from her louder, bangier. And when Sam comes into the kitchen, often celebrating a letter from Miriam, and sharing a soft, lost look with Little Sister. Even when it changes, it doesn't change. And still, it does change. By degrees.

We are all in the hands of God who knows our stories and holds them in great love as we live out the narrative we call our lives, and that is a blessing,

Sr. A.—

9 December 2004
Feastday of St. Juan Diego

Miriam, dear,

In the spirit of Saint Juan Diego, who was given the vision of Our Lady of Guadalupe, when asked about himself, said, "I am a nobody, I am a small rope, a tiny ladder, the tail end, a leaf"—in the same way we as a small community, being small, reflect over this past year, hoping that we form a tiny ladder to God—through burdens and sorrows and returns and healings and the daily prayers we share with and for the world. This remains our hope: to be a tiny ladder, a small rope, a leaf.

All of us in our part: Sister Farm, working hard with her half-working tractor, a half-working truck, 4 hives for honey (with thanks to Frankie), 10 sheep, 2 cows.

And Little Sister in her bakery making all sorts of spice and fruitcakes to send to our friends (we hope you like the package. And unlike most fruitcakes, these cherry almond cakes are edible. I've also given you a small jar of honey and a pair of candles). Little Sister told me last week, "Though no one would believe it, I pray up one side of the day and down the other in this kitchen." I told her that I believed it, though added that she also does take frequent prayer breaks for occasional cursing. "Oh, that's not a break," she said. "That's the praying part."

Then Frankie, with his bees and frames and colonies and broods and cut comb honey. And his ice cream. Frankie doesn't concern himself with what he's not, or even what he *should* be, he simply *does* and *is*. And, unless he doesn't get his ice cream, then always a smile. Showing off his suspenders and understanding his own gifts for joy and ice cream and the honeybee.

Traversing the bakery doors, he will hug whoever is in there, usually me and then Little Sister—if she's in a mood or not—and forage for Neopolitan ice cream, of which the chocolate is first to go, then strawberry, then, dutifully, the vanilla.

A few weeks ago, Tom came into the kitchen for coffee and bear claws and asked Little Sister and me, "So what *is* it about Frankie? Every time he sees one of you Sisters, he gives you a hug and says 'Epet EwYoh [happy new year].'" When he sees me or Father Martinez he just waves his chubby fingers at us or tucks his thumbs into his suspenders like they're better suspenders than mine."

Little Sister, measuring out one of 2 varieties of nutmeg into a shallow bowl said, "He likes breasts. Get some and he'll give you a hug. And the bigger the breasts, the happier he is, the more he likes to hug you."

Tom coughed. Then said, "Nope, I would get new suspenders for a hug, but no new breasts today."

"Guess you're hugless then," Little Sister said.

"Guess I am."

"Well, ok then," she said, which entitles the hearer to about 20 seconds to amble out of her kitchen, as those three words denote the end of a conversation.

Then there's Sister Bird, with her Sister Bird bird books, and her enthusiasms for all things homeopathic, naturopathic, and ornithological. Lugging her thermos and notebooks to the sandy edge of the shore; there she'll put the binos to her eyes and watch the winged creatures of the earth, even on a winter's day: the scattered great blue herons, the brants, American black ducks, horned grebes, and red-throated loons, scaups, and kill-deer. and the sanderlings, and great black-backed gulls, and the purple sandpiper, and all others who fly into our winter skies near these coastal lands.

And Mother Lourdes, wiry and strong to each task, finding the call of God challenging, "And," as she says, "while I'd like a different set of tasks, there are very few others that include bees and donkeys and birds and faith. And those have been surprisingly good, too."

And Sister Patrick Gertrude was given the gift of Telemann Recorder Music for Beginners to help all of us enjoy the sounds more. And only when the smell of cigars has crossed some boundary does she play "Onward Christian Soldiers," which isn't as much as you might expect.

But we keep a little hand in with turmoil, and as you have been so fair-minded in commenting on others of our conundrums, I wonder what you might respond with our latest, which is in some odd way, a Christmas story in need of advice. We've come into Advent season short on extra funds. We don't really need extra funds, but as you know Mother Lourdes has a special place in her heart (as we all do) for those who are shut-in or old, in need of solace, or a little help.

A few days ago Sister Farm came to me in the kitchen and asked, "Does a loving motive cancel a lie?"

Sister Patrick Gertrude walked by just then and as she passed said, "Oh Lord, smells like trouble."

I said, "It depends on what the loving motive is and wherein the lie," I guessed, squinting at her, to discern what manner of things were being discussed.

"Well, the loving motive is 'do Mother Lourdes no harm'—is that enough?"

"I think that's a very sensible and loving motive," I said, "and should wonder if God didn't think so too."

"Oh good," said Sister Farm.

"So, what about the lie?" I said.

"Does a sensible motive still need to admit a lie?"

"Well, *you* were the one who came to me as though to a confessor. Take me or leave me, it seems I'm all you've got until Father Martinez comes for confessions next Friday."

"Ok, ok," she said. "So here's the lie: The money that I got for Mother Lourdes to help old Mrs. Benzag and Mrs. Markovsky pay their December rent?"

"Oh, God, don't tell me this."

"I couldn't help it."

"Well," I said, "actually, you could. You've been clean and gamble-free for three years."

"I know, I know. But I'm so good at it. They needed the money."

"Did you go to Mohegan Sun?" I asked.

"Yup."

"Please tell me you wore civvies while gambling."

"I did."

"And you didn't say, 'Thank you, Blessed Mother' or 'Praise Jesus,' when you won."

"Well, I did say 'Thank God.'"

"Well, at least when you plow into a defiance of the Rule of Saint Athanasius, you take God along. That's heartening."

"That, or I can't shake him."

"How much?"

"$2,187.82. It covers their rent fully, with $37.82 left over for Christmas gifts for them. Isn't that handy?"

"Sister," I said.

"I think I need a smoke," Sister Farm said.

"Well, pray the rosary while you're at it," I said, wanting to be done with the whole conversation. But I went with her to the barn. And while she had a smoke in the chilly cow air, I said to her how glad I was that I wasn't at all talented in any of the dangerous arts like gambling. But I think, off the wagon or not, Sister Farm always returns to us, and speaks the confessive truth to Father Martinez. And then does it again. We all leave and return in our way. Fall, get up, as the Desert Fathers write about.

The days are getting long now, the darkness hovers over so many hours of the day one would believe it wins out—that old struggle between the darkness, the light.

Miriam, I begin to believe in some things fiercely, here in my older age, though they aren't in my list of Loose Rules, there's something here at this monastery: You don't get the answers you want, the character you want, the faith you want, the life you want, or the terms you want. But once you get past that, you get to live faithfulness and you get to live prayer. Enough to help a person in each day's little hours. That's all. No ultimate end, no big win maybe or no major success, but a quiet motion as influential as the tidal pull of the moon.

Faithfulness & prayer answer to faithfulness and prayer. And they are each other's best answer.

And so with hopes that both of these answer to your year's end as well, as I know they have—and also with a hearty wish that you enjoy the cherry fruit cake, the plum blossom honey, and the light of the candles,

Sr. A.—

14 December 2004
Feastday of
St. Bartholomew Buonpedoni

Miriam, dear—

A long while ago you asked me if I heard from my Doctor-Writer again. I surely have. Will you be surprised to know that he became a faithful friend over the years? Always sharp and accusing and direct and humorous in letters and conversation. Often commenting on my vows. And about his vows, which he called as theologically and morally grounded as my Loose Rules. Still, I argued, they are *in process.* You won't be surprised when I tell you my response never was convincing to him.

Maybe I haven't written of him, as it is like writing of the framework of one's past, of childhood and younger years and family. To me it's as though I were talking about air and breathing, sometimes. I don't understand air and breathing, rarely writing of it, and yet it is there, the building materials from which this life in faith and my entire frame emerged.

But you may want to know that his wife ended the marriage, soon after I had left. He had lived so apart for so long, that, as he wrote, "I had moved out long ago, and there was never a vacuum created by my leaving." And he told me later that he'd been faithful ever since. The year following, he sought me out. I remember the day, early May, the garden tilled, the air pure, sharp, and chill.

After lessons with the novice mistress, I was in my cell at prayer when Sister Anne knocked on the door—oh, she also was at the beginning of my religious formation, she was here a long time. She told me that a gentleman was down by the point—

near where our plovers were hatched, Miriam. "Spicy looking," she said—her term for a man who was not quite handsome, but nevertheless had some interest and attraction.

"He said you'd know who was visiting you."

In a moment of great fear, all my runnings away coming to meet me, and not knowing if my calling was indeed mine, I responded, "Must I go?"

"Of course not," Sister Anne returned. "But you will. And don't go by the path of the main house, everyone seems to be out and in the garden." Not that I can ask her now, but I suppose her volunteering that, then, allowed for any response in me: to walk away from the monastery or to stay.

That evening Sister Anne said to me, "And you are staying because . . . ?"

But I could give neither my Doctor-Writer nor Sister Anne good reason why. Even using the word *calling* stuck in my throat, though the phrase the Doctor used to help me speak was *running away.*

"Well then," Sister Anne said that evening, "you'll either find the good reason or you won't. You might find you made a good decision, despite yourself. Time will tell."

Every year hence he sent an annual Christmas card timed to arrive between my birthday and Christmas, so in early December, and I was always glad to see it. And always glad I remained here. And you'll be sorry to hear that this year no card came calling in charm and gruff voice. And his sister wrote to me yesterday that he has passed, writing that Augustine and a prayer book that I had sent him were his two companions. And I will miss him in the years, each Christmas when no letter arrives. I will think of how he was lost and cranky, a man with a good heart toward the world even so, who taught me so many things and how, through him, I ran to faith. And that's a good thing to say about someone you love.

And, Miriam, it comes to me now, in this year of loss, this year of learning my skills and professional works, that years of not knowing the heart of something may simply be the way to learn how to ask questions and wait until a life lived in hesitation and question proves the mercy of God, speaks in the right chords and the right time. And I am tempted to create a Loose Rule here, but in respect to Doctor Breamer, will refrain.

Fitting that there is a trinity of snow geese at the bay. The few who stayed to winter here. And I think of rare timing and of this year's losses and this year's gains and all in the hands of a loving God.

Miriam, all these things I hold close and ponder. And I know you, too, will have a sad heart in the goings of a dear man, and a grateful heart at the snow geese on the bay.

Yours,
Sr. A.—

20 December 2004
Feastday of St. Dominic of Brescia

Miriam,

We are deeply coming into winter. And I write you from the warm, nutmeg-induced lull of a kitchen in winter. The coffee-maker at my left hand, your transistor to my right. The winter sports pages getting slower, talk of Jason Varitek as a free agent, and Schilling's surgery and long-expected healing time. No games. No scores. No stats. Little Sister, as bowl-banging as ever, but also downright chatty.

In our observed silence during the lunch hour yesterday (a wild rice and mushroom soup, with a pumpernickel bread), Sister Bird was reading the Gospel of John. At one point Little Sister caught her eye, getting Sister Bird to read a section again. And then again. This is the reading where Jesus offers his disciples a chance to leave him, but his high-strung disciple, Saint Peter, says in return, "But where would we go? No one else has the words of eternal life."

Later, in the kitchen, Little Sister said to me, "That reading. That's what I feel like, like St. Peter. It doesn't make sense about staying, I mean, but then where else would I go?" I said to her that maybe having it all come down to her leaving explained why she wanted to stay.

"Could you just make us coffee?" she said. "No matter how short your homilies are, your coffee is better." (Newest Loose Rule #58: *Coffee is sometimes preferable to homilies.*)

So we had coffee.

The vows of chastity and obedience, simplicity and prayer, at least this month, the Advent of God with us, small in manger, are some of the hardest and most honest things to witness, day after day.

Wishing you, dear, all sorts of blessings this Advent season and hoping you enjoyed those small gifts from all in our monastery: the cherry fruitcake, the jar of Frankie's honey, and two beeswax candles made from our own buzzing friends.

Yours,
Sr. A—

1 January 2005
Feastday of Bd. Berka Zdislava

Miriam, dear—

Snow falling, fat flake upon fat flake—or as Christina Rossetti put it, "snow on snow on snow." Shall we rest, maybe just today, from our labors of mind and heart and home and community, and you drink your afternoon tea and I my glorious coffee this new day of the New Year? And you watch the chickadees and the house finch at the feeder, pecking through the snow caps down into the seeds. Feather upon feather, small bird next to small bird at a feeder on a winter's day. On a snowy day, that seems enough doesn't it, being a creature in God's big snowed in world?

Miriam, I am re-reading your letter. About Franklin and you there together in a ride in the car in a conversation sparked about your son Brendan being in college, about the changes happening for each of you. How Franklin feels more detached, shifting away from one clear definition of family into this new changing definition.

And you respond. I can almost visualize your yellow walls and the rose-paper wainscoting in the odd light of later night, while you and Franklin continue the conversation in the kitchen at 2:00 a.m. You angry. Franklin tired, but staying awake there.

I should have liked to see that moment when you began to yell, angry at everything: about Franklin (his thin lips, his complete motion toward the dutiful next thing as though he hadn't noticed the past unsolved thing). No more pretending, you yelled, that being a household with a son's room upstairs that only gets filled at holidays is ok. It's not ok, you yell.

"Ok, ok," he says (which didn't really match up with how you hoped a late-night conversation might go.)

I remember you wrote to me once about your early family days, you and Franklin barely slept 2 hours side by side: feedings and babies and work. But that the whole matter seemed settled, a family being a family and sleepless nights. Expected. Average. Good.

Then, a new edge comes again. Your son leaves home, your daughter stays home confused at trying to find her place in the world. You fall ill and then more ill, and then waiting, and less ill. And Franklin shifts over, but who knows where to shift to? And you find yourself yelling at Franklin, who (I say in admiration and wisdom) says little, except "Ok, ok. I know." And, "We've done this before, it's just a new time, is all."

And then he says, "My dear, I don't know what you are asking me to do."—I love that line, so direct. And your response—there in the kitchen with that awful bright florescent light—where you say quietly, "I don't know what I want. I think I want you to be a different person," and you know it was true and you knew how horrible it sounded and how mean and true you felt saying it.

And you went to bed with about 3 feet between you and you thought you would never meet anywhere in the middle. And he thought, he told you later, "It's just the next place two people have to go. We're just not at last year's place anymore." And for every reason to be mad that you have (which is true), there may be reason to keep going and shift around (which may be equally true).

And you wrote that Franklin lit the prayer candles from our monastery, left them on the side table for you, and went to bed. (A kindly intentioned fire hazard.) And you could only howl yourself out.

Aren't we all working hard? Living through the rhythm of days in prayer, work, anger, confusion, hope. Sometimes dismay or disorder show a hand, sometimes we have moments free from untamed recorder notes in the lower meadow from seemingly endless-paged protestant hymnals.

Sometimes the little blue heron alights at the bay, on the barn side of the monastery. And Sister Bird pulls out her binoculars and sketchbook and notes, and tries to memorize the long way its neck reaches over the shallow water to wait patiently for dinner at low tide.

It is days like this, Miriam, that I would love to see you walk up the road and follow the path between the small barn and the monastery and simply knock, and say in the voice I imagine, clear & clean, "I am intrigued by life at the monastery, but I have a couple questions. Is there birdwatching here? And, too, what do I do about my husband?"

At which time the door will swing wide to you, for a visit, to answer at least the birdwatching question, but also to renew your heart.

I remain, your friend. Waiting, dear, for your visit. I'll be here,

Sr. A—

- end -

Gratitudes

Many people—friends and family and colleagues—supported my writing early on. Thank you.

To those Copans who cheered and buoyed my writing, painting, and the creative life, thank you. And to my father and my mother—of blessed memory—who were united in their conviction that the writers, poets, and artists are numbered among the meaning makers.

To those who provided a deep well of friendship along the way: Els Maagdenberg, Janet LaMarre, Vinita Hampton Wright, Carmen Butcher, and Judy Folkerts, who introduced me to Meme and Pepe and their small farm.

To those early readers, editors, agents, inspirers, cheerers-on: Lauren Winner, Mary Martin, Kathy Helmers, Claudia Cross, Donna Kehoe, Chris Wave, Cindy Crosby, Dave O'Neal, Liz Kelly, Brent Bill, Annette Hughes, Regina Hoosier.

LaVonne Neff. I'm indebted to you for bottles of wine and conversations about the Athanasian Creed.

Jana Riess and Kelly Hughes, for providing information, congratulations, resources, and support. Thank you.

Mike Withers. Friend, you introduced me to the community in Petersham, MA, where I met Brother Leo and his Buff Orps. This began a long writing, faith journey for me. Thank you.

Various other religious and monastic communities provided retreat and writing space, as well as faith and baseball animated conversation, and a shared table, but the communities that stand out to me in profound ways are the ones in Petersham: St. Scholastica Priory | St. Mary's Monastery.

Kitchen Table Writers. When I moved to a new city, you provided kindred hearts and writerly goodness, and a safe space for writing. Kate Young Wilder supported this book for years and many pages. And Fran Araujo introduced me to a little spit of green park on the South Shore, which in my imagination became home to the Bings. And Jane Zimmerman celebrated each new pebble-ringed nest and clutch of piping plovers. All the Kitchen Table Writers supported this work, and it was informed by the wonderful, poetic, quirky, joyous, and sometimes seaside writings of the group.

Anne Quinn, who lived in my Dorchester neighborhood and faithfully went to Red Sox games with her husband until he became too ill to go. She would visit him in the hospital, followed by the trek to each game. I would sometimes see her walking home at night, her small, aging, and fragile figure, her little transistor radio in the pocket of her worn Red Sox jacket. Anne went to every Red Sox game (save one) for years, sat 19 rows up from the bullpen, transistor radio on, pencil in hand to score games. Her life and presence were legendary for many in Red Sox Nation. She provided me with Red Sox lore, vocabulary, stats, but it was her enthusiasm for the game and the team that had a radiance all its own.

Kate Campbell granted permission for me to use a line from her song, "Who Will Pray for Junior When I'm Gone," tying in to some of the writing about Frankie.

David E. Clapp of Natural History Services and Massachusetts Audubon Society, who saw early pages of this novel, made suggestions, and offered corrections regarding all things ornithological. Any changes, imperfections, and downright mistakes in this book are my own.

Martha Stout, friend along the way, sharing additional ornithological insight and baseball smarts and exuberance—and manuscript corrections. And some of my life's most important conversations. Bless you.

Paul Oppedisano, whose work in community and advocacy and justice inspires me. And whose support over the years has been a lifeline. Thank you. Your additions to Red Sox and Boston-related sections were perfect.

Susan (Sr. Sarah) Conlin, for thoughtful edits specifically related to monastic tradition. (Let me know how to get your mother the promised copy of the book!)

To those who provided resources and information: retreat masters, ornithologists, nun birders and baseball fans, bird bloggers, website publishers, and to those providing materials about monastic life, baseball, birds, literature, and the liturgy of the hours I owe many thanks. Too many to mention, but a few here: local and seasonal migration info at www.birdnature.com, South Shore Bird Club (SSBC) of Massachusetts, Massachusetts Audubon Society, Cornell Lab of Ornithology, James Weldon Johnson Foundation and Jill Rosenberg Jones, the foundation's literary executor; WEEI and the voice of the Red Sox, Joe Castiglione, St. Mary's Monastery and St. Scholastica guesthouse.

With appreciation to those authors whose books about monastic life found their way to my shelves. Their explorations gave rise to my own curiosities and fueled this writing journey: Mark Salzman, *Lying Awake;* Rémy Rougeau, *All We Know of Heaven;* Ron Hansen, *Mariette in Ecstasy;* Rumer Godden, *In this House of Brede;* Christine Hilger, *A Force of Habit.*

Catherine Kane, early reader who wanted copies to share with friends. You kept the at-points-thinning-flame fanned for this book. Thank you for believing this book is worth sharing.

Mary Kane, publisher, poet, life-time friend. You made room at One Bird Books for this work and created generous space for collaboration. The world is being made into a better place through your spirit, presence, thoughtful considerations, poetry, envelope art, and care. I'm blessed to know you.

Klaas Wolterstorff, the book's designer, who patiently tolerated several rounds of design reviews, tweaks, and queries—and who was always willing to share bird sightings along the way. Thank you. And Jim Morgan, who shepherded this book through early pages and formats. I owe you for your patience over a long set of years.

Mary Horner Collins, thank you for sharing your love for books, for libraries, for words with me. And thank you for providing editing support, proofreading skills—when it was *so* needed.

And you. If you read, supported, and cheered this book early on, and I haven't mentioned you by name, I hope you'll extend some grace (and/or correction!) for the lost bits of paper that carried your name(s).

And Deborah Risë Mrantz, for pushing to get this book to press, for caring about details, always. And for having the important conversations about life, faith, literature, justice, and love.

To all the Bings: To those who are of their Order or feel that the Bings offer you a place in the faith landscape where you might fit, I hope this book provides at least a temporary spiritual home that is sound, true, gracious, odd, curious, and grouchy enough to suit you, welcome you.

And for the baseball fans of those teams who have long losing histories but very big hopes. Thank you for believing that sometimes a big win—the biggest wins—can still happen.

About the Author

Lil Copan is an editor, arts columnist, and painter. This is her first work of fiction and brings together longtime interests in contemplative spirituality, baseball, and birding. A graduate of the University of Connecticut, Lil has degrees in art and creative writing. In addition to a long history in editorial work, she has worked as a curatorial assistant at an art museum, a high school English teacher, and a corn detasseler in Iowa fields. She leads workshops on spiritual writing and creative nonfiction. A long-time Bostonian, she now lives in "the city different"—Santa Fe, New Mexico—with her partner.

About One Bird Books

One Bird Books is a Cape Cod based independent company dedicated to publishing high quality literary writing. We are open to various forms but publish only works we wholeheart-edly wish to bring to the world.

Visit our website at onebirdbooks.com

Made in the USA
Middletown, DE
15 June 2021